Julia,
You made it possible
I am very grateful

Jack Doreen
3/9/09

This is a story of passion for money

WHEN ALL THE BANKS
FAILED

A novel by Jean Doucet

****

How did this financial tsunami happen?

What roles were played by the French Intelligence Agency, the Investment manager of the United Arab Emirates and the President of the largest U.S. bank?

Could all banks fail again?

A compelling love story involving international spies, oil, gold, money, unscrupulous mafiosos, and greedy bankers; written in a steamy style sometimes reminiscent of Harold Robbins'.

It might be true!

This is a story of passion for love

<u>Warning</u>

The graphic description of sex scenes, the use of foul language and the violence depicted in the Vietnam episode may make the reading of this book inappropriate for young persons or persons that are easily offended.

<u>Author's Note</u>

This book is a work of fiction dedicated to all those who believe in the Golden Fleece. Some factual places, incidents, events and institutions have been used in the story to better identify locales, entities and persons that might have been or could be involved in the described financial chaos and extraordinary love story.

Otherwise, all other names, characters, places and incidents are either the product of the author's imagination or are used fictitiously. Any resemblance to actual persons, living or dead, events, locales, organizations, institutions and corporations is entirely coincidental

Order this book online at www.trafford.com
or email orders@trafford.com

Most Trafford titles are also available at major online book retailers.

Note for Librarians: A cataloguing record for this book is available from Library and Archives Canada at www.collectionscanada.ca/amicus/index-e.html

Printed in Victoria, BC, Canada.

ISBN: 978-1-4251-7563-4 (sc)

First Printing: July 2009

We at Trafford believe that it is the responsibility of us all, as both individuals and corporations, to make choices that are environmentally and socially sound. You, in turn, are supporting this responsible conduct each time you purchase a Trafford book, or make use of our publishing services. To find out how you are helping, please visit www.trafford.com/responsiblepublishing.html

Our mission is to efficiently provide the world's finest, most comprehensive book publishing service, enabling every author to experience success. To find out how to publish your book, your way, and have it available worldwide, visit us online at www.trafford.com

Trafford rev.7/7/2009

 www.trafford.com

North America & international
toll-free: 1 888 232 4444 (USA & Canada)
phone: 250 383 6864 ♦ fax: 250 383 6804 ♦ email: info@trafford.com

Also by Jean Doucet

La danseuse était nue
(a new novel in French. Expected winter 2009)

To: Bobbie McCoy whose support and love never failed.

TABLE OF CONTENTS

PROLOGUE

This novel was written in 1975 during the worldwide credit crisis and hyper inflation brought about by OPEC's oil producers when, in 1973, they declared an embargo on shipments of oil to Israel and supporting countries. As I write this prologue, the price of a barrel of oil in July 2008 reached over $140. It was less than $5.00 in 1973.

While the world economy disintegrated, where were the authorities? The Federal Reserve Board, the Federal Deposit Insurance Corporation (FDIC), Central Banks, auditors, finance ministers and other watch dogs? All of a sudden, in a matter of a very few months, some of the events, which bankrupted the world's banking system in my 1975 novel, were being repeated tenfold.

Results? My 1975 novel, "When All The Banks FAILED" has become the story to read in 2009. The action could have happened in 1978. Did it? It could be happening now. Is it? I think so. **Better check your bank accounts.**

"Those who read the manuscript before its publication believe it is on course for a Best Seller label"

"If I had any money I would place it in a big Bank, a strong Bank..."

(From the Northwester, November 1974. Reply to a member's question in the Assembly by Vassel Johnson, Financial Secretary, Government of the Cayman Islands)

CHAPTER ONE
THE WITHDRAWAL

"Do not devour each other's wealth among yourselves through deceit and falsehood, nor offer your wealth as a bribe to the authorities that you may deliberately devour a part of other people's wealth through injustice".

(From the Quran, page 30, a new translation by Muhammad Zafrulla Khan. Curzon Press, London 1971)

On this grey morning of the last day of June 1978, Sheik Ben Said Al-Madir stood, a solitary and grim figure, in one of the high-speed elevators of the Grand American Bank tower on Park Avenue in New York. The Sheik had insisted on an early meeting with the Chairman of the bank in order to avoid witnesses and interruptions. The meeting was the most important step in his long planned road to world power. Soon no one would be capable of stopping him.

In his office, on the 59th floor, overlooking the East River flowing beyond the irregular rooflines of the drab New York office buildings, Peter Hardrock, the Chairman of the Grand American Bank, was expecting his visitor. The Sheik had telephone him the previous afternoon to set up this early appointment. At first, he had tried to steer him to Andrew Robertson, the President of the Bank, who had been the Sheik's friend since Robertson's lengthy stay in the Middle East in the early 60's. But the Sheik had refused. He would accept to see no one but the Chairman because, among other issues, the meeting concerned his personal relationship with Robertson. Reluctantly, Hardrock had agreed to the meeting at this very early hour.

Through the half open door, Hardrock watched the Sheik walking towards his office, his long white robe rustling on the high pile green carpet. It was exceptional for Sheik Al-Madir to wear his Arab clothes. He only did so for official functions and ceremonies. But Hardrock had no reason to be concerned. The relationship of the Grand American Bank with the oil rich United Arab Emirates, of which Sheik Al-Madir was the investment manager, had always been most cordial and was carefully nurtured by Roberston who understood the Arab mentality better than anyone else in the Western Hemisphere. As a result of Robertson's efforts, Grand American Bank, with assets of 121 billion dollars, was now the largest bank in the world, larger than Bank of America and First National City Bank combined. Naturally, Hardrock and Robertson where the highest paid executive team in banking history. For the year 1977, their combined salaries and bonuses had exceeded $1,200,000. While they received individual pay, they also earned a team bonus, 60% of which was taken by Hardrock and 40% by Robertson, although Robertson had always felt that a 50/50 split would have been more equitable.

Hardrock rose and stood by the door of his office, his hand extended. "Good morning Sheik Al-Madir".

"It was kind of you to see me so early in the morning", replied the Sheik as he took the hand of Hardrock and shook it somewhat reticently.

Hardrock closed the door behind them, indicating a seat in the conference corner of his office. He glanced at Germaine Gallibert's masterpiece "La Sortie du Sultan"[1] on the paneled wall behind the Sheik and had a sudden premonition that there was a relationship between the title of his favorite painting from the grand lady of impressionism and the visit of the Sheik. He glanced at his eyes, they told him nothing. He looked at his hands, they rested calmly on his thin briefcase and, when he started to speak, his voice was controlled.

"Mr. Hardrock, when one must do unpleasant things, it is better to do them quickly in order to permit one to return rapidly to the more pleasant things in life. With your permission, I shall skip the polite and social talk and discuss with you immediately the purpose of my visit."

"You are aware that the United Arab Emirates that I represent are the largest clients of your bank. The various deposits of the Emirates have grown substantially since the fall

1 The Departure of the Sheik

of 1973 when we decreed the oil embargo. Today they total many billions of dollars."

Hardrock reached quickly for a computer printout lying on his desk. "My latest report shows slightly in excess of 28 billion."

Sheik Al-Madir raised his hand, impatiently. "I know very well what your computer shows and I know also what it does not show: the billions of dollars deposited by the Emirs and members of their families in your various branches."

"Did you say billions?"

"I did. To be exact, those deposits exceed 22 billion dollars."

"Impossible!"

"Let me continue and do not question my figures. They are correct and I shall let you have full details before I leave."

"But our computer department reports daily to me and Robertson all deposits from Arab sources in excess of 10 million dollars and never..."

"Mr. Hardrock, please! I wish to conclude what I came here to do before the opening of your bank at nine. Therefore, please listen to me carefully and do not interrupt me. The total deposits under my control in your bank at 5 p.m. closing time last night, including the 28 billion dollars of the United Arab Emirates that you know of, the 22 billion of the Emirs and members of their families that you don't know of, and those deposits in the name of other corporations under my control totaled $60,129,834,645."

"That's preposterous! That's more than half the assets of my bank!"

"So it is. The deposits are detailed here on my computer print-out and, with due respect, allow me to tell you that this computer print-out is complete and correct because I personally saw to it that the input in my computer be complete and correct."

"I can't believe 60 billion dollars!"

"Mr. Hardrock, no doubt you will find out eventually how so much money came into your bank over the past five years without you suspecting it. I must admit that I was always surprised that in your message to your shareholders at the end of each of the last four years you could attribute the extraordinary growth of your bank to a general increase in business in all sectors of your activities. It is amazing that it never entered your mind that an annual growth of 20 billion dollars in the assets of any bank anywhere is, to say the least, suspicious. But that is already the past and my concern — and yours also — is the present."

The Sheik continued, "yesterday all bank accounts appearing in the books of your bank in the name of the United Arab Emirates, the Emirs and the numerous members of their families, and the hundreds of corporations under our control were transferred to your main office here in New York into one omnibus account in the name of 'Sheik Ben Said Al-Madir in trust.' There are no longer accounts in any of your branches anywhere in the world in which we have any interest. I have here a cheque drawn on my account in trust and payable to my order in the amount of $60,129,834,645. I wish to withdraw the proceeds".

"That's preposterous! Why?"

"I have decided to close my account."

"You must be joking." That's all Peter Hardrock could say. He realized how inadequate these words were but he couldn't believe what he was hearing.

"There is no joke, Mr. Hardrock. At nine o'clock you can call your own computer department and they will tell you that my cheque is good. Here is the cheque; I have endorsed it as required."

"Is that all?" ask Hardrock incredulously.

"As a matter of fact, it is not, Mr. Hardrock." The Sheik spoke more slowly insisting on each word. "I also wish to be paid in cash."

"But there isn't that much cash in the whole of the United States."

"Then you will have to ask you Federal Reserve Board to print some."

"But why?"

"Ha! Why? I do not intend to discuss my personal reasons with you."

"What do you mean you don't intend to discuss your personal reasons with me?" Hardrock could not help raising his voice. "You come here to tell me that you have managed to break all the internal rules of this bank by placing on deposit with us more funds than any one bank in the world is prepared to accept or can handle; you come here to tell me that having achieved this, you now want to withdraw these funds, in cash, and you don't intend to discuss the reasons of this gigantic and impossible withdrawal? come on now, Sheik Al-Madir, let's be sensible."

"Mr. Hardrock, it is said 'for those who do evil, the penalty shall be in proportion thereto, and ignominy shall cover them, there will be none to shield them from Allah's chastisement'."

"I know. I know. And all sinners go to hell! But at this moment, I couldn't care less about your 'what is said.' What I want to know is what exactly have *we* said or done to you that you have prepared such an unbelievable plot against us?"

"Ask Robertson."

"What has Robertson to do with this?"

"That's all I am prepared to say." Allah knows everything and you know nothing."

Hardrock rose briskly, walked to his desk and impatiently pressed the intercom button linking his office to Robertson's.

"Mr. Hardrock, I do not care to meet or talk to your Mr. Robertson this morning, later on today or ever for that matter, so please don't force me to leave by asking him to your office now, you can always do this after I depart."

Hardrock released the intercom button. Robertson would not have arrived anyway, his train came in from White Plains at 9:08 and it was only 8:30. He returned to his seat, facing his visitor, glanced at the 'Departure of the Sheik' painting on the wall, picked up the 60 billion dollar cheque from the coffee table, read it carefully, checked the endorsement and shook his head as if coming out of a nightmare.

"Sheik Al-Madir, what you have just revealed to me is, to say the least, incredible. So is your demand for closing your account for reasons you refuse to reveal. Whether you like it or not, I need to discuss this extraordinary situation with Robertson as soon as he reaches his office. I must also inform the members of my Board of your mind-shattering decision."

"I had hoped to conclude this business before nine o'clock."

"You know very well that this is not possible. Do you realize the serious implications of your actions?"

The Sheik smiled. "I do. Technically, this places your bank in default, but in view of our past relationship, I am prepared to be reasonable. I shall return at 10:30 to see you – and again, you alone. Keep Robertson out of my way, and remember, I want cash -all of it in cash. May I have my cheque back?"

Hardrock parted reluctantly with the cheque, rose and walked heavily to the door of his office, which he held open. He was sweating profusely.

The Sheik stopped in front of him, bowed solemnly, his face impassive, turned swiftly on his heels and continued to the elevators.

Hardrock watched him leave and beckoned to his executive assistant who was already at her post. "Madame de Rivoli, please come in."

"Coffee, Mr. Hardrock?"

"Yes, bring me a coffee, a very black one. And you may bring yours also, but come quickly."

With the international expansion of the bank, Hardrock had wanted a multilingual executive assistant and had rejoiced when, at a business cocktail, his good friend, René Mathieu, the President of the Compagnie de Suez — the largest French client of the bank — had suggested the French born Baroness Simone de Rivoli. She had lost her husband in Vietnam in 1968 and was eager to start a new life in the US. She held a doctorate degree in Economics from the Sorbonne University in Paris and had acquired banking experience while working at the Bank of France. She spoke French, English, German and

Vietnamese. She was 36, tall and elegant. She knew business protocol, understood international banking and was discreet and reliable.

She had brought a touch of her aristocracy to the office of the Chairman of Grand American Bank and Hardrock was flattered. While she was entitled to be called Baroness, everyone at the bank, including Hardrock, addressed her as Madame de Rivoli. Only Andrew Robertson, the President, called her Simone.

She brought the two coffees to Hardrock's office.

"Madame de Rivoli, as soon as Robertson comes in, I want to see him in my office. Immediately!"

Simone detected his nervous and upset tone. "Then let me alert his secretary." She pressed the intercom button for Robertson's office. "Louise?"

"Yes, Madame de Rivoli?"

"As soon as Mr. Robertson comes in, Mr. Hardrock would like to see him."

"Unfortunately, he has an appointment at 9:15."

"It will have to wait", interjected Hardrock.

"I heard that", Louise said, "I will call you, Madame de Rivoli, as soon as he comes in."

"Thank you, and please sit down, Madame de Rivoli", Hardrock said. He paused as if hesitating, then in an unsure voice said, "You have been a most efficient and devoted assistant for the past eighteen months and I am most satisfied with your services."

"I only do my job, Mr. Hardrock, to the best of my ability."

"I know. I know. Because your position is one of trust, I have always felt free to discuss openly with you the most confidential files that cross my desk. I don't think there is a single business matter concerning this bank of which you are not aware."

"I have always appreciated your trust."

"Then let me brief you on what happened this morning and perhaps you could give me some advice."

"I don't know if I have the competence..."

"I am satisfied that you have. In addition, you may have certain knowledge, which might be useful. Madame de Rivoli, it is no secret in New York's social circles that you have been a frequent escort of Sheik Al-Madir."

"I find the Sheik a charming and witty man, he is also a gentleman."

"No doubt, Madame de Rivoli. As you well know, the Sheik and the United Arab Emirates that he represents are very large clients of this bank."

"The Sheik and I never discuss business..."

"He does not have to tell you. You have seen the daily computer print-outs listing our Arab deposits."

"I don't read them. I only send them to "Confidential Filing". Those have been your instructions."

"Well take my word for it, they are large clients. The largest. There are no larger bank depositors in the world."

"I try to keep my personal life separate from the affairs of the bank."

"I am not concerned about your personal life, Madame de Rivoli, nor do I want to interfere with it, so don't misunderstand me. Nevertheless, knowing your devotion to this bank and, I hope, to me, I felt that I could ask you to let me know whether you have heard or noticed anything recently indicating that Sheik Al-Madir was not pleased with our services or the attitude of the officers of this bank who are handling his accounts."

"Mr. Hardrock, if I had any information that might assist you in whatever problem you seem to face with Sheik Al-Madir, I would volunteer it."

"I thought you would. Already, I feel better about it."

The intercom buzzed.

"Mr. Hardrock's office," answered Simone.

"Louise here, Madame de Rivoli, the 'big man' is on his way."

"Mr. Robertson is on his way, Mr. Hardrock," translated Simone.

"Thank you, Madame de Rivoli, let him right in. I expect

Sheik Al-Madir to return at 10:30, don't keep him waiting. Also, cancel all my calls and appointments for this morning."

Simone left the office knowing that Hardrock's gaze was following her. She walked with her back straighter than usual, her head high, reflecting a touch of aristocratic arrogance, the way she had been instructed to do when she was a young girl and had been told that there were two classes of people in the world: 'you and the others'. Mr. Hardrock, you may be Chairman of the Grand American Bank, she reflected, and a member of one of the wealthiest families in the world, but you will always be one of the others. No real taste, only greed. No real class, only money. No real happiness, only power. She would soon be in a position to show him. There was no way her mission could fail now.

Simone de Rivoli drove her jeep as fast as she could over the narrow muddy road that linked the village of My Lai to the main highway that led to Saigon, the capital of Vietnam. She was zigzagging from shoulder to shoulder trying to avoid the begging potholes left by mines and bombs. She drove tensely, thinking of the unending wars in Vietnam. First, the Japanese occupation, then fifteen years of intermittent battles with the French military forces and now six years of destruction by the US Army. What the French, who knew this territory intimately, had not succeeded in accomplishing in more than one hundred years of presence in Indochina, the Americans were hopeful of doing in a matter of months. And they could not even speak the language! Poor Americans. But they had a simple formula. Take a country like Vietnam, don't learn the language, don't study the history, don't understand the culture, just find a convenient parallel, draw a line across the country and presto! The problem is solved. All residents of the North are declared bad and those of the South good. Forget four thousand years of civilization. Forget history, customs, and traditions. Forget fathers born in the North and children in the South. Just draw a line and shoot. The same technique was used in Korea. Draw a line, shoot all the North Koreans. Those from the North are necessarily the bad ones!

Perhaps the Americans have never recovered from the pattern of their own civil war between North and South. Who were the good and the bad ones then, in America? "Yankees why don't you go home", she hissed to herself.

Simone's knuckles were white from the tension of driving

and her face flushed from despair at the thought of all the terrible, inhuman and unnecessary miseries of wars. She had taken the jeep to Saigon from My Lai two days before in a desperate effort to find medicine for her husband's hospital. For many weeks now My Lai had been cut off from the outside world by the fighting around the village. She couldn't understand why the war had suddenly moved towards the hamlet of My Lai where there was nothing left but perhaps four hundred innocent old people, women and children living around the small hospital where she worked with her husband at mending those poor bodies, undernourished, weakened, exposed to all the horrible diseases of the war.

Baron Antoine de Rivoli had retired from the French Army when France had finally decided to abandon Indochina after the defeat of Dien Bien Phu. A medical officer, he had decided to return to Vietnam in 1963 and had established a small hospital at My Lai. "Someone needs to do something about the terrible ravages of this war," he had explained.

Then, two days ago, dejected, Antoine had said, "Simone, this is the end. We must close the hospital. There are no supplies left. Nothing. All the cabinets are empty. Not even an aspirin."

"My dear Antoine," she had leaned against him and linked her fingers through his beautiful strong surgeon's hands, "I shall find you some supplies."

"Where, where?" Antoine had asked impatiently.

"In Saigon."

"You can't reach Saigon. We are completely cut off from the outside world. Simone, it's the end."

"I don't want to reopen that file," she had said, "your decision was taken when the last French soldier left. You decided to return because you said you had a vocation. More, a duty to build your hospital in this country as your contribution to the reparation due to Vietnam and also to give a purpose to our lives. No more wastage of our talents like we did in Europe. No more lifestyle secured by our titles, our servants and our social success. You wanted to be a real doctor. You wanted me to be a real nurse and a real wife. We chose to come. We stayed and we succeeded."

"Succeeded," cried Antoine, "look at our poisoned river; look at our destroyed rice fields; look at the empty cabinets; look at me, helpless; look at you..."

"Yes, but look also at this hospital," interrupted Simone, "look at those children, your children, our children. Look at the hope in the eyes of these men and women. You are their doctor, their friend, perhaps their only friend in this whole barbarian world. They don't understand what these foreign soldiers have been doing here for generations destroying their country. For more than twenty-five years they have seen them come and go, they have seen them shoot, kill and die. But you, you are the doctor, the only person expressing kindness to them. You don't shout, you protect. You don't kill, you bring life. You don't die, you live and your mission must continue. I shall go and get your supplies."

"But Simone, both the Vietcong and the Americans are entrenched between here and Saigon."

"Antoine, for me there are no such things as Vietcong, friends or enemies, there are only Vietnamese and for five years I have learnt to be one of them. As to the Americans, they can never resist a pretty face," she smiled at him.

"I won't let you, said Antoine."

Simone kissed Antoine, turned quickly and ran to the grove where their jeep was parked. He ran after her. "See you tomorrow," she waved as she gunned the motor and drove off in a cloud of red dust that the wind blew skyward. Had he caught her, he could not have stopped her. She was determined to go.

After her departure, Antoine made a last resigned tour of patients and decided to lie down to rest his exhausted body and forget his mental suffering. He had been dozing for about an hour when the deafening chop-chop of giant helicopters and the screaming of men woke him up. From the window of the dispensary, he saw what appeared to be American soldiers jump from the big army carriers and run crouched alongside the crumbling walls of the village's crude dwellings.

"Empty all these shacks and burn them down!" barked a Lieutenant. He was a brute of a man, looking even taller than his six feet as he stood on top of a knoll by the rice field which bordered the road across from the hospital. "Come on, come on you men, and bring all that scum out here on the double!"

The soldiers were entering and searching every house in the village brutally pushing with the butt of their guns the women and children out of them towards the Lieutenant. Some of them could hardly walk and were shoved hard until they felt, were picked up and shoved again harder. When they were all assembled by the rice field, a soldier shouted, "that's it Lieutenant. What do we do now?"

"What about that long building?" snapped the Lieutenant.

"But it's a hospital," replied two soldiers in unison.

"It might be full of Cong. Either you get them or they'll get you. Go on." By this time the Lieutenant was in a rage.

Antoine rushed to the front entrance of the hospital to be met by six young soldiers, machine guns ready. "What are you doing? This is a hospital."

"Orders," they replied, and started to move the patients out of their beds with the butt of their guns.

"These are sick people. I am the doctor responsible for this hospital; you can not touch my patients."

One of the young soldiers pushed him aside roughly. Antoine protested, "at least let me carry those who can't walk."

"They can crawl," replied the soldier.

Antoine rushed to a bed along the far wall where little Pam Lai lay, her stomach freshly bandaged.

He found her crying last night at the far end of the rice field in front of the hospital. She had been caught by one of the patrols but she could not remember whether it was an American or a Vietcong patrol. She had been beaten and raped at least ten to twelve times until her insides were all torn and bleeding and left dying along the road to Mon Mon Tai. Antoine had worked all night to bring the girl out of her shock and to repair the irreparable damage done to this child of fourteen. In the name of war! In the name of freedom! In the name of democracy! In the name of God! Draw a parallel. Shoot those from the North. Screw and rape those in the South. All in the name of liberty. In God we trust!

Antoine took her in his arms tenderly, covered her with a blanket and marched out of the hospital leading his sick, like a defeated army, towards the Lieutenant.

"What in the hell is this?"

"I am Baron Antoine de Rivoli, retired Captain from the French Army and director of this hospital. What you are doing is inhuman. You are breaking all international conventions."

"Doc, I know only one convention, I shoot first. I kill or get killed."

Antoine reposted, "I order you to leave this village immediately. There is nothing here for you. Only sick old men, women and children. So please leave and let us be."

"Who do you think you are, Frenchman, to order me to leave?" snarled the Lieutenant. "Intelligence said there were Cong here. We came here to rid the place. We came here to finish the job you didn't have the guts to finish, Frenchman." He sneered at Antoine. "Can't you see, Doc, that they are all friends of the Cong, all shit."

"They are all innocent bystanders," said Antoine.

"Innocent my foot! They are more dangerous than soldiers with guns. At least with soldiers you can see the guns; it's an honest fight. But with these, you never know what surprises they hide in the folds of their clothes." As he yelled, the Lieutenant grabbed the neck of the dress of an old woman in front of him, pulled hard and tore the dress from her. She stood nude, her wrinkled skin showing the ravage of her hunger, her disapproving eyes fixed on the Lieutenant, nobly. He spat at her. Her eyes never left his face.

Shocked and disgusted, Antoine interposed himself

between the raging Lieutenant and the defenseless old woman. "Lieutenant, I shall report you to your Commanding Officer."

"You will report nothing, to no one, frenchy. Either you are with us or against us. You choose."

"I swear to you Lieutenant, I will have you court-marshaled for this within days."

"Screw you man! Screw you ten times! Roberts! Prescott! Wienner!" barked the Lieutenant. "Waste this shit!"

"Waste them, Lieutenant?"

"I said waste them, don't you now what it means?" The Lieutenant grabbed the machine gun from Roberts. "If you haven't got the guts, I'll show you." He started to shoot through the ranks of women and children. They fell on the knoll and rolled in the ditch by the rice field, a pile of flesh, brains and blood. He threw the machine gun back to Roberts and screamed, "Now finish the goddamn job!"

He swirled around to face Antoine who was rushing at him and placed his handgun on his belly, "you mind your own business, Frenchman. Court martial, eh?" He raised the gun and, without wincing, shot little Pam Lai through the head and the blood spurted all over Antoine's face and then shouted, "balls to you Frenchman!" and shot Antoine in the face.

"Come on men, let's get out of here," and he ran with his men to the waiting 'copters

As Simone drove out of the defoliated forest and reached the top of the hill at the end of the rice field, she discovered the smoldering smoke coming up from the village and exclaimed, "my God!" Disregarding holes and rocks, she raced the jeep towards My Lai.

Then she saw the bodies blocking her way, lying all over the knoll and in the ditch by the rice field. "Antoine!" The silence of death answered her. And the smell. Not a movement, not a cry, not a survivor!

"Antoine!" Jumping out of the jeep, she ran towards what was left of the burnt down hospital to find only emptiness, destruction, and disaster.

Then she heard a sob and caught sight of young Tom Poi crawling out from under Antoine's steel desk in the far corner of the hospital. She ran to him over the smoldering partitions and mattresses, hugged him to her breast and cried, "Tom, Tom, what happened?"

"The Americans."

"Where are they?"

"They left in their big birds."

"The doctor, Tom, where is the doctor?"

"He was shot also."

"Are you sure?"

"I saw it."

"By whom?"

"A big, bad American."

Sitting on the left side of the DC8 jet, Simone de Rivoli was enjoying her first sight of the French soil in six years.

Nine months had gone by since the murder of her husband and four hundred innocent Vietnamese in My Lai and all of her efforts to have the matter brought to trial had failed. The US Army strongly denied that its troops had ever been involved in a My Lai operation and blamed the Viet Cong. The Government in Saigon claimed that My Lai was an abandoned village used occasionally by the Viet Cong as ammunition depot. It had to be destroyed. If any one had died, no murder had been committed because only enemies had been killed, they said. As each day went by and as each new interview ended in the same denial, Simone gradually realized that she was the victim of a horrifying cover-up against which her only witness was Tom Poi. She had become a powerless woman alone with a twelve-year-old boy against the powerful US Army and its puppet Government in Saigon.

Government officials who had known her and Antoine and who had visited their hospital, started to say, "Madame de Rivoli, c'est la guerre! You can't expect the Government to believe the story of a twelve-year-old sick boy. You can't expect the US Army to distinguish between North and South. It's the war. Soldiers shoot people, what do you expect?"

"I expect justice."

"There is no justice in war. Why don't you forget it and return to France? You should have never come here anyway".

"But we were needed", Simone insisted.

"You know very well that you were barely tolerated. We

Vietnamese want our independence. We can't accept the Americans' occupation and we will never forgive the French. You remain an enemy. A painful reminder of the colonial days."

She pleaded with her best friends. They said, "Simone, you know it's useless. No, we will not get involved. Go back to France, start a new life. You have a name, friends, and connections. Go back and forget you were ever here."

Defeated, angered at the Americans and revolted by the unfairness of the situation, she decided to go back, but she swore she would never forget. She would find a way to revenge the murder of her husband. That became the ultimate purpose of what was left of her life.

The Seine River and the suburbs of Paris appeared through the rising silvery fog and, in the distance, emerged a series of high-rise residential structures built since the last time Simone had seen Paris. They looked misplaced in the surrounding landscape. More like a series of mistakes. How could anyone live in such horrendous apartments? What has happened to the good taste France has always been so proud of, Simone asked herself.

As the big plane made its last turn before landing at Orly Airport Simone tightened her belt. She opened her purse and read again the cable reply she had received from Pierre Beauchamp. "Come immediately. Will meet you at Orly. You can stay with us. As always, Pierre."

Pierre Beauchamp had been the best friend of Antoine and Simone before their move to Vietnam. They were then an inseparable trio. Pierre and Simone had met at the Lycée a few years before Antoine had entered her life. Antoine had courted her for only six months and on the day she told Pierre that Antoine had asked her to marry him, he had said, "Marry Antoine, Simone. You are young, beautiful and intelligent, you need a husband. I am not ready for marriage and I don't know if I'll ever be. Antoine can give you his illustrious name and, what's more important, he loves and needs you. We will remain good friends, forever. I love you more than I thought I was capable of loving anyone, Simone. Don't cry, dearest, I am sure you will find happiness with Antoine". She had married Antoine. She was only twenty.

Pierre had remained their closest friend. They cherished

his warm relationship with Antoine and she knew that he would always be supportive, eager to help her always in a correct and proper manner. His love would never falter. Pierre spent many nights with them in Paris in their apartment on Marbeuf street, around the corner from the Georges V Hotel. Most of their summer weekends and the month of August, when most Parisians escaped the heat of the city, were spent in Mougins on the Côte d'Azur where Pierre had inherited a large provincial villa from his father. He had never married and seemed content to share their happiness.

Pierre lived in Paris with his mother in an apartment on Rue Berri. He worked for an inconspicuous government financial service, which required him to be away frequently on what appear to be secret assignments. He had never discussed his work with them. Either it was too boring or too confidential. The mystery had remained and, being good friends, they had never tried to pry.

The plane had landed. Simone gathered her personal effects. The stewardess had taken her post by the exit and unlocked the door. Soon it opened and the passengers started to disembark. As usual Orly airport was bustling with thousands of passengers. Simone read the various indications making sure she was following the arrows reading 'Paris' and placed her hand luggage on the rolling sidewalk, which brought her from the gate to the center of the terminal. She presented her passport to the immigration officer who looked absentmindedly at her and her photo, flipped the pages nonchalantly and returned it to her. She identified her luggage to the custom inspector who waved her through. And then she saw Pierre, on the other side of the custom gates. She rushed towards him, the parting tears of six years ago already forgotten.

He drove her to Rue Berri where his mother greeted her with great enthusiasm and during the following days helped her renew her acquaintance with Paris. At the end of the second week Pierre told her, "

"Simone, why don't you go to my villa in Mougins for a few weeks? After everything that has happened to you recently, the death of Antoine, the miseries of war, your fight with the US Army and the Saigon Government, you must be exhausted and in need of a change of venue".

"That's very kind of you, Pierre, but after the jungles of Vietnam, I rather like Paris, its mad traffic, its people, its lights and its noises. There is excitement in the air that I find exhilarating. I'm not sure I want to leave it and be alone again".

"You won't be alone, my caretakers, Joseph and Lila, are still there. They will take good care of you and perhaps I can rearrange my schedule to spend a long weekend with you."

"But Pierre, you and your mother have already been so kind to me. I feel I am imposing".

"Nonsense! Friends never impose. Let me call Air France. Tomorrow is Friday; we could leave on the noon flight."

"Really, Pierre, I have so much to do here in Paris. I need to reopen my apartment, buy new clothes and look for some means of livelihood."

You can do all that later after you are well rested. As to the job, why do you need to work?"

"Antoine left me the apartment on Marbeuf Street and I receive his army retirement benefits but that's very little. While

I am a Baroness, my dear Pierre, I can't live on my title and charm alone." "If I were you, I would try", he said teasingly. "Pierre, let's be serious." "All right! Let's spend some time in Mougins together. This is April, all the flowers are in bloom and the tourist crowds have yet to arrive. Let's do it for old time's sake. Let's do it for your own good".

"Doctor, I am your patient," said Simone laughing gaily. There was something about Pierre that Simone found reassuring. She had always felt comfortable in his presence. He was solid, dependable and kind. You could look at his eyes and see the intelligence but never the superiority.

If he placed his hands on you, it was always a pleasant gesture, sort of protective never provocative. Pierre was a good man and such a good friend. She realized that she had always loved him.

"Simone, stop gazing at me this way, mother will start worrying!" "Children, as long as you are only gazing," replied Pierre's mother. "I'll help you pack your bags, I know you will enjoy your stay at villa Belle Simone and I envy you."

"Is that what the villa is called?" asked Simone. "Sometime after you went to Vietnam, Pierre decided to change the name from villa 'Beaux Champs' to 'La Belle Simone'. You know, you were his first love and perhaps his only love and while he rejoiced at your happiness with Antoine and shared it, for him you were always the woman he loved".

Pierre, I didn't know you had named your villa in Mougins after me. I am really flattered".

"Wait until you see it, you will agree that the name fits it perfectly. It's beautiful, like you."

"You are always so very gallant, Pierre that perhaps I should hesitate about spending a long weekend alone with you in Mougins. It might be dangerous".

"Since when have you been afraid of danger, Baroness?"

They all laughed.

The white and blue Air France Boeing 727 banked slowly to the left. Over the intercom, the Captain's voice pointed out the fishing village of St. Tropez, made famous by Brigitte Bardot, and further along the coast, to the towns of Fréjus and St. Raphael sloping graciously into the ocean.

Simone took her sunglasses out of her purse and rediscovered the enchantment of the Côte d'Azur as the plane started its descent towards Nice seaside airport.

Pierre leaned towards her and watched with her as the white, ocher and beige houses and villas with their orange tile roofs flowed by against the green and grey mountain background and the red soil of the Cap d'Esterel.

Within minutes, Cannes appeared, a colorful cement fantasy decorated with plane tree lined streets moving up towards the medieval village of Mougins; and behind, clinging to the foot of the Alps, the perfume city of Grasse. "What beauty", whispered Pierre. "Every time I land in Nice, after flying along this coast, I can't help thinking that this air route was designed purposely by the Côte d'Azur Tourist Board to make sure each plane exposes its passengers to this magnificent scenery that spreads from St. Tropez to Monaco."

The plane landed and quickly reached its parking position on the tarmac. The steps were moved against the front entrance of the aircraft. Pierre and Simone said "au revoir" to the stewardess and alertly came down the steps and walked the short distance to the terminal, under the warm afternoon sun.

Simone and Pierre followed the other passengers through

the entrance marked "National" and into the terminal itself. In the opinion of many, "L'Aéroport Nice – Côte d'Azur", as it is known, with its terminal surrounded by flower beds, is the most pleasant in the world.

Pierre's caretaker, Joseph, was there awaiting their arrival.

"Bonjour Monsieur, vous avez fait un bon voyage?" "Merci Joseph. Vous reconnaissez sans doute la Barone de Rivoli. Elle séjournera quelques jours chez nous."

"Soyez la bienvenue, Madame, il me fait grand plaisir de vous revoir. Puis-je avoir vos talons de bagages?"

Joseph took the luggage tickets and went to the conveyors where bags were already starting to accumulate.

Soon they were on the Esterel Autoroute driving west towards the Cannes exit that leads to the village of Mougins. "Thank you, Pierre, for having convinced me to come. I feel better already, just being here. What a contrast with Vietnam."

"Please don't think about it. That's all in the past now."

"There are things, Pierre, that one can never forget. The murder of my husband is an unpunished crime. I cannot forget it. I will never forgive the Americans. The ultimate purpose of my life is to revenge Antoine's murder".

"It was the war".

"A war is no excuse for murdering old women, children, defenseless sick people and an unarmed doctor."

"Simone, let's agree that during the next ten days, we will not talk about these ugly things. You are here to rest and enjoy yourself. Please listen to me. I know what's best for you. If you do what I say, if you forget Vietnam while I am here with you, I promise you that I will give you the opportunity to avenge the murder of your husband."

"You will? "How?"

"I'll let you know in due time. Just trust me".

"I have always trusted you, Pierre, you know that."

La Belle Simone was a magnificent villa up on a hill across route Notre-Dame de Vie from Mougins. On one side, the villa afforded a view of the old town up on a peak governing the sight of Cannes to the South and that of Grasse and the foot of the Alps to the North. Large french doors opened from the living room and dining room onto a tile terrace overlooking the manicured garden, where evergreens and olive trees provided a feeling of privacy. There were flowers everywhere and red stone footpaths leading through the property and surrounding the swimming pool. Far below, the orange and beige tiled roofs of Cannes brought a touch of reality to the scenery.

Simone surveyed the living room, gazed at the panorama from the patio and swirled around, her eyes sparkling, and a smile on her face freeing her ivory teeth and creating, below her left cheek, that dimple which had always fascinated men.

"Pierre, you have done miracles with this property. I remember it from our youth. Look at those trees and flowers. It seems that the whole property has blossomed."

"So have you", said Pierre, as he joined her on the terrace and leaned close to her against the ramp. He placed his arm around her shoulders, a gesture full of tenderness.

"That's why I changed the name of the villa to "Belle Simone". His arm pressed her against him playfully.

For a moment, Simone let her head touch his shoulder, then suddenly she whirled away to the end of the patio, "let's have a swim. Is it too cold for a swim?"

"The pool is heated".

"Oh! Come on, Pierre, let's go for a swim. I'll race you".

Simone was first at the pool. She threw her white terry cloth robe on a lounge chair, revealing a clinging one-piece blue and white swimsuit. At 27, childless, she had kept her 20-year-old waist. She had straight ballet dancer legs, and like most French women, narrow hips, a flat belly, smallish but high firm breasts and that straight back and aristocratic high head. She turned towards Pierre who was emerging from the house and with a burst of laughter taunted him. "Catch me, old man!" She ran to the board and dove perfectly, arms and legs stretched like a bird in flight.

Pierre ran to the other side of the pool and dove under where she was surfacing. Her slowly moving legs touched his back. He turned around, grabbed her ankles and brought her to the bottom of the pool before kicking firmly to propel them back to the surface. She shook her head and brushed her blond hair away from her face, "You nearly drowned me!" Placing her hands on his shoulders, she pushed him under water while encircling his waist with her legs.

He grabbed her hips and brought her down with him until they touched bottom, both of them standing on their toes, face to face. He tried to kiss her but she was gone, kicking the water furiously, until she surfaced at the end of the pool. She lifted herself to the edge and sat, feet still dangling in the water.

Pierre raced after her and reached for her feet, which he suddenly brought to his mouth.

"Pierre, stop it, you are acting like a schoolboy."

"It's so good to have you here, Simone. Remember how we used to go to the Palm Beach Club in Cannes and race on the beach until exhaustion or the day we rode our bicycles to Vallauris, without telling anyone. My mother, worried about us, called the Gendarmes. The police brought us back home, two unrepentant sixteen year olds. Those were good days."

"We were young and foolish."

"We were young and happy," said Pierre as he pulled hard on her feet and made her fall into the pool while he swiftly swam away. "Eh, catch me, if you can."

"I will, one day," and all of a sudden she meant it.

The next day, they drove through Valbonne and Biot and turned left towards the mountains. They stopped at St. Paul de Vence, parked the car outside the walls, and walked through the gate into the walled city built by the Romans two thousands years ago.

She told him proudly, "did you know that Pontius Pilate at one time had a summer residence here, in St. Paul? I read that he would sail from Rome to Nice and then come up to St. Paul on horseback. How amazing!"

"It is. Just think, today we are walking on the same cobblestone narrow streets and looking at the same scenery, as he must have done. What a heritage we have in this beautiful country of ours!"

They were holding hands and leisurely stopping at each store window. Over the years, St. Paul had become an enchanting strolling area for visitors to the Côte d'Azur. Every doorway led to a boutique, an art gallery or an artist studio displaying just about everything from colorful Vallauris pottery to curious sculptures carved out of the thousand year old olive trees found on the surrounding hills.

"I must confess, Simone, that I have not walked like this with anyone for a long time. The Sunday afternoon walks that the three of us used to enjoy before you and Antoine moved to Vietnam were the highlights of my weeks. I guess I have missed them and had not realized it until now."

"What about all those elegant Parisian girls? Don't they go after the most eligible bachelor in the Government service?"

"Perhaps they do, but I have never walked with them".

"Then, what do you do?"

"Now you are being indiscreet, Madame la Barone."

They drove back, talking about the old days, forgotten friends, remembering the pleasures of their youth and the happiness of their friendship.

In the evening, they stopped at one of the South of France's three star restaurants, 'La Bonne Auberge' on highway 7 linking Nice to Antibes. The chef came to their table to greet them and recommended his Ragoût de Turbotin and Canard au Citron. Pierre ordered a bottle of La Doucette Pouilly Fumé. As they sipped the white wine and ate the superb food, they never stopped talking, remembering so many happy events, forgetting the tragedies of Vietnam, the secret and mysterious demands of his office, the death of Antoine, and the loneliness of her widowhood.

Later, they drove back to Pierre's villa using the Autoroute as if eager to return home rapidly.

"Thank you, Pierre, for a very beautiful day and an excellent dinner. You have guaranteed my pleasant dreams for tonight".

"Please don't retire now, Simone. Look! Joseph has lit a fire. Join me for a cognac. I have Monet, your favorite, and I will let you select the music. This has been a day filled with pleasant memories. Don't end it yet."

Simone sat on the thick shag carpet waiting for Pierre to bring their cognacs. They rolled their glasses slowly in their hands to warm the cognac and raised them religiously to their lips, their eyes closed, savoring the smoothness of the liquor.

The red, blue and orange reflections from the fire threw a luminous glow on Simone's face. The heat started to penetrate her and she moved away slightly and placed her back against an armchair. She put her glass on the floor next to her and raising her knees, linked her arms around them, her eyes fixing the strange dance of the flames.

Pierre rolled on his side and leaned on his elbow close to her.

"The last time we sat like this", reminisced Simone, "was nine years ago when we went skiing at Mégève and your parents retired early on New Year's eve, leaving us to dream in front of the fireplace. I still remember because it was the first time we had ever kissed as man and woman."

"And at that time, it troubled me", recalled Pierre, "I thought perhaps I had offended you."

"You lay next to me as you are doing now and placed your head on my knees."

"And when you ruffled my hair," said Pierre, "I knew you had accepted my kiss."

"Your kiss…I had accepted all of you," exclaimed Simone, "we were so inexperienced."

"I am not sure one finds more pleasure or more happiness with experience."

"Perhaps you are right, Pierre, as you acquire experience, it seems that the pleasure of wanting and the mystery of discovery fade away."

Pierre moved closer to Simone and placed his head on her knees, his face turned away from her, studying the fire. His hand moved to her feet, his fingers gently stroking her ankles.

Simone playfully messed up his hair. "Think of how afraid we were that your mother would come out of her room and catch us."

"After the second kiss, Simone, you stopped all thinking."

"I was still scared to death."

"You were melting with desire."

"Now you are going to tell me that I seduced you!"

"You did nothing to stop me."

"I said nothing to encourage you."

"But you kissed me a third time, our longest kiss ever."

Pierre lifted his head and looked at Simone. She bent and kissed his forehead and then his cheek, her lips lingering there, close to his ear, feeling his warmth on her face.

"It was such a long time ago, Simone."

"For me it was yesterday."

"Nine years of our lives have flowed by," said Pierre, "like a torrent rushing down the mountain and throwing itself into the oblivion of the ocean."

"All of my life has not gone into oblivion. I have kept some precious memories of Antoine, a wonderful husband, and of you, his favorite friend. You both made me very happy."

"Because we both loved you."

"Perhaps Antoine knew of your feelings for me, but he never expressed any jealousy."

"I was the jealous one, although I knew he made you a better husband."

"Perhaps you would make a better lover." She smiled, her dimple taunting him. "Let me refill our glasses."

She bent her head again and this time kissed him on the mouth like the brush of a butterfly wing and then bit his lower lip and smoothed the bite by taking his lip between hers, wet and soft. "Now let me go, lover boy."

She kicked off her shoes and glided barefoot to the bar dividing the living room from the dining room. She refilled their glasses with Monet cognac. She smelled one of the glasses. "I have not had Monet since I left France".

"I think of you every time I drink it."

"And how often is that?"

"At least three time a week."

"You drink too much," said Simone, dropping to her knees in front of him and offering him one of the glasses.

He brought the offering hand to his lips and kissed three of her fingers, took the glass and raised the inside of her hand to his mouth. He kissed it and the tip of his tongue traced a circle on her palm. She withdrew her hand with a knowledgeable look in her eyes.

"That tickles". She stretched on the carpet, her back to the fireplace, and her head in the cradle of his arms.

"Then I shall try to kiss you without tickling," and he quickly kissed her ear and his tongue flickered inside.

"Pierre! You know I can't stand that. It makes me shiver and covers me with goose pimples".

"Show me".

She threw her head back exposing her throat. For a moment, Pierre gazed at the reflection of the flames on the mirror of her creamy skin. He could see an artist standing there with his brushes mixing reds, oranges and yellows, whites and blues and expertly applying the hue of colors to her throat. He started to kiss her in the hollow below her shoulder bone and his mouth slid up the side of her throat gently until it reached the back of her ear.

"Don't you dare," she warned him.

His mouth followed the contour of her ear to her temple, remaining there for a short while and then his half parted lips drew the pattern of her eyebrow and followed the ridge of her nose until he found her lips. He kissed her upper lip and drew it out very slowly between his. With the tip of his tongue he wet his mouth and this time took her lower lip. She bit his exposed upper lip.

"No violence, Baroness" and he kissed her fully on her waiting mouth, but not hard, just fully with wet lips. She turned her body, accommodating his caress as her arms encircled his shoulder with her fingers reaching the back of his hair. She ran one nail up and down his neck provocatively and opened her mouth just enough to permit his tongue to touch hers, moving very slowly.

He was the first to pull away. Her eyes were still closed. Nine years of suppressed tenderness rushed from his heart to his mouth, his eyes, and the tip of his fingers. His hand formed the shape of her shoulder and followed the line of her body while feeling the softness of her breast under the silky blouse.

She opened her eyes and read through his. His hand continued its caress, holding her close, as he rolled on his back without either of them letting go their embrace. She stayed on top of him, her face buried in the hollow of his shoulder. "Take me to your room," she begged.

On October 15, 1966 Andrew Robertson completed his first two years of service in Dubai for Grand American Bank. It had been his idea in 1962 that the bank expand in the Middle East although, at that time, there was little to indicate what importance this part of the world would eventually play in the international monetary game. Or was it war?

Like many other international banks, Grand American Bank had established a branch in Beirut in the late 50's. It was while he managed that branch that Robertson frequently reminded New York that Beirut was only a depository city, a transient point for funds moving from various Arab countries toward London or Switzerland.

Robertson had watched with envy the tremendous growth of Beirut's Intra Bank from a few million to a billion dollar organization, with substantial interest in Middle East Airline, French Shipyards and real estate in New York. But Robertson knew also how vulnerable Intra Bank was because most of its funds came from a limited number of Emirs and Sheiks who managed their fortunes in accordance with their whims and wishes and paid little attention to the daily course of monetary events. They showed little loyalty to their bankers and banked with Intra Bank because Intra was a success story and it was chic in Middle East circles to say, "I bank at Intra".

Robertson's argument with New York had been that Grand American Bank had to expand in each one of the Arab countries and establish direct on-the-spot relationship with the Emirs and Sheiks in order to control funds at the source before they reached Beirut or Switzerland. This is exactly what the British had done decades ago and it explained why the bulk of Arab money was still entrusted to British banks.

As a first step Robertson had strongly recommended the establishment of a branch in Dubai. Already in 1960 there were signs that Dubai would play an important role in the export of gold and other precious metals to India and China, particularly. Even then, its small ports were being used for a substantial import and export business. He had had an opportunity to meet the Ruler, Sheik Roshid Ben Said Al-Maktoum, who in 1958 had succeeded his father, Sheik Said. He had listened carefully to the development plans laid out by the father that were now expected to be implemented by the son. Robertson had observed with great interest the efforts and moneys expended to find oil offshore by the Dubai Petroleum Company, a wholly owned subsidiary of Continental Oil Company of Delaware, a client of Grand American Bank in New York. They all knew that there was oil there and soon it would be found and Dubai would take its place among the oil producing states.

Finally, in 1964, New York had approved a Middle East expansion program on the condition that Robertson moved from Beirut to Dubai and agreed to stay there for at least three years while in charge of the bank's business in the Trucial States. Two year had gone by and Grand American Bank showed little results for his efforts. Robertson knew that he needed to produce quickly a tangible proof that his judgment had been correct and that Grand American Bank, by being at l'avant garde of the US banks invasion of the Middle East, stood to reap millions in profits.

Robertson's next promotion to the International Banking Division at head office, a first step to his ascendancy to the presidency, depended on his performance in Dubai today.

Using Dubai as his base, Robertson had established precious contacts across the United Arab Emirates. As a result, he was entertained frequently in the palaces of Sheiks from Bahrain to Qatar and from Ajman to Fumairah, but little business had come to his bank because the British had preceded him everywhere and what deposit business didn't go to the British banks still went to Intra Bank.

Robertson was an impressive looking banker. He stood six feet four, had unusually large square shoulders. He displayed the aggressiveness of a former college football player and the ruthlessness of an ex-sergeant in the U.S. Marines. Hard hitting, selfish and extremely ambitious, he understood two things: money and the power it buys.

Everything else was a waste of time. A solid drinker, he had little respect for fine food, books, music or any type of cultural activities. They were a waste of energy. During the week, he read the Wall Street Journal, Barons, the American Banker, Times, Newsweek and the International Herald Tribune. Weekends, he glanced at Fortune and Business Week. That was his culture. At the bank, they referred to him as the "big man", not only because he was physically big, but also because he handled people in an arrogant and domineering manner. Sex was an animal need which he felt daily, satisfied often, quickly, without the pleasure of foreplay and without the tenderness of the aftermath. "Buy them, screw them and send them home," he used to say. He always kept a few dollar bills in the top drawer of his bed side table to pay for the taxi fare of his visitors.

At 39, Robertson felt ready. Ready to move to the headquarters of Grand American Bank and ready to exercise the power of money. He also felt impatient. He had been transferred from branch to branch since joining the bank sixteen years ago. He was given an assignment to the branch in Hong Kong because of his knowledge of the Far East acquired during the war. Then on to London "to broaden his field of experience", they had said. He still hated his brief stay in Paris. He called Parisians snobs, taxi drivers rude and found French women too romantic and expensive. He had enjoyed Nassau in the Bahamas, where he learned to drink gin and tonic, discovered the intricacies of tax haven operations and qualified for his transfer to Beirut.

Had he made a mistake in assessing the banking business

potential of Grand American Bank in the United Arab Emirates? Had he risked his whole future at Grand American Bank by accepting the vice presidency of the Middle East region? He could not have. He still remembered the words of Steve Blackburn, who was soon to retire as Chairman of the bank to be replaced by his nephew, Peter Hardrock, the grandson of the founder.

"Andrew, we are depending entirely on your strong and persistent recommendations. Most board members discard the Middle East countries outside of Israel as unimportant. We already derive a good volume of business from that region through the various American oil companies that are our clients in the US and that operate there. We enjoy this business without having to establish local branches to cater to all those difficult Arabs and camel riding Sheiks. But I trust your judgment. I always have. I also believe that a man like you should be prepared to support his own recommendations and, therefore, I am asking you to move to Dubai as Vice President, Middle East. For us, it's a new department; it's a new branch, a new region. For you, it's a new challenge. You want it, it's all yours. You don't take it, we don't open in Dubai. That's the Board's decision. I agree with it, so does Hardrock."

"What's in it for me?" Robertson had asked.

"The International Division...if you succeed."

That meant one of the three senior posts in line for the presidency of the bank and it came directly from the mouth of the Chairman! No banker can refuse such bait. Robertson didn't. "When do you want me to go?"

"As soon as you have made a full review of the US corporations that are clients of ours here in New York and that do business in the Middle East. Business Relations Department will brief you. We also have a somewhat outdated list of who's who in the Arab world. I want you to study it carefully, it should be useful and you can update it from Dubai. Finally, I want you to join me for lunch tomorrow in our executive dining room. I have invited Sheik Al-Madir and Hardrock to join us."

"You had already invited..."

"Andrew, I have known you for a long time. I know the type of man you are. I was sure you were not going to turn down this challenge. You never have in the past, and in this case, after all, it's your recommendation. Anyway, you should find our guest most interesting and he can be very useful to you."

"Who is this guy, this Sheik?"

"Sheik Al-Madir is an astute merchant from Dubai who at one time worked for the CIA. I don't know whether he still does. I believe they paid him by securing for him some exclusive franchises for the Middle East, such as Coca Cola and Westinghouse. He is one of the few Arabs I know who has a US university education – Harvard '48, I believe. His connection with Coca Cola brought him to us as a client. We financed his first bottling plant. We have also enjoyed some of his other banking business but not all of it. He banks extensively with other banks in Beirut and naturally, in Switzerland. I have already told him of our plan to open in Dubai. For him, it is very important. He wants to go back to his Ruler and take credit for the opening of a branch of Grand American Bank in Dubai. Let him have his pleasure. It might bring you dividends."

As soon as Robertson had arrived in Dubai, he had contacted Sheik Al-Madir and appointed him his personal adviser in the Trucial States. The Sheik had found him a house, had vacated half of the ground floor of his own office building for the bank premises, had introduced Robertson to most worthwhile businessmen in Dubai and surrounding States and had got him invited to the palace of the Rulers. It became known that Robertson was a friend of the Sheik and that he enjoyed his protection.

Robertson had to pay for this friendship. The Sheik's lines of credit were increased substantially. He built two new office buildings in Dubai and the bank provided the mortgages. He wanted a private plane and the bank bought a DC9 and leased it to him at favorable terms. He knew that oil would soon be found in Dubai and he decided to order two large tankers, the bank financed both. In the mind of Robertson, these loans were not made in appreciation for the sponsorship of the bank in Dubai by the Sheik. After all, when you are Grand American Bank, whose sponsorship do you need? These loans were favors to the Sheik and one day the Sheik would have to repay. Robertson would see to that. Meanwhile, Robertson needed the Sheik.

"Get me Sheik Al-Madir on the phone," shouted Robertson. Robertson's American secretary jumped in her chair and within minutes buzzed him. "He is on line two, Mr. Robertson".

"Ben? Andrew, here. How are you?

"I am well, thank Allah. And you?"

"I am great but I have no Allah to thank. Only my doctor

and my daily jogging in this awful climate of yours. Say, Ben, I have something rather confidential that I would like to discuss with you."

"You know that what you tell me in confidence dies with me. It is said..."

"Ben, keep Allah and your religion for yourself. I would trust you even if you were a Jew", Robertson laughed.

"Andrew, you should respect my religion and not mention the name of my enemies".

"Sorry if I hurt your feelings. Say, why don't you join me for dinner at home tonight? The wife is gone to Geneva to take the children back to school and I am alone at the house. I'll provide the dinner and then send the staff away. You bring the usual entertainment. We can talk business for one hour and then play until morning".

"I must go to Abu Dhabi early in the morning".

"After our talk tonight, you may want to change your plans. Is nine o'clock all right?"

"It's fine, Andrew, but are you sure you would not prefer to discuss this business matter now and keep the entire evening for pleasure?"

"This business cannot be discussed over the phone or in my office and I have never known you to mind mixing some business with your pleasures".

"See you at nine."

"Thank you, Ben. See you then."

Robertson placed the phone back on its cradle, leaned forward and shouted again, "Margie, bring me the Intra Bank file". Margie walked in with two thick manila folders.

"Put them here". Robertson cleaned the right side of his desk. As Margie leaned to deposit the files, Robertson nudged her breast with the tip of his fingers.

"Andrew! Please."

"Come here."

"I have work to do."

"Come here, I said."

"The report to New York will never be ready today".

"Margie", his tone had a warning sound.

She came around the desk. She leaned against it, standing to his right, staring at the city over his shoulder.

"Are you mad or something?" he asked.

"Andrew, you have a dinner reception tonight with entertainment, remember?"

"You were listening on my phone?"

"You did not close your door and your whispering was rather loud."

"So?"

"So keep you energy for tonight and leave me alone."

Robertson placed his hand between her thighs touching her wet crotch.

"Don't be so vulgar. It is hot here. That's all."

Robertson brought his hand to his nose, smiled, kissed it, then put it back between her legs. "Margie, you will never be able to refuse me".

Once again she knew she could not resist him. "Let me close the door, at least."

Margie was married to Jack Phillips, a petroleum engineer on loan from the Continental Oil Company of Delaware to its subsidiary the Dubai Petroleum Company. Phillips was in charge of their offshore exploration program in Dubai. Bored at home during the day, with no children to keep her busy, bored at night with a husband always too tired or too drunk, Margie had been the first employee to join Robertson in Dubai. She had also been his first affair there. The office was their refuge. For both work and sex.

Dubai is a small territory of 2,500 square miles with a population of less than 60,000 people. Dubai, the capital, is even smaller and there are few places where couples can go to satisfy their sexual impulses without being seen, especially foreigners.

Robertson felt safer in his office, so did Margie. Within their second week of working together, Robertson had returned from lunch one day with a bottle of gin and six bottles of tonic. "Margie, let's close the office early and celebrate."

"Celebrate what?"

"Our success. The fact that in less than one month, with your help, we have this office running smoothly. The fact that you are here, I am here and it's too goddamn hot to go outside. Bring some ice."

They had sat on the couch for a while drinking gin and tonics, Robertson reminiscing about his stay in Beirut, his winnings and losses at the casino, his adventures in Hong Kong, his escapades in Nassau, his boredom in Paris. Suddenly Robertson had asked her, "how is your sex life, Margie?"

"Mr. Robertson, really! I don't think that's any of your business."

"Margie, from now on you can call me Andrew. As to your sex life being my business, you can bet your sweet little cunt that it is. I have a theory and it has never failed. If you are unhappy at home, you are unhappy at the office. If you are sexually frustrated at home, you will frustrate me at the office."

"Mr. Robertson, I don't have to listen to such talk. This is not part of my job".

"Andrew to you, I told you. This is part of my job. I need to make sure that you are happy. So, my question about your sex life is quite appropriate."

Margie had deposited her glass on the coffee table and risen from the couch. "I'm leaving. Find yourself another secretary."

Robertson had stepped over the table, grabbed her, wheeled her around and kissed her hard. Very hard and very long. She had fought him at first but then his kiss had soften her, the violence also. He had pressed further against her and she had felt him hard against her thigh. He wanted her! And darn it, he was right. She was frustrated and she was bored. Jack had gradually moved away from her and lost interest in their sex life. He was always too tired. She had begged him for a while, then let it go.

"I don't want another secretary," Robertson was murmuring in her ear, "you are doing fine, very fine." He kissed her again while his hands were traveling all over her. He raised her skirt and touched the flesh of her bare legs. She trembled, out of control.

"I hate you, Andrew Robertson!" and, despite herself, she was kissing him back and holding one of his legs between hers. His hands were inside her panties and he was pushing her towards the couch and undressing her, his pants now open. Without further preambles, he had taken her.

This had been two years ago. She now called him Andrew and he took her every time he felt like it. She always submitted to him, not so much because she wanted him, but because she had no one else to turn to, no one else to sleep with, no one else to love. The "big man" had become her whole life, work and sex. But recently he seemed to have tired of her. They had quarreled frequently. Like today, after she had locked the door of the office.

"Andrew, I don't want to have sex with you today."

"Margie, don't start that again. I just showed you, you are all wet and ready."

"Why don't you marry me, Andrew?"

He looked at her, shocked. It had never entered his mind. He was married and had children. His wife had passed all the tests of a good corporate wife. She never interfered with his career. There was no more love between them but they maintained a good public image. He supported her generously and in return she let him have his ambitions, his activities, his business, his travels and his adventures. "Make sure you are clean when you come home", had been her only request. But now this secretary is a bit too fat, a bit too sexy, and a bit too ambitious.

"Why don't you Andrew? You don't love your wife. You spend more time with me than you do with her. We work well together and you like screwing me. So why don't you?"

He had answered her cautiously. "That would be foolish, wouldn't it? If I married you, you would have to stay home. Being my wife, you would not be permitted to work with me.

It's against the rules and, as a matter of principle, I would not let you work. Certainly not with me. So you would lose what you have and I would have to find myself another secretary."

"Another cunt, you mean!"

"Margie, really, you are being unreasonable. Come here. Open your legs again"

"Don't touch me. Don't you ever touch me. You don't need me anyway. So go to your Sheik and his entertainment. They can't read, they can't write and I hope they can't fuck either. I hope they are a bunch of faggots!" She had walked out and slammed the door.

I have enough problems now, mused Robertson, without this sex crazy woman on top of everything. She will have to go. And then he looked at the couch and remembered all the pleasant afternoons they had spent on it. He raised his finger to his nose, sniffed, and smiled.

Robertson lived in a house that Sheik Al-Madir had built for his brother, Mohammed Ibn, but the brother had decided to move to New York permanently. Robertson found himself enjoying the true oriental decor. The house was built for living and entertaining, especially the living area that covered nearly half of the house and opened into a large landscaped terrace with a pool and a fountain. As a firm believer in the teaching of the Quran, Sheik Al-Madir never drank nor gambled at home. "Satan desires only to create enmity and hatred between you by means of liquor and gambling", said the Holy Book. But the same book said, "Allah requires not of anyone that which is beyond his capacity," and Sheik Al-Madir felt that outside of his home he could not refuse the offerings of his friend, Andrew Robertson. So they sat in Robertson's library, sipping gin and tonic while the entertainers waited outside.

"Ben, since my arrival in Dubai, you have been most helpful to me. You have guided me, assisted me and protected me. If it were not for you, my bank would not have achieved the success it has met since we came here and my reputation in New York would not be as good as it is now."

"It is said, "No one can bear the burden of another"."

"Please Ben leave your funny religion aside for one night. What I wish to discuss with you is of the utmost importance for you. I am not the type that wastes much time in expressing appreciation for services received, so it is difficult for me to say what I am trying to say. Ben, I like you. I owe you a lot and I want to say thank you."

"Andrew, you are getting sentimental."

"I'm not getting sentimental, goddamn it, I am only trying to help a friend, but in doing so, I have to breach all secrecy pledges that are binding me to my bank."

"What do you mean?"

"I mean that I possess some information that concerns you. A lot of you. Millions of dollars that belong to you and some of your friends and associates. But my information is totally confidential. Top secret. Nobody is supposed to know".

"How do you know?"

"I know because I have this report that came to me as Vice President in charge of the Middle East affairs of Grand American Bank before it being dispatched to our New York headquarters. I have stopped it here. It's in this file". Robertson flipped the cover of a file folder in front of him. It read "Strictly Confidential". As he turned the cover, a white sheet marked in red faced Robertson. "This file contains confidential information, Code 1000. Do not read unless you are an authorized officer within the 1000 Group. If you are not, return this file to Confidential Filing immediately."

"Ben, I am going to walk out of this room for fifteen minutes as I need to check the arrangements for dinner. I am leaving this confidential bank file on my desk. Beneath this top sheet there is a fifteen page report that should interest you greatly."

"Why do you want me to read it if it is confidential? Are you not taking a personal risk?"

"It's my way of saying thank you, but swear to me, in front of Allah and everything else that's dear to you, that you will never divulge the existence of this report and its content to anyone, anywhere, at anytime."

"Andrew, you know very well..."

"Swear it!"

"I do, in front of Allah, most Gracious, ever Merciful."

"You've got fifteen minutes."

Robertson left and Sheik Al-Madir reached anxiously for the thick file, looked at the cover and front page and turned to page one.

October 15, 1964

From   – Vice President, Beirut
To – Regional Vice President, Dubai
Subject   – Intra Bank, Beirut (STRICTLY CONFIDENTIAL
– Code 1000)

We have serious reasons to believe that Intra Bank is in deep trouble. Yesterday, their senior Vice President in Beirut came to our offices asking us to increase our correspondent balances with them by at least one and a half million dollars. We declined...

The report went on for fifteen pages describing the liquidity problems of Intra Bank, its commitments, and its cash flow requirements. It commented at length on its unconventional investments in Middle East Airline and the French Shipyard Company. It covered the assistance granted by Grand American Bank in the past, the strength of its management, the small   number of large depositors and concluded:

In our opinion, Intra Bank has become a bad risk. We have today decided to reduce to the minimum our funds on deposit with them. We are also thinking of demanding the reimbursement of all our advances. We don't think Intra Bank would survive such actions. Their position is hopeless.

> *Arthur Thompson*
> *Vice President, Beirut*
> *Grand American Bank*

Sheik Al-Madir closed the file and placed it back on Robertson's desk. He was greatly distressed. He and the Ruler of Dubai were substantial clients of Intra Bank. So were a number of their relatives. He could hardly believe what he had just read. The President of Intra Bank had visited him less than two weeks ago. No concern had transpired. But now there was this report. The irrefutable proof that Intra Bank was in trouble. If Grand American were withdrawing their funds from Intra Bank, he should quickly do the same and also tell the Ruler. He had sworn to Robertson not to tell anyone but the Ruler would not tell. He would have him swear by Allah to keep the secret. He could also trust his brothers. They would not betray him.

Robertson returned, looked at him, placed the report in the top drawer of his desk, locked it, and announced, "dinner is served."

"Andrew, wait".

"Sorry, Ben, dinner can't wait. Come my friend. The only thing I am going to say to you is remember your oath of secrecy. Otherwise there is nothing to say. The file is closed. It's time for pleasure."

"Andrew, please allow me one word. I had planned to visit Abu Dhabi tomorrow. I have just at this instant remembered some urgent business in Beirut. With your permission, I would like to leave now. The entertainers will stay."

"But there are no more flights out of Dubai airport tonight," said Robertson.

"There is a late flight out of Sharja. It is only ten miles from here. The road is not good but I could be there in half an hour."

"But Ben, I was looking forward to our dining together."

"Another time, Andrew. Believe me, this is an emergency."

"What do I do with the entertainers? I can't command them. I don't speak Arabic, yet."

"Just clap your hands, they are well trained."

With a smile on his face, Robertson watched Sheik Al-Madir drive away. His plan was working. The Sheik had believed what he had read. It was a brilliant idea. There was no other way to fight Intra Bank. You had to destroy them. They were too close to this Arab world. Too aggressive. Taking decisions on the spot, as needed, without having to write lengthy reports to head office and without having to wait for a senile board of directors to make up their mind. By the time they did, the business opportunity was gone. They invested in too many local industries and businesses, adept at assessing profit-making transactions quickly. "I'm going to get the bastards and their cockeyed flamboyant President, if it is the last thing I do," hissed Robertson.

He had manufactured the report entirely. Sure, some of Intra Bank's investments were rather unconventional when seen from New York, but this did not make the bank imprudent. Unlike Grand American Bank in America, intra Bank was not subject to the authority of half a dozen regulatory bodies. Therefore, it was freer to do banking as banking should be done. In fact, its officers were pretty good at their trade and Robertson, who admired no one, always felt a twinge of respect for them. But now the successes of these bastards were undermining his future and his chances of acceding to the presidency of Grand American Bank.

His friend, the Sheik, was going to put a halt to that. His friend, the Sheik, was going to repay his debt for favors rendered, unknowingly.

He called his butler, "take that food away, I am not going to eat." The Arab servant looked at him and then at the food hesitantly. "Did you not hear me? Take this goddamn food away and bring me a bottle of gin and lots of tonic water. After that, you can leave and tell the maid to go also. I want to be left alone."

He moved to the living room and sat uncomfortably on the oriental cushions spread on the floor. "I am too darn big to sit on these sissy seats," he thought. "One day, I'll buy myself a real Lazy-Boy". He clapped his hands awkwardly.

Immediately six dancers emerged from the shadowed terrace moving to the rhythm of their finger cymbals. Three girls and three boys, young, healthy and exciting behind the diaphanous veils which were attached to their waists, flowing in the air under the movements of their legs. The girls wore mini bras decorated with glass jewelry. The boys wore a large gold medallion over their bare chests.

At first their dance was slow and enticing but as the rhythm increased, the boys started to perform acrobatics around the hip-twisting girls. "I don't like acrobatics," said Robertson aloud. The dance went on. "How do I stop it?" he asked himself.

He stood up, took three steps towards the dancers and clapped his hands. The dancers stopped, uncertain. Robertson snatched the bra from one of them. She looked at her nude breasts, then at Robertson and spoke softly in Arabic to her partners. They rushed behind Robertson and started to throw cushions where he was standing, in the center of the room. The first dancer placed her hands on his shoulders and pressed him down. He understood and dropped heavily on the pile of cushions.

"Me Ladya," she said.

The other dancers sat in a half circle on the floor, their legs folded in front of them, their finger cymbals clicking over their heads. Ladya started to dance lasciviously to a new rhythm. She danced close to him, so close he could smell her and, when she turned, she threw beads of perspiration at him. "Eh, you're spoiling my drink," he said half drunkenly as he finished his glass. One of the male dancers fetched the bottle of gin and the ice and tonic and placed them next to Robertson who helped himself copiously. "This is the life," he thought. Ladya was bending over him, her erect nipples tracing the part in his hair. He tried to grab her. She threw her veils over him and pulled slowly while moving in waves in front of him, until his head was between her fast approaching legs. Before he had time to raise his hands, she had rolled away, laughing loudly, and one of the male dancers had jumped from his sitting position to replace her. Robertson had never paid attention to a eunuch before and he wondered what they looked like undressed. What was left there? He looked through the veils but could not discern anything. He wanted to touch, but the dancer lay with his back on the floor, his legs bent at the knees under him, twisting and moving towards Robertson, his body sliding on his shoulders. Over his head, his hands were interpreting a ballet of their own, undulating, the long fingers moving the cymbals in unison with the rhythm of his body.

His shoulders were now touching the cushions where Robertson sat and his hands kept dancing as they moved closer, so close that the cymbals touched Robertson's pants.

"Get away from me, you goddamn faggot," he shouted. The dancer misunderstood him. He clinked his cymbals enthusiastically and rolled away towards his companions. They all rose and resumed their dancing together. The other two girls had removed their bras and as they passed in front of Robertson, they dropped them on his lap. He hurled the bras back at them screaming, "leave me alone!" and poured more gin in his glass. Robertson was drunk, happily drunk as he thought of Sheik Al-Madir now on his way to Beirut. Madly drunk, he felt the pleasurable touch of the cymbals of the boy, who was now pirouetting, the gold medallion flying, his skin gleaming from sweat in the subdued light of the room. "

Simone de Rivoli stood in the glass elevator of the Hyatt House Hotel in Atlanta and scanned the approaching ground floor searching for Andrew Robertson, who she expected to find at the bar. She could not decide whether the design of this unusual hotel was an architectural accomplishment or a monument to bad taste. Seven years after its opening, the hotel was still the center of attraction, not only of Atlanta, but also of the whole South East coast of the United States. Shooting twenty-seven floors above Peachview Avenue, the lobby of the hotel was an enclosed cavernous room extending to the glass-covered roof. From the inverted pyramid bar or the open terrace restaurant on the ground floor, guests constantly lifted and lowered their heads as if nodding their acceptance, while they watched the nineteen century style glass elevator zoom up and down the twenty-seven floors in the center of the begging void over the lobby.

As expected, Simone found Robertson at the bar. "Mr. Robertson, there you are. I have been looking all over for you. If you are free now, Mr. Hardrock would like to glance at your speech."

"I'll be right up," replied Robertson. "What room is he in?"

"Suite 2702."

"Let me sign this bill and I'll come up with you, Simone."

Peter Hardrock, Andrew Robertson, Simone de Rivoli and a number of senior officers of Grand American Bank had arrived from New York late in the afternoon to attend the 1977 Annual Convention of the American Bankers Association scheduled to open the next day.

Andrew Robertson had been elected President of the Association at the 1976 convention in San Francisco and, as retiring President, he was scheduled to address the three thousand delegates on the opening day of the new convention, during which a new President would be elected.

Simone had joined the Bank eight months earlier and had been asked by Hardrock to accompany the group to the 1977 convention where her assistance would no doubt be required.

As they walked to Hardrock's suite, Robertson turned to Simone, "what are you doing for dinner?"

"I have made no plans as I don't know how late Mr. Hardrock will want me."

"Just remember that we brought you to Atlanta to assist me also if I needed you," retorted Robertson.

"But Louise is here."

"Louise is only a secretary. You are an executive assistant. You certainly don't expect me to ask Louise's opinion on my speech?"

"She typed it. She may have some helpful suggestions."

"I prefer yours," grinned Robertson.

Simone knocked at the door of Penthouse suite 2702, "Come in," said Hardrock. "Thank you for coming up so quickly, Andrew. I thought that perhaps we could review your speech together before we get involved with the entertaining of our guests. I understand that our courtesy suite is already crowded and a number of bankers are looking for us."

"I have an extra copy of the speech here," said Robertson. "You want to read it or do you want me to rehearse it in front of you?"

"Will you need me, Mr. Hardrock?" asked Simone. Hardrock looked at her and then at Robertson who nodded. "Yes, please stay, Madame de Rivoli, we want your opinion and you can also take note of the last minute corrections."

"I am at your disposal," replied Simone. She took a seat discreetly at the far end of the room.

"A drink Andrew?" asked Hardrock.

"I'll need one if I am going to go through this whole speech with you. Gin and tonic, as usual."

"Madame de Rivoli, will you fix us some drinks. You should find what is necessary on the table there. Call room service if you need anything else. I'll have a scotch and soda. Let's go Andrew."

Robertson's speech had been written by Jack Wannamaker, the bank's senior economist. Robertson's only contribution had been an introduction joke and a "Gold bless you" ending — a pun on God bless you — otherwise it was an economist's speech.

It reviewed the year 1976-1977 in depth, from the election of a new US President in the fall of 1976 to an unacceptable increase in the inflation rate. Led by Barry Hardrock, the brother of Peter, the Democrats had won the November 1976 contest. President Ford had had no chance, but he never admitted that his administration had been a failure.

He had faced unsolvable economic problems at home, including the highest unemployment rate since 1933, an economy which could not be primed up, a fast growing inflation rate, despite the slump in industrial production, and an international monetary mess fueled by the irrational flow of the petrodollars and the refusal of Government Heads to take the electorally unpopular steps needed to balance their budgets, discipline their politicians and restore some sense of law and order in international trade.

President Ford and Vice President Rockefeller had tried to give the country some leadership but the politicians derailed their efforts. The Democrats controlled both Houses and they were not prepared to let a Republican President save the country. That's a Democratic prerogative anyway. If the country must suffer in the meantime, who cares? "Politicking before statesmanship" that's the motto of the old and new politicians.

When, at the insistence of Rockefeller, President Ford hardened his position, the press attacked his plans or his nominees or his commissions and criticized and demolished his best-drawn plans before giving him a chance to implement them. "It's for the good of the country and in the best interest of the public," they claimed in one-inch high headings across the nation's newspapers front pages.

Barry Hardrock's presidential election had been assured before the voting day because he was rich. In times of high prices and unemployment, the public felt that it needed a rich man in the White House. Perhaps he would distribute some of his wealth. Who knows, part of it might fall into the hands of each elector. Anyway, poor Presidents were known to be poor risks. Look at Nixon's performance.

Then, remember the success of the wealthy Kennedys. Hardrock had proven to be a reassuring man. Older, dependable, above petty politics, experienced in business and in Government affairs, he offered hope against all odds.

After praising President Hardrock for his State of the Union message and his imaginative, no nonsense, internal policies since acceding to the presidency, Robertson's speech dwelled on the international monetary scene and its effects on US banking.

The flow of money from the Western countries to the oil producing States and, more particularly to those of the Middle East, had increased continuously since the oil embargo in the fall of 1973. The earnings of the members of the Organization of Petroleum Exporting Countries, known as OPEC, had since reached more than 175 billion dollars. By mid-1978, they were expected to exceed 300 billion dollars. Close to 60% of these funds were held by banks in short term deposits. That was a most dangerous situation that had brought about the failure of some twenty banks in the US and elsewhere in 1974, nearly fifty in 1975, sixty-six in 1976 and forty-one in the first six months of 1977 alone.

Oil producing Arab states refused to place their funds in long-term deposits. They did not trust any of the host countries. They never knew which country would suddenly decide to freeze all Arab deposits, or their assets for that matter, in retaliation for the upsetting effects of the high oil prices on the world economy. For that reason, very little of their funds were invested long term in oil importing countries.

Banks tried, for a while, to turn away the short-term deposits. They refused to pay interest but the Arabs were not seeking interest. "Allah has made buying and selling lawful and has made the taking of interest unlawful" said the Quran . And when one sensible bank turned away a deposit, it went to a "more aggressive" bank and through the system very often ended up in the refusing bank as a correspondent bank deposit. Bankers are taught that the business of banking is the business of accepting deposits and investing them by way of loans. Bank management is judged and paid on its performance. Shareholders always expect record earnings and record dividends. If your bank accepts Arab deposits, it is assured of establishing records in growth of assets and earnings. Don't talk about the ominous presence of those short-term liabilities! Just accept the dangerous deposits and cross your fingers.

If everyone does it, the practice will be established and accepted. The danger will not go away but no one will mention it and everyone will feel secured in their insecurity. More banks will collapse when suddenly substantial deposits are withdrawn but that's always the problem of the other banks. It never happens to your bank.

So the Arabs' multi billion petro-dollars went on short-term deposits with banks throughout the world and multiplied as banks re-deposited their surpluses with each other. A billion dollar deposit with a Swiss bank was re-deposited by them with a British bank that re-deposited it in a New York bank who would re-deposit it with a California bank. From there, the California bank fed funds to a number of its smaller US correspondents. The original billion dollars had multiplied four to six times, the same billion increasing the balance sheet of each bank along the way, setting up a chain. A chain of unavoidable disasters.

"Our banking system is sounder than ever," Robertson would proclaim in his speech. "Total assets of all US banks increased by more than fifty-five billion dollars last year. Those of Grand American Bank by more than twenty billion for the second consecutive year and we expect a further similar growth in 1978. For the first time in banking history, the assets of one bank have now reached the hundred billion dollar mark." There would be applause. Robertson would look at Hardrock, who would nod with a contented smile on his face, and then Robertson, the President of the largest bank in the world, would survey the room slowly as if looking individually at each of the three thousand applauding members of the American Bankers Association of which he had been the most successful President in terms of growth of assets and earnings. But no one would mention the "chain of potential disasters" or the eight hundred odd banks known to be under the daily surveillance of the Federal Reserve Board because of their illiquidity position. No one would dare tell one hundred million American depositors that they stood on the verge of loosing their life savings.

The economist of Grand American Bank had then written into Robertson's speech some comments on the Eurodollar Market, that uncontrollable, unruly market where external US dollars were being traded. "From eighty billion dollars in 1974, this market has grown to more than two hundred and fifty billion dollars in 1977," they had stated. Robertson would add: "It is a solid evidence that the international banking community is in good health and the recycling of petro-dollars as set up in early 1975 is working to everyone's satisfaction." Nobody would dare say that the word "recycling" was an elegant term for "further indebtedness of the oil importing countries to the oil producing states, either directly or through the International Monetary Fund." But it erased the unpleasant statistics of the commercial trade deficits of the importing countries. The correction of a statistic, that's all the "recycling" accomplished. In fact, it compounded the problems. The borrowing country, having borrowed enough money to erase its trade deficit, would now have to repay, plus interest. At eight percent over ten years, you repay double what you have borrowed. So you double your problems. But that's a problem for the future. Don't face the problem now. Wait. It might go away, anyway. No one was prepared to tell the world that it was bankrupt.

The speech commented on gold and the success of the US operation to demonetize gold despite the protests of France. Gold was now an ordinary metal like copper, steel, and silver. No more. No less. It was listed in the report of wealth of the US Government as an ordinary asset with other stockpiled metals, office buildings and furniture. No longer was it providing backing for the issue of money. No country issued money based on gold reserves anymore. No. Why, that's a restraint on the amount of money you can print. If you did, you would have to avoid deficits in your budgets. You would have to control your expenses. You would have to eliminate handouts. You would have to discipline politicians and government heads. Who wants to do that? Disciplined politicians never get elected.

"The 1975 removal of the prohibition for US citizens to hold gold," Robertson would say, "has proven a wise decision. After uncertain steps, the gold market has now stabilized and gold trading on the Chicago Mart and other exchanges is today a matter of routine, like any other commodity. The French are still accumulating gold. Let them be. Gold earns no interest. Gold does not work. Gold does not contribute to the economy. Gold is only an idol. A god for fools. We have won the gold war. The world is now free to trade and governments have been liberated from the harness of this capricious metal. On this victory note, I wish to leave you. My Presidency has been most rewarding because of you. You will soon elect a new President to lead your Association. I leave the books to him in balance. I leave them, confident, that whomever you choose, he has a golden future ahead of him. Gold bless you all – I mean God bless you all. (Smile) Thank you."

"Andrew, it's a great speech," exclaimed Hardrock, "short, to the point while all encompassing, and you managed a plug, the mention of the rise of our assets to the one hundred billion dollar mark."

"Peter, I'm scared to death," replied Robertson as he presented his glass to Simone for a refill.

"Why?"

"I'm afraid that some smart clerk will rise on the floor and start questioning the increase in short term liabilities of the banking system. You know, some young university punk with a big degree in economics or some other obsolete nonsense and the title of Vice President of some obscure bank in the Appalachians. Our bank is safe as we have our own internal regulations limiting Arab deposits to thirty billion dollars or twenty-five percent of our total assets, but what about the others? Those who have not set limits on their exposure? The smaller banks, eager to grow, to impress their neighbors, to overcome their competition by overloading their books with these fragile deposits, placing themselves at the mercy of the whims of camel riding Sheiks. Something is bound to give, Peter. And while each time a small bank fails, we benefit because depositors get scared and move their funds to the big banks, each time we become weaker because the whole system is endangered. The Federal Reserve admits to eight hundred banks being under its close surveillance. I would be prepared to bet the figure is closer to two thousand. We know. We can tell by the number of requests from our correspondent banks for short-term accommodation. Once we grant it, they never repay. They roll the amounts over at maturity and ask for more. They are all over exposed. And I'm sick to death knowing it and not being able to say or do anything about it.

"All that crap about a gold victory! We are old-school bankers, you and I, Peter, and we know that on the day we were freed from gold reserves as the store of value, we abandoned all discipline. Governments are now free to overspend, to mismanage their budgets year after year with larger and larger deficits and there is nothing to restrain them. They print money, as they need it. It is only paper. Peter, the whole goddamn fucking world is bankrupt and no one dares say so. Not even I and I am the President of the largest bank in the world and the retiring president of the American Bankers Association."

"Have another drink," said Hardrock, "and you will feel better. Simone what's your reaction?"

"I think the speech is well written but I know so little about banking and economics."

"I thought you had a degree in economics from the Sorbonne and years of experience at the Bank of France," retorted Hardrock.

"Yes, but as Mr. Robertson says, such degrees have now become an obsolete nonsense."

"I didn't mean your degrees," interjected Robertson, "come on, let us have your honest opinion."

"My honest opinion is that the speech will be well received as is. It needs no correction. The French press will dislike you for your comments that gold is the god of every Frenchman and that every Frenchman is a fool. But they already dislike you and, being French myself, I don't feel I can be impartial in judging that part of your speech."

"Perhaps we should review the gold segment of your speech carefully," said Hardrock. "Why antagonize the French..."

"Fuck the French. The speech stays as it is," said Robertson.

Simone rose from her seat and looked at the skyline of Atlanta unrolling for miles away from the Hyatt hotel.

"I am sorry Madame de Rivoli, I am sure Andrew did not mean this literally."

"Maybe I did, maybe I did," laughed Robertson.

Simone turned and her eyes met his, contemptuously, while addressing Hardrock. "Will there be anything else, Mr. Hardrock?"

"No, that is all for now, Madame de Rivoli. You may go and change. See you in the courtesy suite in say, half an hour."

Robertson followed Simone out of the suite. "I did not appreciate your last remark, Mr. Robertson."

"Toutes mes excuses, Madame de Rivoli," he replied in his broken French, derisively.

She pressed the button for the elevator and kept silent until she reached her room on the twenty-sixth floor, three doors away from Robertson's suite.

"See you later," said Robertson.

"I'm not sure I like you," replied Simone.

"One day I will take that goddamn aristocratic tone out of your voice, whether you like me or not," Robertson muttered to himself as he headed toward his own room.

When Robertson entered Grand American Bank's courtesy suite, it was overflowing with bankers from all over the US, mostly Chairmen, Presidents and Senior Vice Presidents. Ever since Robertson had become its President, Grand American Bank had set up the largest courtesy suite at the yearly American Bankers Association convention. It was looked at as the welcoming suite of the convention and it gave an opportunity to the Grand American Bank officers to establish contact with the delegates before any other banking institution. Initially, the Big Suite (as it was known) had paid handsome dividends, bringing hundreds of new correspondent bank accounts to Grand American Bank, but now that Grand American Bank had become the largest bank in the world, mostly every bank who maintained an account in New York had to have an account with Grand American Bank, if not for the prestige, at least for the convenience of dealing with the most extensive network of branches, agencies and correspondents in the world.

The "Big Suite" was no longer a place to recruit business. It was now a meeting place where bankers met friends and associates to exchange gossip over free drinks. The bars opened at noon and never closed before 2 a.m. Every officer of Grand American Bank attending the convention had to spend at least three hours a day at the Big Suite, entertaining visiting bankers. The bars ran the length of the room. Two large photos of Peter Hardrock and Andrew Robertson hung on the wall behind the bars under two bright spotlights. Visitors never waited for a drink nor missed food. Whatever they did or said in the Big Suite was always under the overwhelming presence of their hosts, the Chairman and the President of Grand American Bank, the most successful management team in banking history.

Robertson walked briskly to one of the bars, ordered a gin and tonic, took a sip, asked the waiter for more gin, and only then started to acknowledge the greetings from the visiting bankers.

"Good to see you, Michael, how are things in Wichita?" "Eh, Stevenson, haven't seen you in ages. How's the cattle business down your way?" "Hello, Henry. Where is that good-looking wife of yours? Best skier in Colorado." "Excuse me, Henderson, I'm just trying to reach White before he leaves." Robertson had spotted Patrick White, the Chairman of the Federal Reserve Board, walking towards the exit.

"Patrick, you are not leaving?" White took his pipe out of the corner of his mouth and greeted him.

"Good evening, Andrew, nice to see you again. Big success your suite, as usual. How are things?"

"Couldn't be better."

"All set for the big speech tomorrow?"

"I think so. I believe you will like most of it."

"You are going to talk about gold no doubt?" White puffed on his pipe.

"This is one time when you and I disagreed and I was proven right," boasted Robertson.

"Time will tell. Time will tell, Andrew."

In 1974 White had insisted that President Ford veto the bill authorizing Americans to buy gold. Ford understood nothing about gold. Other members of the Cabinet thought the prohibition to hold gold was a repression of the freedom of Americans to own property. All the newspapers said it was essential to "demonetize" gold, whatever that meant. Robertson had made a public statement to the effect that Grand American Bank was in favor of the bill and intended to buy, store and trade in gold.

President Ford had signed the bill over the continuous protest of White. Everyone now rejoiced that gold had been "demonetized" without the world being hit by any of the calamities predicted by the Federal Reserve Board. White knew better. He could see the tragedy building up in the weekly statistics published by his Board. But it was not politically acceptable to spread such black prophecies and White would have been a voice in the desert, as always. So he took to smoking more and talking less, waiting for his term as Chairman of the Federal Reserve Board to expire and praying dear God that it would expire before those calamities hit the world.

"Andrew, thank you for your hospitality. If you will excuse me, I would like to retire early."

"Anyone we know?" asked Robertson laughingly as he slapped White on the back. "Have a good night, Patrick and don't miss my speech tomorrow."

At the other end of the room Hardrock was introducing Simone de Rivoli to a circle of bankers.

"Gentlemen, Baroness Simone de Rivoli is my new assistant. We found her in Paris with an impressive Doctorate in Economics and hired her away from the Bank of France. She has been with us now for nearly nine months. I don't know how I could run my office without her. Or for that matter, run the bank. Madame de Rivoli, let me introduce these eminent bankers to you. There are a lot of names to remember."

"I have a good memory," said Simone, while distributing her most engaging smiles to the admiring circle.

"Jack Thorton, Chairman of Phillips Bank from Philadelphia, Peter Black, President of the State Street Bank of San Diego, Michael...Michael, oh yes, Michael Cashbox — with a name like this how could I forget it? Michael is Vice President, International, of the Sugarland Bank of Houston. Texas used to have all the oil money but, since the Arabs took over the oil business in 1973, they are the ones with all the money and they are all our clients." Everyone laughed. "Here is Oliver Starr. He is the big boss at Chicago Second National. James Cooper. He owns all the banks in Minnesota..."

"Except one," interjected Cooper.

"And which one is that?" asked Simone.

"The Suburban Bank of St. Paul. It still belongs to the Hardrock family. I have been trying to persuade Peter to sell it to me for years. But no go."

"It's good for you to have competition," said Hardrock "Keeps you on your toes. Why don't you be courageous and buy control of Grand American? I'll soon be ready for retirement."

"My goodness, there is not enough money in the whole world and furthermore, I don't speak Arabic." New laughter.

"Gentlemen, it is indeed a pleasure for me to make your acquaintance," said Simone. "I am most impressed. If you ever need anything from Grand American Bank and you can't get through to Mr. Hardrock, please telephone me." She smiled, "At times, a woman's way..." Simone shook hands with every one of them. The assembled bankers took her words as an invitation and quickly, in their minds, invented reasons to fly to New York on business to visit the glamorous Baroness.

One of them rolled his eyes suggestively at Simone and pushed Hardrock, "you son-of-a-bitch."

When the Baroness offered her hand to Michael Cashbox, he did not shake it. He looked at her, bowed slightly and raised her hand to his lips in a very continental manner.

"Whew! Michael, where in the hell did you learn that?" they roared.

"I went to Paris once. We wanted to buy the Eiffel Tower and install it on top of our headquarters in Houston!"

By eleven o'clock, the party was in full swing. Most guests had already drunk too much and the "Big Suite" was now a noisy, smoky room, exploding with bursts of laughter, challenges of dirty jokes and too much backslapping. Simone felt ill at ease in front of this lack of decorum. "French bankers would never behave this way, she thought".

Hardrock joined her, "You look tired," he said.

"I feel fine. It's the smoke and the noise mostly."

"Well, I guess I have enough of this for tonight also. The PR boys can finish the job and eventually send these people to bed. What about some food?"

"Isn't it rather late?" replied Simone.

"Never too late to eat. Ask Robertson whether he wants to join us."

The three of them soon left the suite and rode the glass elevator to the ground floor.

"We had a good crowd," said Hardrock.

"But little business to be had. They are already clients," said Robertson. "They now come for the free booze and because they know we have all the Arab money. These little country bankers hope we might share some of our deposit business with them."

"Where do we get food at this late hour?" asked Hardrock. "Andrew should know. He has a black book with a list of all the good places."

"What about the Mouse Trap?" suggested Robertson.

"What an ominous name," said Simone.

"It's right around the corner — we can walk," insisted Robertson.

They walked the short distance to the restaurant that specialized in broiled steaks and giant salads with Roquefort dressing. It was part of a well-known little chain with successful outlets in Fort Lauderdale and Miami. They sat in the piano bar lounge and a Playboy Club type waitress, minus the ears and the tail, was soon at their table.

"What will it be, folks?"

Robertson looked at the high cut red leotard which exposed the leg all the way to the hip bone, placed his arm around her waist, and said, "I don't know what you have on the menu or what my two friends here will choose, but my mind is made up, honey. I'll take you without dressing right after you close this joint."

The girl disengaged herself by rolling out of Robertson's arm, as she had been taught to do, and walked to Hardrock's side of the table while blowing Robertson a kiss and a smile. "You want me rare or well done?"

"Come on children," interjected Hardrock, "food comes first. Let's order, I'm famished."

They placed their orders and Hardrock suggested a bottle of California wine, which Simone declined.

"I'll stick to gin and tonic," said Robertson.

"Go easy Andrew, you have to give that speech tomorrow."

"I can take care of myself and tomorrow is tomorrow. Let's live tonight. Eh! Buddy," addressing the pianist, "give us some fun music."

Somewhat embarrassed, Simone looked at Hardrock who leaned forward and placed his hand on Robertson's arm. "Andrew, Madame de Rivoli is slightly tired..."

Robertson rose from his seat, "Toutes mes excuses, Madame la Baroness," he sat down again. "I have already said that once earlier today. Jamais deux sans trois!"

They ate their steaks, skipped the thick chocolate cake and deep apple pie offered as deserts and ordered coffee. Hardrock soon rose, "think I will call it a day. Tomorrow will again be a long day. Are you two coming?"

"I'll stay for a while and have one for the road," said Robertson.

"Madame?"

"I'm coming."

"Stay!" Robertson pressed her arm on the table preventing her from leaving.

"Mr. Robertson!"

"Andrew, if Madame de Rivoli wants to leave..."

"But she does not want to leave, does she?" asked Robertson.

Simone looked at Hardrock unsure as to what to do, torn between her duty to her employer and her need to retire. She had no desire to stay with Robertson. She questioned Hardrock again with her eyes. He did not seem to care.

"Make sure you bring him home early and in good shape. We need him in top form for that speech tomorrow."

It sounded like instructions. Simone stopped trying to leave and Robertson relaxed his hold on her arm. Hardrock was already gone.

"All right, Mr. Robertson, I'll have one cognac with you and then we go home."

"Promise?"

"Promise what?"

"To go home with me."

"Mr. Robertson, look at that bunny girl, she is much more interesting than I am and much more your style."

"You don't know my style, baby. Irresistible! That's what they said in Paris when I was stationed there."

"I have resisted more attractive men than you, Mr. Robertson."

"You don't like me, do you?"

"I could easily dislike you."

They walked back to the Hyatt House silently, Simone leading the way, two steps ahead of Robertson as if to build a distance between the two of them. As they crossed Peachtree Avenue, the traffic lights changed and Simone quickened her pace. "Eh! don't run away," let out Robertson.

"I wish I could," replied Simone coldly, "I find no pleasure walking in public with someone who has drunk too much."

"Don't be such a snob," he said as he overtook her and placed his hand under her elbow. "Let's walk in this hotel elegantly. People might be watching."

"They will watch anyway," replied Simone, disengaging herself.

They took the elevator. Simone turned her back to Robertson and surveyed the nearly deserted lobby where tired guests were having a late coffee or drink before the closing of the restaurant and bars. She glanced at her watch. Nearly one o'clock in the morning. She felt very tired and very bored with the big American. How far did she have to go to answer the call of duty? This was her first business convention in America and she did not like it, she did not like the atmosphere, the drinking, and the loud jokes.

These so called serious businessmen appeared to her as a bunch of students let loose after class away from the supervision of their teachers and parents. "Americans never grow up," someone had written. Perhaps they never do, thought Simone.

They got off on the twenty-sixth floor and walked to

Simone's door. "Good night, Mr. Robertson, try to have a good night's rest".

"I'm coming in for a nightcap."

"Oh! no you don't."

"Where is your sense of hospitality, Madame la Baroness?"

"One has the right to choose one's friends, Mr. Robertson."

"I have chosen you!" Robertson pushed the door open, walked in, waited for Simone to follow him, which she did reluctantly, then closed the door behind them. He went to the bedside table, picked up the phone and dialed "5" for room service.

"God dam it, there is no answer." He lifted the phone and dialed the operator. "I'm dialing room service and nobody answers. Could you find them for me, please? I'm in room 2604. What do you mean, they are closed?" He looked at his watch. "It's only 1:05 in the morning. Give me the manager."

He turned to Simone. "Can you imagine a hotel like this closing its room service at midnight?" A voice came over the phone. "What can I do for you, sir?"

"I want a drink."

"I am sorry, sir, our room service is closed for the night."

"Then reopen the damn thing."

"I can't do that, sir."

"What do you mean; you can't do that, sir? Do you know who I am? I'm Andrew Robertson. I'm the President of the ABA and we have three thousand delegates in your hotel, so don't tell me you can't keep your room service open for us."

"Mr. Robertson, it does not matter," interjected Simone, "you have had enough to drink anyway."

Robertson placed his hand on the mouthpiece. "Mind your own business." Returning his attention to his interlocutor, he raised his voice, "who are you anyway?"

"My name is Simon, sir, I'm the night manager."

"What the hell do you manage, if everything is closed? Listen Simon, I'm in room 2604, my name is Robertson, and I want two, double gins and tonic. I want them now and I don't give a fuck what you do to find them for me. So get off your ass, Mr. Night Manager, otherwise you better start looking for another job." He slammed the phone down. "Imagine, these little no-good punks telling us when things are open and closed, when we can drink or eat or piss. Everything for the convenience of employees and screw the clients. Christ, if I ran my bank this way, we would be out of business in a month."

"Mr. Robertson, I think we are both tired and we should forget the drinks and go to bed."

"That's a good idea", said Robertson taking off his tie.

"Please go to your room, Mr. Robertson, and let me rest. I am really very tired."

Robertson dropped his jacket on a chair, stepped to the other side of the bed, where Simone stood, and seized her by the shoulders. "You can't chase me away now Simone, you promised to come home with me."

"I never meant...."

"A promise is a promise."

She turned her head away as he tried to kiss her. His right hand left her shoulder, enveloped her chin and brought her mouth to his.

"You are hurting me. Take your hands off me", she protested.

"Then stop fighting me."

There was a knock at the door. "Go away", shouted Robertson.

"Room service, sir, your drinks."

"I don't want the goddamn drinks, go away."

"But sir...."

"Fuck off, man."

Simone had moved away from Robertson. He looked at her. "Buy them, fuck them, send them home!" he thought.

"Let's go to my suite, we will be more comfortable."

"No sir!"

"Then I'm going to stay right here. God I need a drink!"

He grabbed the phone. "Give me that night manager again."
There was a click, "Simon? Where are the fucking drinks?"
"Sir...."
"Send the fucking drinks up, do you understand?" This time he slammed the phone so hard that it fell to the floor.
"You will wake up the neighbors", whispered Simone. She bent to pick up the phone. Robertson slapped her rump so hard that Simone nearly lost her balance and tears came to her eyes.
"Mr. Robertson, please leave my room immediately, otherwise I shall call the manager."
"That guy Simon? You must be kidding, he is so scared of me, he is shitting in his pants."
Then he looked at her face, rushed to her, took it in his hands, "you are crying. I didn't think it was possible!" He started to kiss her eyes, her cheeks and her neck and finally he took her mouth while pressing his knee against her unresponding body. "Let's fuck!" He pulled hard on the collar of her blouse and buttons came off.
"Mr. Robertson, I don't want to fight you."
"So don't fight me and call me Andrew."
Simone tried to move away from him. He reached for the elastic band between the cups of her bra and with a snap broke it. "Please stop it, Mr. Robertson, you are hurting me."
He pinched her nipples between his thumb and forefinger. The pain hardened them. "You see, Simone, you body betrays you. You want to fuck as much as I do." He lifted her and threw her roughly on the bed cover. He pulled at her belt but could not undo it. He got up and undressed throwing the balance of his clothes on the chair where he had dropped his tie and coat. He turned towards the bed, his penis erect despite his drunkenness.
Simone had not moved. She lay there motionless, her blouse and bra torn open, otherwise she was still fully dressed. Her eyes were closed. She was exhausted. When she felt the weight of Robertson on the bed, she murmured, "at least you could undress me."

"What for?"

There was a knock at the door. "Room service!"

"Go away", shouted Robertson. He turned on top of Simone, tore her pantyhose with his fingers and lunged into her.

"Simone slowly kicked off her shoes.

As usual, the ABA convention had been a great success. The newspapers throughout the country hailed Robertson's speech. Their headlines read, "Retiring President of ABA praises White House." "International Banking System Sounder Than Ever, Says Retiring ABA President." "International Banking Community In Good Health." Time Magazine ran a special story "We Have Won the Gold War."

Patrick White, disgusted, had thrown the newspapers and magazines in his wastebasket.

He should resign. All this was madness. But they would not let him. "It would endanger the faith of the people in our system", they said. "The public would think that you disagree with my policies", the President had said. "But I do. I have told you a thousand times that the system is sick. The only remedy suggested by your financial advisers is "print more paper." It can't last, Mr. President. The house of cards will collapse. But you won't listen to me."

"I have listened to you, Patrick," the President had said, "and you have all my sympathy. But I can't let you go because it would not be in the best interest of the country, at least, not at this time."

Patrick White had returned to his office in a sweat. "I'm sitting on a time bomb. The fuse has burned out but for some unexplained reason the bomb has yet to explode and I can't run away from it."

On October 3rd, one week after the convention, he picked up the report on banks under surveillance and read: "During the month of September, 1977, eleven more banks were added to those under surveillance and two were removed. One because it failed, the other because it merged with its main competitor. The competitor has been added to our list. The number of banks under surveillance now total 1827 — we have only admitted to 800. There are 193 on the most critical list. Both are record highs. Short-term liabilities of banks (under 90 days) have increased another 1.40% during the last month. Demand deposits and short-term liabilities now represent 71.55% of total liabilities. Grand American Bank shows the highest ratio with 78.90%, substantially above the average. There are no explanations but we suspect it is due to unusually large Arab deposits."

White stopped reading, reached for his intercom, "Sally, get me Andrew Robertson at Grand American."

"Right away, sir." In less than a minute he had Robertson on the line. When the Chairman of the Federal Reserve Board called, everybody jumped.

"Andrew? White here."

"How are you, Patrick?"

"Fine, Andrew. That was a great speech last week at the ABA. I did not have the opportunity to congratulate you as I had to leave the convention early."

"Thanks. What can I do for you?"

"I'd like to have lunch with you."

"My place or yours?"

"It might be more discreet at mine. Tomorrow, twelve thirty?"

"Meet you in your office?"

"O.K. bye Andrew."

"See you tomorrow, Patrick."

Lunch had consisted of the usual platitudes served in most executive dining rooms in America. Robertson had his two gin and tonics, skipped the clear consommé, ate half a chicken potpie, made with cubes of mock chicken, and drank an insipid coffee.

"Patrick, I know that Government cooks are no better than those in private enterprise but at least they could use real chicken in their chicken pot pies."

"We are on tight budgets."

"I thought you printed money as you needed it."

"Don't rub it in, Andrew, it's a most unpleasant situation. I don't know where we are going anymore. That is incorrect. I know, but I can't convince the White House to change course." White filled his pipe for the second time since the butler had removed their plates.

"Want a cognac, Andrew?"

"No thanks, not when I am working. That's the one drink that paralyses my brain and I presume that you invited me here for work."

White sucked on his pipe furiously, lowered his glasses on his nose slightly, and stared at Robertson. "Anything wrong with your bank, Andrew, that I should know about?"

"We are doing fine, Patrick. Greatest year ever. Another twenty billion dollar increase. You heard me mention this figure at the ABA meeting."

White's eyes had not left Robertson's face. "Andrew, you and I have known each other for a long time. Long enough to have become friends and enemies. Long enough to have had our fights and disagreements. But also long enough to tell each other the truth. Andrew, I believe your bank is in serious trouble."

Robertson did not flinch. White continued. "I also believe that you have overextended yourself with your Arab friends."

"That's pure nonsense. We are the largest bank in the world and naturally some of our figures and transactions are pretty large. You should not let large figures upset you, Patrick."

"Don't worry; I'm used to dealing in billions."

Robertson leaned towards White and with a very reassuring voice said: "Let me tell you something, Patrick. I have built Grand American Bank to what it is today. The largest. When I became President, we had barely forty-five billion dollars of assets. Now we have more than one hundred billion. It's an amazing growth but I can assure you that it was accomplished within all the most conservative criteria of prudent banking. Hell! We were the first bank to voluntarily limit the amount of Arab deposits we would accept. You know the figure. I have discussed it with you before. Thirty billion dollars or twenty-five percent of our assets. It's a reasonable figure. It protects us against sudden large withdrawals. I only wish more banks would adopt similar prudent policies."

"How do you explain that you show the highest ratio of short term liabilities?" asked White.

"We are up to 78.9% as of last week." Robertson always knew this one statistic. He watched it daily. It worried him. It grew daily but he was unable to trace the source of these demand and short-term funds. "General and well spread increase in business", his Vice Presidents would explain. He knew that Sheik Al-Madir had some ten to twelve billion in various sundry accounts, which were not shown in the computer listing of Arab deposits, but this was not enough to explain the continued increase in that dangerous statistic — 78.9%.

"I don't believe one should worry about this figure, Patrick." Robertson tried to keep his voice natural and steady.

"What needs to be done is to break down the figure. We do so regularly. A lot of these so-called demand deposits are in fact rather permanent funds. They are not all to be withdrawn at the same time. There is no way you can even think of that. Look at our Arab deposits. Somewhat more than twenty-eight billion dollars last night — Robertson did not mention the additional ten to twelve billion dollars not shown on the report — no one can expect the Arabs to walk in one day and say, "we want our twenty-eight billion!"

"They could", said White dryly.

"Where would they go? Even if they did withdraw, they would have to transfer these funds to other banks that in all probability would be correspondents of ours and the funds would come right back to us."

"I don't like it", said White.

"When I think as an old-fashioned banker like you, I don't like it either", said Robertson. "I remember 1960 when we were so worried that we ran to you for your assurance of support when our ratio nearly reached fifty percent."

"Do you need my support now?" asked White.

"Christ, right now we could support you and the whole Government of the United States. In fact, we do." Robertson laughed loudly. "Patrick, believe me, Grand American Bank needs the support of no one."

The 30th of June 1978 had started well for Andrew Robertson. Most days did if he slept at his apartment in New York instead of waking up in White Plains next to his wife, Pat, pushing him out of bed with her "you will miss your train." No "good morning", no smile, no "hello". Just "you will miss your train", as if she wished to get rid of him. She did the same thing to their two children, Bobby and Andrew Jr. "Hurry up; you are going to be late for school." Every morning at his house in White Plains was "get out of here". "Go to work, slave. Bring me the money. Don't touch me. You will miss your train". A merry-go-round. A morning of hurry-ups.

At one time Robertson had the bank limousine drive him to work every morning but it took twice as long as by train and he had to rise at six to get to the office by nine. Now he rose at 7:30, caught the 8:10 and arrived in New York at 9:08. But trains are always inconvenient at night. You must always finish your work or play around a train schedule. Work you can adjust, but sex does not always answer to an "all aboard" call. So he had taken the apartment in New York on 54th street, between Fifth Avenue and Madison. He slept there most of the time.

Robertson loved to wake up alone. Stretch and yawn as he wished. Piss, scratch and fart at will. No one else to consider, no one else to upset. That's why he had developed a personal policy "buy them, fuck them, send them home." It didn't matter who they were. Whores, call girls, friends or lovers. Make sure you send them home before morning. Must wake up alone in the morning. Some of them protested but eventually, they all went. Even the Baronesses, thought Robertson, as he remembered the comments of Simone last night.

"I feel like a whore when I dress to go home while you lay there contented", she had said.

"You'll sleep better in your own bed", he had retorted.

"And I suppose you will wake up in the morning without any feelings of guilt."

"Why should I feel guilty? Pat is at home more worried about her children, Bazaar's, clothes and her country club than about my work or me. As to you, I have never forced you. You came of your own free will. You are a merry widow. No attachment."

"You forget the Sheik."

"Balls. So the Sheik has found you in my bed...."

"You in my bed", corrected Simone.

"Me in your bed, you in my bed, what's the difference? It's all the same fucking. What's the big deal? You are not married to him."

"He has asked me."

"You have yet to say yes. So meanwhile, you are free game."

"I thought he was your friend."

"He is my best client. Otherwise, he has no friends. Only people he uses."

"Are you talking about the Sheik or yourself?" asked Simone sarcastically.

"I don't use anybody. I pay well for services rendered. The Sheik has been good to me. In return, he received more help from my bank than he deserved. He would not be what he is now if it had not been for me".

"And what about me, Andrew? How do you repay me?"

"You, that's different".

"Tell me more".

"Simone, you are an aristocrat. You play at society games. You have charm, intelligence, beauty and elegance. With those qualities you've earned a good life. You understand power, like I do, and you know where it rests. You are the assistant to Hardrock but you understand that I run the bank and that soon, very soon, I'll be the new Chairman. So you work with me. Smart girl. I asked you to help me find out what Sheik Al-Madir was up to. You became his friend, and you slept with him to get the information. Bravo! You are good. You are an expert. Now, we've had an accident, the Sheik knows about me and you. So what? Screw him. Thanks to you, I have now learned all I needed to know about him anyway. You can leave the Sheik alone and come back to daddy. I was good last night, wasn't I"?

"You were irresistible", snorted Simone as she walked out of the apartment hoping to find a taxi before getting mugged at this early hour of the morning. Irresistible! She dried the tears in her eyes with the back of her hand and thought of Pierre Beauchamp.

When Robertson walked into his office, Louise was waiting.

"You're wanted upstairs immediately."

"What's the rush? Don't I have an appointment with the President of Dow Chemical at 9:15?"

"I canceled it." He looked at her. "Instructions from upstairs."

"I'm on my way."

Robertson stepped off the elevator and walked towards Hardrock's office. He stopped by Simone's desk and asked, "what's up?"

"I don't know", replied Simone, "but he looks excessively nervous."

"Any clues?"

"The Sheik was here."

"When?"

"Early. He was leaving when I arrived. He is coming back at 10:30."

"Did Hardrock say anything to you?"

"Yes."

"What did you tell him?"

"Nothing."

"Do you think he knows?"

"I don't know."

"Shit!"

He opened the door to Hardrock's office and closed it behind him as Simone heard him say jovially "Good morning, Peter, what's up?"

Simone's eyes remained for a long time on the closed door.

She could hear the sounds of conversation but could not discern the words. One of the two executives started to shout. No doubt Robertson, but she could not understand what he was shouting about. Then the voices were subdued again.

She picked up the computer print-out analysis of Arab deposits of ten million dollars and over, walked to the Xerox room, copied the summary, returned to her desk and placed the original in a large manila envelope upon which she affixed a red label "For Confidential Filing".

She opened her purse and discreetly dropped the photocopy in it.

Peter Hardrock was walking back and forth behind his desk while addressing Robertson. "Jesus, this is a catastrophe! Sixty billion dollars! What do we do now? Sixty billion dollars that we haven't got. I guess I should call Patrick White."

"Don't get panicky", retorted Robertson. "Let's review the facts calmly."

"The facts have been the same for the last half hour and you don't seem to understand them. Your Sheik is going to walk in here at 10:30, less than an hour from now, present us with a sixty billion dollar check and demand payment in cash, that we haven't got. Now can you put that in your head?"

"Sit down, Peter, for Christ sake! How can we think when you are jumping around like an old maid who has just seen the devil?"

"It's more than the devil, its complete hell. How can you keep so calm?"

"I am not calm. I am just trying to quiet my mind and calm my body. I am trying to compose myself in order to face this problem like any other ordinary..."

"You call a sixty billion dollar cash problem an ordinary problem?"

"Peter, please! Let's start from the beginning. As I understand it, the situation is as follows. Sheik Al-Madir telephoned you yesterday and insisted on an early morning appointment without witnesses. As agreed, he came this morning, told you that he never wanted to talk to me or see me again — and I honestly don't know why such an old friend would suddenly turn against me, but I'll find out — and asked to close all his accounts amounting, according to him, to some sixty billion dollars."

"Half of our assets", moaned Hardrock.

"Our computer print-out shows that only twenty-eight billion dollars on deposit belong to the Sheik and his friends. He is coming back at 10:30 and he wants to be paid in cash. That's it?"

"That's it."

"Have you checked with our Computer Center whether the claims of the Sheik are correct?"

"I have." Hardrock presented to Robertson a slip of paper upon which he had written $60,129,834,645. "I got these figures just before you came in. They match the amount of the check presented to me by the Sheik this morning."

"Where does it all come from?"

"From all over", replied Hardrock. "I have a computer report on that also. He and his friends held deposits in every one of our branches. Some openly, some under disguises, so our people in the field would not know. Therefore, our computer center was never fed this information. You and I never knew. From twenty-eight billion to sixty billion dollars, that's a thirty-two billion dollar gap! How could they do it? It's an impossible feat. They must have been working on this scheme since 75." He looked suspiciously at Robertson. "Did you know anything about this, Andrew?"

Robertson remained silent. The fucking double-crossing Sheik! Many months ago, he had told Robertson of his desire to deposit more money with Grand American than the thirty billion dollar limit established by the bank. "Why should I deposit my money with other banks when you are my friend", he had said. Robertson had seen an opportunity for an even faster growth of the bank and more prestige for himself. He had set up a series of bank accounts, which he had directed to those branches where he knew the Vice President in charge would welcome new business and not ask too many questions because the business came from Robertson. The accounts were all in the assumed names of US individuals or corporations with US addresses and therefore would raise no suspicion that they might be connected to Arab funds. However, there was one mandatory signature on all the accounts, whether directly as an officer of the depositing corporation or as an attorney of the individual effecting a deposit: a certain Ben Madir. No one noticed. No one questioned such a neutral name. No one connected the name to Sheik Ben Said Al-Madir. Ben is mostly a Jewish surname anyway. Sheik Al-Madir and Robertson had been in agreement that no more than ten to twelve billion dollars would be placed on deposit in such convenience accounts and no more than five billion in any one year. The double-crossing fucking bastard! In less than two years, the Sheik had managed to deposit secretly with the bank an additional thirty-two billion dollars.

"Andrew, you are not answering me", insisted Hardrock.

"Well, to be frank with you, I knew of a few billion dollars..."

"A few billion? How many exactly, Andrew?"

"Oh! not many, ten, maybe twelve."

"You call ten to twelve billion dollars not many? But why, Andrew?"

"The Sheik said that forcing him to place his funds with other banks was embarrassing him. We were his friends, after all. He remembered his more humble days, when I was of great assistance to him in Beirut and Dubai, and he felt guilty about taking his money elsewhere. I knew how adamant the Board was about the thirty billion dollar limit so I took it upon myself to authorize another ten to twelve billion without reporting it. I felt that we could safely accept another ten billion, that it would help us reach that magic one hundred billion-dollar asset figure earlier. He screwed me. I take full responsibility."

"You take full responsibility?" said Hardrock. "Great! Where is the cash to reimburse that "not many" ten to twelve billion dollars?"

"You don't have to get sarcastic with me, Peter. We are both in the same boat whether you like it or not."

"I don't like it a damn bit. We need to report this to the Board immediately and then I must call Patrick White."

You will do nothing of the sort", answered Robertson, coldly.

"But that's the only logical course of action to follow."

"We are not dealing with a logical problem. Peter, if you talk to the Board, we are dead. They will sack me for my actions; they will fire you because you are my superior. Furthermore, knowing how we always work as a team, they will never believe that you did not know."

"I guess you are right", said Hardrock, dejected, "but surely we must inform the Feds."

"Within fifteen minutes after you call Patrick, he will have an army of investigators here scrutinizing our books. In our present illiquid situation, that would mean the end of this bank. He is already suspicious enough about us."

"What do you mean?"

"I never told you because I did not want to worry you unnecessarily but White called me about a year ago. It was at the time when our ratio of short-term liabilities went over seventy-five percent. He invited me to his private dining room and told me bluntly that he believed that our bank was in trouble and that we were overextended with our Arab friends. Those were his exact words."

"You should have told me", insisted Hardrock.

"What for? To have you shake all over every time you encountered White?"

"What did you do?"

"I denied his accusations, mentioned to him the thirty billion limits on our exposure, and explained to him that most funds withdrawn would no doubt be re-deposited with us anyway by other banks."

"Did he buy that?"

"Whether he did or not is not important. He never raised the subject again. But I know that he did not like it. I remember him saying so and asking me whether we needed his support."

"And you turned him down, naturally."

"Naturally. How can Grand American need support?"

"We need it now, damn it. I still think I should call him." Hardrock reached for the intercom.

"Then you will kill your brother", stated Robertson flatly.

"What has my brother to do with this?"

"Peter, sometimes you amaze me! You don't seem to understand that everything you do affects the President of the United States whether you want it to or not. Jesus Christ! He is your brother after all and this is the family bank, founded by your grandfather. What do you think White is going to do if you call him? He will convene his Board and rush a confidential memo to the President. Within an hour some son-of-a-bitch from the press, like Anderson, will be given secretly a copy of this memo and all hell is going to break loose. And when the Feds come to our rescue, the President will be accused of rescuing his own brother."

Hardrock jumped from his chair and marched to the sitting corner of his office. Lifting his fist towards 'the Departure of the Sheik', his favorite painting, he screamed, "you goddamn bastard!"

Robertson was immediately behind him and placed his hand on his shoulder. "That's the spirit, Peter. You don't often swear. It will do you good. I never like this painting anyway. It has offended many of our Jewish clients. The Sheik is a bastard, a double-crossing bastard. After all we have done for him. But we'll get even, you have my word."

"I would rather have sixty billion dollars."

"All right, here is what we are going to do. Have you a copy of our latest cash position?"

"It's on my desk, but you won't find any cash there. I have looked. We have about fourteen billion dollars available but

I don't think we can spare much more than ten billion out of that. The balance we need for our day-to-day operations.

Robertson looked at Hardrock. "We are not going to use our cash. We must get out of this bind on OPM."[2]

"How do you expect to do that?"

"First, you must tell the Sheik that we can't pay him."

"He will go out of here screaming and he will run straight to the bankruptcy court."

"No he won't." said Robertson. "First, because he stands to lose too much, second because you are going to offer him an alternative."

"I can't see any."

"Listen to me carefully and take notes, you will need them."

Robertson was now in his element, juggling with balance sheet figures, juggling with billions. They are only figures anyway. They don't mean much. You can move them about at will, provided the total always comes out right. That's all the auditors want to see. They will place their usual caveat on their report and using the magic words: "in accordance with acceptable accounting practices, this report represents fairly the position of the bank." Follows the name of their firm, handwritten. No signatures. No one wants to take the personal responsibility. "Acceptable accounting practices." That's the secret formula. Acceptable to whom? The auditors? They are only concerned with their fees. The shareholders? As long as they receive their dividends, they are happy. The depositors? They don't care. A bank is a bank is a bank. To whom then? The Feds? Internal Revenue? The International Monetary Fund? The world? By the time you find out, all the figures are obsolete anyway. Months behind. Dead figures. Auditors are morticians. They only deal with dead things and they are scared shitless of the future. Try them. Ask them to make projections! Who cares anyway? All the rules of the

2 OPM – "Other People's Money" a term used frequently by entre-preneurs and bankers when the public's money is used instead of the capital of the principals.

game have been changed. They are still changing as you play. The Arabs rule the world. Screw the Arabs!

Robertson brought his attention back to Hardrock. "The alternative is as follows."

"We are going to transfer to him twenty-two billion dollars of US Treasury Bills. We have thirty-one point four billion of them on our balance sheet. They are all in bearer form, they all mature within ninety days. He can cash them in as they come to maturity or buy new ones in replacement. It's his problem. But they are as good as cash. They are issued by the same Government and probably bear the same signature as our dollar bills, anyway."

"You think he will take them?" asked Hardrock.

"The Sheik knows Treasury Bills. He probably has his safety deposit boxes full of them. Now, what's important is to buy time. Once he has accepted the bills, you tell him that you can't deliver them before next Wednesday. Your reasons are that it will take that long to assemble them. Some are in our vault downstairs, others have yet to be received from the Treasury. Some we have bought from brokers and they have yet to deliver. You see the picture?"

"Yes, but I don't see what a couple of days will do?"

"Don't be stupid", snapped Robertson. "Monday is reporting day to the Feds. You don't want us to show a drop of twenty-two billion dollars in one week on our return, do you? I'll fix up the books. We'll take out say seven billion this week and fifteen billion the following week. Who knows, something else may happen next week and we won't have to take out that much. It's a big crap game. You never know what your next throw will bring. I might also manage to get some large depositors to move some funds to us from other banks. I'll call the usual gang. General Electric, General Motors, IBM, Xerox, Continental, Standard Oil. Christ! Standard Oil must have billions sitting with other banks and you are their largest shareholder. You should call them yourself."

"It's a family policy never to interfere with their

management", stated Hardrock coldly. "Unless there is a crisis. A few years ago, you forced them to fire their President".

"That was my father, twenty years ago!"

"Its about time you showed them who is boss again. I leave Standard to you. In any event, I don't foresee problems with our using Treasury Bills the way I say."

"I wish I had your confidence. So, assuming he accepts, we have settled twenty-two billion dollars. That leaves thirty-eight to go. What miracle do you hope to pull?"

Robertson pushed the cash position report back towards Hardrock. "Take your cash position back. We won't need it any longer. For the balance of the funds, we call on OPM.

"Where do you expect to find thirty-eight billion dollars of OPM?"

"Right under your nose, my dear Peter. But I'll only tell you if you agree to revise my share of our performance bonus. You get sixty percent, I get forty percent. I think it's unfair".

"Why".

"I do all the thinking. From now on, we go fifty/fifty."

"No way, Andrew, our split was set up six years ago and I see no reason to change it."

"On the contrary, Peter. I see a very good reason. Thirty-eight billion good reasons. You agree or I leave you alone to fight the Sheik."

"It's unfair. At a time when..."

"At a time when you need my brain, my imagination and my ability, I think it is only fair, on the contrary, that we talk of my reward." Robertson was glowing. For six years he had felt cheated by this arrangement. Last year, for instance, the performance bonus had reached $775,000. After Hardrock had taken his sixty percent – $455,000, Robertson's share had amounted to only $225,000. But he was the one who was responsible for the performance. Not Hardrock. He was too damn busy with his Foundation and his art and music committees to pay attention to the business of banking. He did not play the game anymore. Most of the time he sat on the bench and Robertson had to carry the ball. "This is my opportunity", thought Robertson. "It's now or never."

"Peter, we are wasting precious time. The Sheik will soon be back."

"All right, Andrew, you have a deal but only on the condition that the Sheik goes along and accepts your alternatives, as you say he will."

"Don't worry about that. I know him well."

"Apparently not well enough to have prevented this crisis."

"Well enough to take us out of it", said Robertson sharply. "So let's continue. Your second offer to the Sheik will be an eighteen billion dollar transfer to a Swiss bank — to Swiss International Bank to be precise."

"Why would he accept such a move?" asked Hardrock.

"Again because you will convince him that he has no choice. Also because I know that he owes Swiss International for some special favors which they granted to the rulers of the Emirates, particularly those of Bahrain and Abu Dhabi. The time has come for him to repay. He has never dealt with Swiss International. All of his Swiss banking is conducted with Swiss Credit and Swiss Union and a small private bank in which I believe he has a personal interest."

"And I suppose you know a way to ensure that Swiss International will re-deposit this eighteen billion with us?" suggested Hardrock.

"Exactly!" Robertson looked triumphant. "You know Dr. Shermer, their new Chairman. You met him last December at the cocktail party we threw for IMF members after that meeting during which they tried to force us to accept more short-term Arab funds and re-lend them on long term basis to developing countries. Recycling, they called it. Christ! Those poor countries will never be able to pay back. We take all the risks, suffer all the losses and the Arabs waltz away with no risk, their capital and interest on top. We killed that one quickly enough."

"I remember that and I remember Dr. Shermer", said Hardrock.

"Shermer owes me a few favors. Leave him to me. I'll make the deal with him while you are talking to the Sheik."

"Will you be able to reach him in Zurich before his bank closes? It's already 4:15 there."

"By sheer coincidence, our good Dr. Shermer is right here in New York. I know exactly where to find him – in the arms of Judith."

"Not Judith Watson?"

"Why not? The good doctor was lonely last night and prepared to forget his Protestant upbringing, "you shall not commit adultery." I called Judith and asked her for a very special treatment for a very special friend. Knowing her as I do, he should still be in her bed, unable to believe that any woman can be that good. Not only do I know where to find the doctor this morning, but also within hours my dear Judith should have a juicy little report for me on what's on the mind of the dear old doctor these days. Give me two Judith Watsons you can sack the whole of our Business Development Department."

"I am not impressed by the quality of your management", said Hardrock.

"It works. That's what's important. Furthermore, you should not be so fussy about the methods I use to run this bank. Some of those used by your grandfather, fifty years ago, would make interesting headlines."

"Leave my family out of this and let's come back to Swiss International. I suppose you intend to effect the transfer from the account of the Sheik to the account of Swiss International in our books by way of a simple book entry?"

"That's it. We debit the Sheik's account for eighteen billion and credit Swiss International for the same amount. We notify them by telex that we have placed this credit to their account by order of Sheik Al-Madir who wishes to establish a new account with them."

"And then?"

"Then, by return telex they will give us instructions to place these funds on seven day call deposit until further notice."

"How do you know that?" said Hardrock.

"That's the deal I will make with Shermer."

"How long will the funds stay with us? It won't help if they start drawing on this account within a matter of days."

"The funds will stay with us. Don't worry." But Robertson was gambling. He was gambling on the size of the deposit and the impossibility for Swiss International to place such large funds elsewhere quickly. He was also hoping that the rate of interest which he would offer Swiss International would be attractive enough to discourage them from shopping elsewhere. "I'm gambling with nothing to lose, we are bankrupt otherwise", he thought.

"That settles forty billion dollars. Where do you expect to find the last twenty billion?" asked Hardrock.

"We are going to borrow it", replied Robertson

"Where?"

"In Zurich."

"From whom?"

"From the same Swiss International Bank. The amount is too big for them. They will need to form a syndicate, which they will lead. That's all right. We have done enough for them in the past; it's time they show some gratitude."

"You think they will do it?"

"I'll tell Shermer that there are two conditions to be met if he wants the eighteen billion deposits from the Sheik. First, he leaves the funds with us on a seven day basis and a gentlemen's agreement that the funds shall remain with us as long as feasible. Second, Swiss International must lead a syndicate of Swiss banks to raise twenty billion dollars for us on a five year basis."

"They will want to know why?"

"Christ, they are not going to ask many questions. They all have surpluses of funds. They will be pleased to place them on five-year basis with the world's largest bank. They all know that we average a twenty billion dollar growth per year and that theoretically we could pay them back within a year. We'll tell them the Feds are getting sticky about our ratio of short-term liabilities and that we wish to borrow on medium term — five years should do it — to readjust this ratio and satisfy the Feds. They hate government controls as much as we do. They will understand our position and will be happy to help."

"I hope so", Hardrock sighed. "How do we get these funds to the Sheik?"

"He wants cash. He will get cash. Tell him he gets his last twenty billion in cash in ten days."

"He won't wait that long."

"He will. He knows as well as we do that there is not that much cash available in the whole US and that we will have to ask the Federal Reserve to print some."

"Won't the Feds question such a large order for bills?"

"We won't ask them for the whole amount. We can probably gather nine to ten billion from other banks and draw temporarily from our working supply. We have ten days to obtain the balance from the Feds. That's three to four billion every five days. I think we can do it without creating too much furor."

"Where are we going to store it? Do you know how much space we will need?"

"Peter, why do you always worry about details? We pay people to look after our vaults and the storage of our cash. Let them worry about it."

Hardrock completed his notes and swung his chair around to face the windows of his office. The morning fog had lifted and he could now see clearly the East River flowing into the Hudson River and beyond into the Atlantic Ocean. "We are all going to drown", he reflected. "The whole world is going to drown in an ocean of Arab money. No one can resist its tides. Since 1973, the whole financial community has been swimming in its waves and after five years we are no closer to shore. On the contrary, we are on the brink of crashing on a giant reef and drowning. And you, Andrew Robertson, you are responsible for our mess. You are the friend of the Arabs. You fought to establish us in the Middle East in the early 60's; since then you have nurtured our relationship using your schemes, favors, and unwarranted loans, higher than necessary interest. Also your Judith Watson and other whores. Robertson, I hold you responsible and this time I won't let you go unpunished." Still gazing out the window, he heard himself say aloud "Thank you Andrew, I know what to say and you have me nearly convinced that it will work."

"It will."

"But let me tell you something, Andrew, when we return from Zurich with our twenty billion dollars and if we save our skins from this dreadful mess, I shall have you fired."

"You wouldn't dare", replied Robertson, cockily, "you can't walk without me."

He rose to leave, "I'll have Madame de Rivoli make our reservations to Zurich. You want her to come along?"

"No."

As he was leaving Hardrock's office, Robertson looked at his watch. The Sheik was expected to return at 10:30, in less than five minutes. Robertson stopped at Simone de Rivoli's desk.

"Simone, please book Peter and me for Zurich on this Sunday's noon flight. Leave the return open. Also, reserve two suites at the Dodler Hotel, say for three nights. Check Peter's appointment schedule and rearrange it. He should be back Thursday morning. Finally, phone the El Morocco, we shall be two for dinner. You and me."

"Are you asking me or telling me?"

"Just be there. I'll meet you at the bar at 7:30."

"The Sheik might walk in. It's one of his favorite places."

"It's also mine, so let him! If he wants to scream, we will give him reasons, the fucking bastard."

"Andrew, watch your language", suggested Simone.

"I said the fucking bastard and that stands. I'll tell him to his face, if you want me to."

The doors of the elevator had barely closed behind Robertson when the other car stopped on the Executive Floor. Sheik Ben Said Al-Madir stepped out, his traditional robe contrasting sharply with the modernistic decor of the large waiting room and its collection of Picassos. Simone met him promptly.

"Good morning again, Sheik Al-Madir. Mr. Hardrock is expecting you. Please follow me."

"I know the way. I have been here before." His tone was sharp and biting.

"You could at least give me the opportunity to explain", whispered Simone.

"There is nothing to explain. Allah has spoken. 'He who goes astray does it to his own loss'. I have nothing else to say to you. Nor to Robertson."

They had reached Hardrock's office. Before Simone could knock, Sheik Al-Madir had already grabbed the doorknob and was walking in.

"Sheik Al-Madir", nodded Hardrock glumly. "Have a seat", and he indicated the chair across from his desk, instead of the conference corner of his office where they had sat earlier. *Might as well re-establish certain distances,* he thought. *I must also have that Gallibert painting removed from my office,* he resolved silently.

The Sheik sat, erect. "I'm ready, Mr. Hardrock and I am listening."

Hardrock scrutinized the face of the Sheik. He could discern no sympathy, no concern. He sat erect, enrobed in his official attire, a costume from another world, his hands resting on the thin briefcase on his knees. Under his Arabian headgear, his black eyes seemed revengeful, with a cruel glint flashing back at Hardrock. He leaned forward, "where is my cash?"

Hardrock lowered his eyes and glanced at his notes in front of him. The Sheik opened his briefcase and pulled out the check.

"As you can see, Mr. Hardrock, the amount has not changed."

Hardrock knew it by heart. $60,129,834,645.

The Sheik continued. "I presume you have verified the status of my account with your computer division and found everything in order."

Hardrock nodded.

The Sheik placed the check in front of Hardrock. "Will you please then honor my check."

No more stalling was possible. No more hesitation. There was no other way to go. Hardrock had to jump. "I can't", he stated flatly.

"Mr. Hardrock..."

"I can't", interrupted Hardrock, "and if you persist with your demand that we honor your check now and in cash, you will leave me no alternative but to close the doors of this bank immediately."

"You could never do such a thing. You are the largest bank in the world!"

"I would have no other choice."

"This is a shock to me", said the Sheik. "Please explain. Why can't you repay my deposit? It's unheard of...a bank of your size."

"Your deposit represents half of our assets. There is no way we can convert those into cash to repay you."

"Why not?" asked the Sheik.

"Because our assets comprise little cash, perhaps twelve percent of the total. That's a fair average. Most banks maintain the same ratio. The balance of our funds is invested. Some in Treasury bills and other securities issued by the US Government, but the bulk are loaned out to our clients. We can't call in these loans."

"Why not?" repeated the Sheik.

"You have borrowed money from us previously. You know that our loans have maturity dates varying from thirty days up to five years. You know also that most lines of credit are extended for a period of one year. So, we can't call in our loans before maturity and, if we did, most of our borrowers would not be able to repay us."

"I must conclude that you are telling me that your bank is bankrupt."

Hardrock replied quickly. "Certainly not. But your demands are creating a serious liquidity problem."

"How much of my deposit can you repay?"

"No more than twelve to fifteen billion."

"That's completely unacceptable and I must conclude that you have solicited and accepted my funds on deposit with your bank under false pretense. You have always advertised the safety and the strength of your assets."

Hardrock saw his first opening. "Let me remind you, Sheik Al-Madir, that it is you who has taken undue risks by depositing more money with us than what our regulations permitted."

"Your thirty billion limits was a figure taken out of thin air."

"No sir, it was not", replied Hardrock. "That figure was dictated by our prudent approach to banking and dictated also by our experience. In the last few years, it has been established that a bank could operate safely with a liquidity position of say, fifteen to twenty percent of its liabilities. It meant that a bank could sustain a drop of fifteen to twenty percent in its deposits without having to call in its loans. In practice, such a drop would mean a run on the bank, a panic amongst depositors. You don't see those often anymore because most deposits are small, less than twenty-five thousand dollars, and those deposits are fully insured by the US Government. So, most depositors don't worry and they don't start runs on their banks."

"You are talking about insignificant amounts", commented the Sheik impatiently. "I'm dealing with billions".

"Exactly", said Hardrock. "In 1973, when you people decided to hold up the world for ransom and quadrupled the price of oil, the rules of the game changed. In fact, they did not change so much as they vanished. Nobody knew what to do or what was going to happen. We all had to play by ear. So our limit of thirty billion dollars was set when our assets reached one hundred billion. We estimated that no more than fifty percent of our Arab deposits would be withdrawn at any one time. Even that was a remote possibility, which meant that our extreme exposure was fifteen billion dollars or fifteen percent of our assets. Certainly you must understand this logic."

"I only understand that you were gambling", retorted the Sheik, "and you were gambling without knowing the hand of the other party", he added sarcastically. He then paused and the glints of cruelty in his eyes appeared to flash more brightly". It is said: "Everyone must bear the consequence of that, which he does."

Hardrock decided to attack. "Sheik Al-Madir, your religion, which I respect but don't understand, is not going to solve our problem. You say that we gambled, but you forget that the real gambler is you."

"I never gamble. Allah forbids it."

"You did when you placed on deposit with us more funds than a prudent man would have done. Do you realize that you have deposited with us ten times the amount of our capital and reserves? You are a businessman, Sheik Al-Madir, you were educated at Harvard, you know that you would have taken an undue risk even if your deposit had only matched our capital, roughly seven billion dollars. What do you think the Rulers of the Emirates will say or do to you when they find out what excessive risks you have taken, you their financial adviser, you their wise and knowledgeable investment manager?"

"How would they know?" The glints faded somewhat.

Hardrock kept punching. "I'll tell them!"

The Sheik rose and dominated Hardrock, still sitting. "I will bankrupt you first."

"If you did, you would lose everything", stated Hardrock positively.

"That's where you are wrong", replied the Sheik. He sat down again. "You were right to remind me of my US education. Under your bankruptcy regulations, my claim of sixty billion dollars would no doubt assure me of the majority vote at the creditors' meeting. I would immediately vote to accept a proposal, my proposal, that ordinary shares of your bank be issued to creditors in payment of their claims."

"What good would that do you?" asked Hardrock.

"I'm already one of the largest shareholders of your bank. Perhaps the second largest, right after your family, Mr. Hardrock. This move would give me control of your bank, the largest bank in the world. Not bad for a camel driver, as your sidekick Robertson often describes me."

Hardrock ignored the caustic accusation. "You seem to forget, Sheik Al-Madir, that we have laws and regulations here prohibiting the ownership of more than twenty-five percent of the capital of a US bank by foreigners."

"Mr. Hardrock, laws are made by men and can be amended by the same men or others. I believe you will agree that I possess sufficient money to have any law of the United States changed to suit me."

Hardrock slammed his fist on his desk. "Not as long as my brother is President of the United States!"

The ringing of Hardrock's private phone broke up the duelists. Hardrock lifted the receiver and lowered his voice. "Yes?"

It was Robertson. " Is the Sheik there?"

"Yes".

"I have just talked to Shermer. Found him where I thought, still in bed with Judith. She is priceless. We have a deal. He will take the deposit and leave it with us on a seven day call basis as long as he can."

"How long is that?"

"Should be long enough. Have your made your proposals?"

"No."

"You will?"

"Yes."

"Good luck". Robertson was gone and the duel had to resume. Hardrock decided to put everything behind one big final thrust. "Sheik Al-Madir, it appears to me that we have reached a deadlock here. If I inform your Rulers of your actions, they will destroy you and in the process they are bound to destroy my bank. If you insist on your sixty billion dollars cash payment today, you will destroy my bank and yourself with it. How do we resolve this stalemate?"

"It seems to me it's your problem and your decision", said the Sheik icily.

"I rather think it's your decision and, with your permission, I would like to suggest that you turn to your most Gracious Allah and ask for his advice. You always invoke his name and his sayings anyway."

The Sheik stared at Hardrock and watched him push his chair back, pull the middle drawer of his desk, take out a sheet of paper. Hardrock glanced back at the Sheik, lowered his eyes and started to read solemnly. "It is written: When a loan is taken, the date of repayment should be agreed upon. If on due date the debtor be in straitened circumstances, then grant him respite in respect of the repayment of the capital sum till a time of ease. In the name of Allah, most Gracious, ever Merciful." Hardrock threw the sheet of paper to the Sheik. "You want the reference? You want the verse number?"

The Sheik looked at Hardrock confounded. "I did not know you were interested in the Quran", he said flatly.

"This quote was given to me many years ago by the then Chairman of Intra Bank of Beirut. He told me that the teachings of the Quran were the source of all the policies of his bank. As a matter of fact, I never understood why his fellow Arabs turned against him and bankrupted his bank."

Sheik Al-Madir managed to remain stoic while the memory of Robertson's confidential file, and his own betrayal of the secrets it contained, rushed to his brain.

"All right, Mr. Hardrock, I am prepared to listen", he said flatly.

Hardrock took his notes from his desk. "I am going to offer you one solution, one unique and total solution within the spirit of your Quran. My solution is not open for discussion. You take it or you leave it. But I wish to remind you that if don't accept it, it is the end of you and me. And in addition, the wrath of Allah shall be upon you!"

Sheik Al-Madir winced. "I'm listening."

At the end of the day, Simone decided to walk to her apartment. She needed to breathe after the tumultuous hours she had just lived through in the office. The two visits of the Sheik, the meeting between Hardrock and Robertson, their sudden decision to fly to Zurich on Sunday, the number of officers called to Hardrock's office throughout the day, bringing with them lined pads covered with figures. Another two hour meeting in the afternoon between Hardrock and Robertson. All appointments canceled until next Thursday. All phone calls refused. Hardrock bossing her, ordering her impatiently, his nervousness spreading to her and everyone else on the executive floor. She sensed that a drama was being enacted in Hardrock's office. She knew that she was playing a role in it, but she was not sure of her own lines. Hardrock asked her to cancel her lunch hour, but he agreed to grant her ten minutes to make a personal errand. She had rushed downstairs to the Western Union office and had dispatched a cable to Pierre Beauchamp under their agreed upon code.

> *"Mme Germaine de Beauval, P.O. Box H224, Paris France. Dear Mother regret news death grandmother please advise day and place of funeral. Simone."*

As she reached her new apartment on Fifth Avenue, she eagerly opened her mailbox. His reply was already there. She had not seen Pierre in six months.

"Please, God, please make him say yes in his cable. I don't

think I can stand it any longer." She nervously ripped open the yellow envelope.

> "Baroness Simone de Rivoli, 780 Fifth Avenue, New York.
> Grandmother's funeral Montreal Saturday 3pm
> Cathedral Marie Reine du Monde. Love, Mother."

She nearly jumped from joy but saw the doorman glancing at her. She turned towards the elevator, and when she was sure that nobody could see her, she brought the cable to her lips and kissed it. She then entered the elevator and pressed her floor button. She had only one hour to bathe and change before meeting Robertson for dinner at the El Morocco.

He was already at the bar when she walked in. At least Robertson had that one quality: he never kept you waiting in bars...or bedrooms. He rose.

"You look beautiful, as usual, although I know what a terrible day we have all had."

"I am completely exhausted", replied Simone.

She took his seat at the bar and he stood behind her. She heard him say. "This place is really full tonight. Let's have a quick one and move on to the dining room. Bartender! Make it two".

The bartender knew Robertson's favorite drink well. He was pouring gin into two glasses when Simone intervened.

"I would rather have a cognac with Perrier."

"Cognac before dinner?" queried Robertson.

"I have just received some bad news." She showed him Pierre's cable.

"I didn't know you had family in Canada."

"My maternal grandmother moved to Montreal many years ago. She raised me when I was very young. I had not seen her for more than twenty years when I visited her six months ago. She was very old."

"Are you going to the funeral"?

"I must. As you can see by the cable, mother is coming from France. I'll leave tomorrow morning on Eastern; they have a flight at 10:30. That should put me in downtown Montreal by 12:30 giving me time for lunch before the funeral."

"Where will you be staying?"

"At the same hotel as my mother. She did not mention

which one in her cable. I'll meet her at the cathedral. The last time I stayed at the Bonaventure hotel. I like their Japanese garden on the roof and their outdoor heated swimming pool. Would you believe I swam there last December."

That was also a lie. Simone and Pierre had walked through the lobby of the hotel on their way to the restaurant and stopped to contemplate the daring swimmers. But she knew that Robertson had often stayed at the Bonaventure Hotel and that he would believe her.

"If I did not have to fly to Zurich, I would come with you. We could spend the weekend in the Laurentians. Wouldn't that be great?"

"You forget that my mother will be there", replied Simone with a conspiratorial smile.

"When are you coming back?"

"Tuesday evening or Wednesday on the early morning flight. I should be at the office by 9:30"

"That's right; I had forgotten that Tuesday is the 4th of July. Independence Day. Does Hardrock know that you won't be in the office Monday?"

"No, I only found out about my grandmother when I reached home".

"I don't think he would want you away while he is in Zurich. At least not under the present circumstances."

"What's wrong?" asked Simone, pretending not to know.

"It's that goddamn Sheik of yours again", exclaimed Robertson.

"Not so loud, Andrew", whispered Simone, "and let me remind you that he was your Sheik before I met him. You are the one who pushed me into his arms..."

"All right! All right! Don't get mad."

"I'm not getting mad. I just want to set the record straight and to remind you that we are in a public bar."

"I know as well as you where we are, so don't get on your high horse! Let's go and eat."

"That's a very good idea," said Simone as she pushed the stool back and took her purse from the bar.

"Si Madame la Baroness veut bien m'accompagner", mimicked Robertson as he offered his arm reverently.

The Maitre d' bowed to both of them. "Your table is ready, Mr. Robertson. Madame la Barone".

After they were seated and had ordered, Simone broke a piece from her bread and while spreading butter on it asked in a matter of fact voice. "At the bar you were swearing at the Sheik. What has he done now?"

"He tried to screw the bank."

"Andrew, I wish you would watch your language, especially when we are dining in public."

Robertson ignored her. "But he won't get away with it, the bastard, the filthy camel driver. Do you know what he did?"

While Robertson recounted the details of the events of the morning, Simone kept watching the room to make sure nobody was listening. Twice she placed her hand on Robertson's arm and reminded him "keep you voice down." When he was finished, Simone's only comments were, "now I know why Mr. Hardrock was so nervous. He even raised his voice to me today. First time in the nearly two years that I have been working with him. He also shouted at Murray from Computer Division. Not like him to display such manners. He is always such a gentleman."

"Now you know why you should stay close to the office", commented Robertson.

"I'll phone first thing Monday and let Louise know where I can be reached. I can be back in New York within two hours. Under the circumstances, I owe it to my mother to spend at least two or three days with her. I am sure that Mr. Hardrock will understand despite our problems."

"Problems! When I return from Zurich, we will no longer have problems. But I promise you something, Simone, your Sheik will have a fucking big problem. If you want to tell him, be my guest."

"You forget that he has refused to see me. You have now soiled me in his eyes."

"That's a lot of crap. He's got the hots for you and all his money won't buy him a fire truck big enough to douse his belly dancer fucking cock."

"Andrew, sometimes I have difficulty thinking of you as a banker. You can be more abusive and cruder than the lowest echelon dockworker. "As she spoke one of the waiters brought a dozen roses to the table. "For Baroness de Rivoli", he said, "from Sheik Al-Madir."

"You see", exulted Robertson, "what did I tell you?"

Simone took the envelope from the spray of flowers and removed the card. Robertson took it away from her. "Let me read that", he said.

"The other night I found him in your bed; tonight would I find you on his lap?"

"Andrew, take me home, please," was Simone's answer.

"Your place or mine?" Robertson joked.

"Home, Andrew, and I mean home."

"Come on Simone, you are not going to let this tribesman stand between us. Let's go to my place and let's fuck. We both need it to forget our problems."

"Andrew, how can you even suggest?"

"What's wrong now?"

She raised a handkerchief to her eyes and walked ahead of him out on the street while crying, "Andrew, I am mourning my grandmother."

CHAPTER TWO
THE FILE

"Somewhere in the dim past, someone discovered gold. And for some reason lost in the mists that surround mankind's early history, gold became the most valuable thing on earth. Ever since, gold has stimulated and haunted the human race. The desire to possess it has moved men to commit crimes, make war and explore new worlds. Most systems of money have been tied, in one way or another, to gold as the standard of value...Gold is back in the news now, haunting the United States, because the government is moving again in an effort to try and break the hold this metal has had on the hearts of mankind throughout history...we do believe that the government has embarked upon the only intelligent course".

(From US Gold Rush in 1974. The Washington Post. December 1974)

Simone's flight terminated smoothly and arrived on time at Mirabel Airport, Montreal's new giant supersonic international airport, the largest in the world. She cleared immigration quickly and soon located her luggage on the oval carousel. She reflected on her vanity that made her bring two suitcases and a makeup bag for a three- day stay in Montreal. An overnight case would have been sufficient. But she had not seen Pierre for six months and women in love do foolish things.

It was only 11:40. She had more than three hours at her disposal before meeting Pierre at three o'clock at the cathedral. She decided to have lunch at the airport, placed her luggage in a locker not too far from the exit to the taxis platform and rode the escalators to the "Le Mirabel Restaurant". She was met by a pleasant maitre d'. "Le restaurant n'ouvre qu'à midi, Madame. Vous désirez attendre au bar quelques minutes?"

She chose a table in the bar by a window overlooking the runways and ordered a Dubonnet with a twist of lemon. Suddenly, a great lassitude invaded her, took possession of her physically and mentally. While she wanted to experience beforehand the pleasure of loving Pierre again, she could not chase from her body the exhaustion from the efforts exerted during the last eighteen months in New York, nor erase from her mind the repulsion of her intimacies with Robertson and Sheik Al-Madir. She heard herself whisper, "how much longer Pierre? How much more?"

A sleek Air France Concorde had landed and was taxiing to its parking position on the tarmac below her. Her eyes followed the Bleu, Blanc, Rouge shield of her country on the fuselage and she felt a tremendous desire to rush to the gate and fly back home forever. But how could she? She was trapped in history. To a certain extent, she was helping to shape it. She, Baroness Simone de Rivoli, super French agent for the French Intelligence Agency.

The last nine years of her life unfolded in front of her vividly, the first seven, a bath of happiness in France, with Pierre never far away, and the last eighteen months, alone in New York, with no contacts with Pierre other than by coded messages, except for two glorious weeks at Christmas, spent with him here in Canada, six months ago. She was alone in New York, her heart with Pierre in Paris and her body in the bed of Robertson or on the couch of the Sheik, her soul tormented by her actions, feeling soiled, naked, and sometimes obscene. For the glory of France? For avenging the murder of Antoine at My Lai? Or was it now out of devotion to Pierre? The Sheik had accused her of being an idolatress. Perhaps she was. She worshipped Pierre. She blindly admired him. She adored him. She would do anything for him or with him. He was the ultimate source of her happiness.

She remembered the night in Mougins after her return to France from Vietnam. She had awakened in the incredible sunlight of the Cote d'Azur, her body perceiving again the extraordinary sensations of the previous evening. Pierre rested next to her, his body still transmitting to her the response of their rediscovered love, her happiness covering them both in a mantle of gold, floating in a spray of diamonds towards the morning sun. She had turned to him and kissed his left nipple with devotion. His skin tingling and his eyes still closed, he had brushed away a lock of her hair from his face. She had knelt and let all of her hair caress his head. He had awakened and had kissed her lips delicately. She had been unable to contain her renewed happiness. She had raised the covers and laid slowly on him, warm and impassioned, and once again, in a repressed scream, she had worshipped his body.

Monday had descended upon them like a black cloud. "When are you leaving?" she had asked.

"At noon."

"Can't you stay longer?"

"I am already overextending my stay here." He had become again the mysterious government official. Tears had come to her eyes. "Don't leave me."

"I must. I can barely make a four o'clock appointment at the Ministry of Finance."

"Take me with you", she had pleaded.

"No. You need to stay. You need to rest. I'll return on Friday to spend another weekend with you." He had added teasingly with a smile on his face, "and if you have been a good girl, if I find you rested and in a happy disposition, I'll take you back to Paris on Sunday."

She had looked at him for a long time, more tears coming to her eyes and descending slowly on her cheeks, "you have given me happiness to last all my life."

She had driven him to Nice airport and had waited until his plane had disappeared over the Alps before starting her solitary return to Mougins.

She had spent the week in the garden enjoying the splendid weather, either lounging by the swimming pool or tending to the grounds, adorned with flowers. She looked with tenderness after the roses as if each one was the expression of a year of love, and having counted thousands of them, she slept contented every night dreaming of roses, love and Pierre.

He returned Friday as promised and they replayed together the scenes of the happiness they had found during the previous weekend but in a different key. Their craving was replaced by a matured expectation. They were not disappointed. She wanted to be alone with him for their remaining hours of ecstasy.

She prepared breakfast and discovered a forgotten tranquility in her newly found freedom from doubt, fear and the miseries of war. He complimented her on her breakfast suggesting teasingly that as her culinary talents matched her amorous behavior, she had finally acquired all the qualities of the ideal housewife. She hated him for using the word but also felt flattered that it could have entered his entrenched bachelor's mind.

They went for a long walk in the forest, moving silently until they reached a large pond well hidden by old plane trees. They looked at the reflection of their faces amongst the branches on the still water, their hands interlaced as young lovers. She will never know what made her break the mood. "I was thinking of Vietnam earlier this morning. It must have been the contrast between the tranquility I found here and the horrifying blood and deafening noises of war."

He turned away from her and leaned against a large tree, his eyes on the ground. "You still want to avenge the murder of your husband?"

It was her duty. While her hatred had diminished with time and distance, her sense of loyalty had grown. "More than ever, Pierre, even if it takes me my whole life."

"Can you hate that long?" he had asked.

"Do I need to hate? Or is it sufficient to be imbued with a sense of justice that lives beyond time and men?"

"You still will not accept that Antoine's death was the result of war", he had questioned sadly.

"I will not and I cannot because it is not the truth. Antoine was not killed at war. He was murdered by Americans who happened to wear army uniforms. They were murderers in disguise." Her voice had taken the sharp, nearly metallic tone she easily mustered each time she felt her morality outraged, her honor abused.

Pierre's eyes had not moved from the ground as if a feeling of guilt had lowered his head in repentance. "I can help", he stated flatly. "I don't want to, but if it is your wish, I will help you."

He had then for the first time divulged to her the mystery of his work. Pierre Beauchamp was the head of the French

Intelligence Agency. A master spy. Not a war spy. A spy in time of peace in the never ending economic wars between nations.

"There is no physical violence in what we do. No doubt from time to time we break the industrial espionage laws of certain countries, such as those of Switzerland for instance, that have been enacted to protect their economy against us and other nations, but most of the time, I can say, we act peacefully, secretly...and then we escape before getting caught." He had snorted, no doubt remembering an amusing episode in his career.

"How can you help me?" she had asked.

"I need you for my agency." Only then had he raised his head, their eyes had met and she had thrown herself in his waiting arms. He had caressed her hair tenderly. "Let's walk back slowly. We will need to start packing soon. I will explain my plans for you. From now on, we work together."

They had returned to Paris in the evening and on Wednesday morning she had registered at the Sorbonne University for a course in Business Administration and Economics. She, Barone Simone de Rivoli, a trained nurse. It took her four years. One day she rushed home radiant and never stopped kissing Pierre until he had wrestled her arms behind her making her drop a large envelope. He had finally let her go and had picked up the envelope. She had looked at him, prouder than ever, while he had read its contents. "L'Université de la Sorbonne a l'honneur de décerner à Madame La Barone Simone de Rivoli un doctorat en sciences économiques avec mention très honorable."

She had gone back to his welcoming arms reacting as a young collegian. "Pierre, I have made it. I have my doctorate. Isn't it great? Let's celebrate."

"Oui, docteur", he had answered, a satisfied smile on his face.

Paris had never looked more exciting to them. They dined at l'Etoile de Moscou and joined in with the Russian singers during the show, clapping their hands or shouting happily at the acrobatic dancers. In the early morning, drunk with pleasure and champagne, they walked gaily down the Champs Elysée and hailed a taxi to take them to Brasserie Lipp where they had each ordered an onion soup. "It absorbs the alcohol," they had shouted in unison. They had also ordered a carafe of red wine, "to chase the soup down!"

"When do I start?" Her question had seemed to destroy the euphoria of their evening.

"I don't think you are ready, yet."

"But Pierre, I have just completed four years of intensive studies. I have worked hard for my doctorate. I received it with great honors. What more do you want of me?"

"Experience. Practical experience."

"Don't I acquire it working with you?"

"We can't take the risk. When you receive your first assignment you will need more than a fancy diploma."

Tears of disappointment had replaced the sparks of her happiness and she had closed her eyes hoping to hide them from him. "I want to work with you, now."

"I have arranged for you to enter the next and final stage of your training. I am giving you ten days of rest, with pay. After that, you will join the Bank of France as an economist."

"The Bank of France? I'm going to spy on the Bank of France?" Simone had asked, incredulously.

"You know very well that you will not. We have an understanding with them. They train every one of our agents in the high acrobatics of finance, both internal and international. You will now see the practical applications of the gold theories you have learned at the Sorbonne. Gold. It's our most precious asset. Without it, there is no commercial world. Without it, France will never enjoy freedom. I want you to become my specialist in gold." And with the usual tempting smile, "I shall call you my golden spy. It suits you perfectly."

"How long will that take?"

"Not long."

"How long is not long, Pierre?"

"A few years."

It had taken exactly three and a half years. Then, one night, while they were resting after their love making during which Pierre had seemed more affectionate and more possessive than usual, he had announced, "I have an assignment for you."

"Pierre, I can't believe it. I was on the verge of losing all hope. Do you realize I returned from Vietnam eight years ago?"

"I thought it was only seven."

"No. It can't be. Antoine was murdered in '68. I came back in early '69 and the day after tomorrow we will celebrate the arrival of 1977." She had rolled over him taking his face between her hands and kissed his mouth, "that makes me a very old woman, so take me, take me again before I become too old for you."

It had been their farewell. A week later she had left for New York to join Grand American Bank as an executive assistant to the Chairman, Peter Hardrock. She had been met in New York by Georges Monti, a vice consul at the French consulate, who had been designated as her contact in the US. Pierre had explained, "No one is going to question why you, as a French citizen, would frequently visit the French consulate. If you feel uneasy about it, date Georges a few times. Have lunch with him openly in well patronized restaurants. You will find that Georges is a most knowledgeable person. He loves art, particularly classical music. He will take you to the opera, if you wish to go. Georges is a Corsican who relishes his work both as a vice consul and as a secret agent. He is no doubt under surveillance in the US and you will have to be prudent."

"Why take the risk of seeing him in the open?"

"That's the idea. See him openly, pretend you like him, want his friendship; it should diminish the suspicions that the two of you are working together. You can trust him implicitly. I do. He is our best contact man."

Georges had found her an apartment on East 56th street, a good residential district and had been most helpful during her first days in New York. Pierre had told her that she would find her operative instructions at the consulate. Georges would give them to her only after her hiring by Grand American Bank had been confirmed. She was interviewed by Hardrock on the third day of her arrival, spent the following two days completing forms, passing medical tests and obtaining photos to complete her personnel records. She was finally told by the Personnel Department that she had been hired. She had phoned Georges. "I have made it, I'm hired."

"When do you start?" he had wanted to know.

"Monday morning."

"OK, that leaves us three days to brief you. Your instructions are in the safe in my office here at the consulate. They can't be taken out. You will have to read them here and when you are finished they will go back to my safe. No copies can be made. You can always consult them here later. When can you come?"

"I'll be there in half an hour."

Georges had handed her a voluminous file, one of those red accordion filing folders with a strong rubber band holding it tightly closed. "You can use that desk in the corner. If you have any questions, feel free to ask me."

She had untied the file with great expectations. At last! After eight years of training, of studies, of waiting. As she took the first document out of the file, the beat of her heart increased considerably.

*"Instructions to Baroness Simone de Rivoli
from Pierre Beauchamp."*

TOP SECRET

Your Assignment — *You have been employed by Grand American Bank as an executive assistant to Peter Hardrock, the Chairman of the bank. You were recommended to Mr. Hardrock by René Mathieu, President of La Companie de Suez. They are friends. You are to remain in your position with Grand American until your mission is accomplished. You cannot resign. Don't get fired. We expect your mission to last two to three years, depending on your efficiency and allowing for the human reactions of the other persons against who your actions are directed. Read carefully what follows. Don't question your instructions. Do as you are told. Vive La France!*

Your Mission — Your mission is twofold. One, you must bankrupt Grand American Bank. Two, you must make the United States recognize gold again as the ultimate money, as the only true store of value. Well executed, the first should condition the second.

"My God! Bankrupt Grand American Bank!" Despite her indoctrination, Simone was shocked by the amplitude of her task.

Grand American Bank — It's the largest bank in the world. Established in 1892 by Winnifred Hardrock, the grandfather of Peter Hardrock, the present Chairman. The bank progressed steadily until 1960 when it reached the 20th rank amongst US banks. Its growth continued at a decent rate after that until 1966 when it experienced a sudden surge in its total deposits, no doubt the result of funds moved to its Dubai branch from Intra Bank, Beirut (see below). At the time, the Dubai office and the whole of the Middle East operations of Grand American were under the supervision of Andrew Robertson, an ambitious Vice President. Robertson was appointed President of the bank in 1969. Since 1974, the bank has undergone extraordinary changes. It has become the largest bank in the world, its assets growing recently at a rate of twenty billion dollars per year. Should that growth rate be maintained, the assets of the bank should top one hundred billion dollars by late 1977. The bank is now as big as Bank of America and First National City Bank combined. It is larger than all French national banks put together.

The latest balance sheet of the bank (December '76) shows the following: (in billions)

Assets		Liabilities	
Cash & due from banks	12.4	Demand deposits	11.1
U.S. Treasury Bills &		Short term deposits	
other US Securities	14.6	(less than 90 days)	45.5
Other Investments	12.3	Savings deposits	10.3
Loans	47.0	Fixed term deposits	14.2
Letters of credit		Letters of credit	2.0
(contra)	2.0		
Other Assets	.3	Other liabilities	.2
		Capital	5.3
	88.6		88.6

A close analysis of this balance sheet reveals its vulnerability. Ratio of short term liabilities (demand deposits and deposits with a maturity of less than ninety days) have reached 65% of total assets. Cash on hand is only equal to 13% of total liabilities, although twelve billion dollars is a substantial sum. Cash and US securities combined represent only about 30% of total assets.

We know that Robertson has a close relationship with Sheik Al-Madir (see below) and we suspect that Sheik Al-Madir, who controls in excess of one hundred and forty billion dollars of cash and other assets belonging to the United Arab Emirates and its Rulers, has placed on deposit with Grand American in excess of twenty billion dollars. The bank has an internal rule limiting Arab deposits to twenty-five percent of its assets with a maximum of thirty billion dollars. We don't know how rigidly this limit is applied. In any event, the deposits held by the Sheik with Grand American Bank have reached an unmanageable size. The Sheik is taking an undue risk by depositing such large sums with one banking institution. We don't know what his motives are, if he has any. The agent will have to find out.

Should the Sheik decide to withdraw the bulk of his funds from Grand American, it would force the bank to call for a moratorium on the repayment of its deposits and the

Federal Reserve Board and the Federal Deposit Insurance Corporation would have to step in, support the bank financially and supervise its management. It would be such a terrible blow to the banking industry of the United States, and more importantly to the US dollar, that we believe it would immediately bring the Americans to the negotiation table at which time the proposition of the French government to re-establish the monetary value of gold would no doubt be accepted forthwith.

The Gold Problem – From the day man created money to facilitate the exchange of goods, gold has been used as the ultimate method of payment. When substitutes were used such as paper money, they were always created against the security of the gold reserves of the issuing Government. If a state ran out of gold, its money became valueless. If a country ran out of gold, it no longer had "real" money to pay for goods it imported from other countries. This was a well known situation until after the second world war when the massive help distributed by the United States, to Germany and Japan particularly, but also to other countries, created a huge supply of US dollars. Soon it established that currency as the currency of trades. Other currencies, such as the pound Sterling and the French franc, saw their usage as international currencies disappear quickly.

The world accepted the US dollar for two reasons: first, because it was being distributed rather freely and most countries, during their reconstruction period, had other problems to solve then those predicted in the warnings of their monetary specialists. Second, because the dollar was convertible into gold at any time, it permitted a country to ask the US Government to convert their US dollar holdings into gold. France did that consistently in the early sixties. It was de Gaulle's policy. The Americans hated him for undermining their gold reserves. In retaliation, some even stopped buying French perfume as if there was a relationship between money and perfume.

"Perhaps there is", Simone joked. "The sweet smell of money!"

The US gold reserves continued to drop during the sixties when the US kept printing money freely,stating that gold was no longer important. The true reserves of the US was its industrial capacity — read its military might. The net effect of printing more money to finance the recurring deficits in its budgets and its foreign wars, particularly the six year futile exercise in Vietnam, was to depreciate the value of the US dollar to a point where no foreign trader nor government wanted to accept it in payment. When they did, they rushed to Washington to convert it into gold. By June 1971, the gold reserves of the US were down to a paltry eleven billion dollars. President Nixon closed the Washington window and declared that the dollar would no longer be convertible into gold. The dollar, which was a promise by the US Government to pay a dollar's worth of gold to the holder, became a promise to pay nothing. There followed a series of futile monetary actions and decisions taken by central banks, the International Monetary Fund, Ministers of Finance, etc. Rates of exchange, fixed to that date, were left to float. No one knew the true value of anything. There was no longer any basis for issuing money. No restraints on government spending and on budget deficits. Money became worthless. Inflation quickly stepped in.

While economists were still debating whether or not a three percent or four percent rate of inflation was acceptable to maintain production and full employment, the rate of inflation in the US, fueled by worthless money printed in always larger quantities by irresponsible politicians, zoomed to seven percent in 1973 and twelve percent in 1974. It kept on growing in 1975 despite the fact that the economy went into its worst slump in history in terms of the size of the drop in the volume of industrial production and consumer spending. The world was definitely bankrupt.

To add to the headaches, the Arabs in late '73 and early 1974 quadrupled the price of crude oil. The result was a massive transfer of funds and purchasing power from the oil importing countries, mostly the western world and Japan, to a few individuals, the Sheiks and Kings of the Middle East. The institution of controls to reestablish some sense of order in international monetary affairs became impossible. Too much money was controlled by too few men who did not understand the problem and who did not care anyway.

The sums accumulated by the Arabs since 1973 are expected to reach two hundred and fifty billion dollars by the end of 1977 and three hundred and fifty billion by the end of 1978. By 1980, the total will exceed six hundred billion dollars. These are staggering figures. The mind can hardly understand them. No one can manage them under the present system unless discipline is again returned to the monetary system, unless governments balance their budgets, unless politicians stop printing paper to finance their handouts, unless gold becomes again what it has always been: The ultimate money, the only permanent store of value.

France's Position – France owns substantial reserves of gold. In excess of five billion dollars. In addition, its citizens who understand the real value of gold, having lost their paper fortune through two wars, are the largest gold hoarders in the world. We estimate their hoarding at eight billion dollars. It is possibly much more.

France wants to return gold to its true function. When trading, France wants to pay and to be paid in gold. France wants to reestablish order in international monetary affairs. France wants to discipline the world's politicians. The mission of the agent is to make this possible and quickly before the end of the world hits us all.

Peter Hardrock – Male, white, age 56, 5'11", about 180 lb., light brown hair, brown eyes, married to June Hasslet

*of Newport 1947, three children, Peter Jr. 17, Rosalie 15
and June 14. Marriage apparently stable. Exterior physical
marks: none. Other signs: Badly crooked little tow on left
foot. Circumcised.*

"How could they find this out?" wondered Simone.

*Religion: Protestant, but practices only when necessary to
maintain his social image.*

*Chairman of Grand American Bank. Director of Hardrock
Foundation (assets three billion). President of American Art
Society and known as the foremost patron of arts in the US.
Spends little time managing the bank, leaving the day to day
operations to Andrew Robertson, the President.*

*Peter is the son of Robert Hardrock, grandson of Winnifred
Hardrock, the founder of the Hardrock fortune. Railroads,
whiskey and oil. The grandfather founded Standard Oil of
Maine. The family is still the largest shareholder. The family
also controls Grand American Bank. Peter has succeeded his
uncle, Steve Blackburn, as Chairman in 1968.*

*Barry Hardrock, a bother of Peter and former Governor
of Vermont, was elected President of the United States
following the elections of November 1976. Brothers are not
very intimate but will close ranks if reputation of family
name is endangered.*

*Peter Hardrock is a pleasant man, a far cry from his ruthless
grandfather. His money and education have brought him a
certain savoir-faire. He admires and respects class, elegance
and good taste, a rare combination that our agent possesses.*

"Thank you, Pierre", thought Simone.

While employed by Hardrock, agent should avoid any type of romantic involvement with him. He would not appreciate it nor would he respond.

"How can you tell?" A smile came to Simone's lips. "I rather resent that remark. Are you daring me?"

Andrew Robertson – Male, white, age 52, 6'4", about 205 lb., dark brown hair, slightly balding, dark brown eyes, married to Paulette Brownsberry of Frankfurt Germany 1949, two children, Bobby 15 and Andrew Jr. 13. Marriage broken but no divorce, to protect his position. He maintains an apartment in New York, and to save face frequently visits his home in White Plains. Exterior physical marks: Short scar left side of forehead from a brawl in a bar in Frankfurt over his wife, then his fiancée. Other signs: Not circumcised, unusual for an American. Right testicle lower than left one, also unusual.

"I wonder what they say in their reports about me" thought Simone. She started to laugh. Georges looked up from his desk.
"What's funny?"
"I can't say."
"He's got right hanging balls," guffawed Georges. "I know, I laughed also when I read it. I sometimes think the agency goes overboard in these reports. But that's the way Beauchamp runs the agency. He knows that a minute detail might make a difference."
"Does he expect me to ask Robertson to take his pants off to establish his identity?"
"You may have to", was Georges' only comment.
Simone returned her attention to her file.

Religion: Protestant but never goes to church. Robertson is the man to watch and the man to use in this mission. While he has a very strong character, he has also many weaknesses: His drinking, his lust for women, his relationships with

*persons of lower standards. One Judith Watson, for instance,
a well known call girl, last address 860 First Ave., apt. 1504,
New York. Not only does she meet Robertson frequently,
he is known to use her services to entertain visiting clients
and bankers. Probably uses her to gather information
from his visitors. Robertson has been seen frequently at
Club 82 in Greenwich Village, a rather shabby run down
transvestite club. He seems to know all the "boys" but there
is no evidence that he has homosexual tendencies, although
he would probably try anything for kicks. Probably did in
Dubai where such practices are current among Arabs.*

*Joined Grand American Bank as a management trainee shortly
after Pearl Harbor, was loaned by bank to US Marine Corps
in 1943. Went to Far East until end of the war when he was
honorably discharged. He was then a sergeant. Worked in
Hong Kong, London, Paris, Nassau and Beirut, climbing
slowly the ladder of management. Then his career took a
sharp turn towards higher management. He was sent to
Dubai in 1964, as Vice President, Middle East. While there
he met Sheik Al-Madir (see below) who acted as his sponsor
and his guide.*

*In 1966, Robertson provided the Sheik with confidential
information on Intra Bank, Beirut. It is our opinion that the
information was false, entirely manufactured by Robertson to
demolish Intra Bank to the benefit of Grand American Bank.
He succeeded. Sheik Al-Madir is known to have started the
run on Intra Bank. His brothers and cousins also closed
their accounts at about the same time. Then the rush was on.
Within three weeks, Intra bank had to close its doors. In its
best days, it had been a billion dollar institution. We believe
that Robertson was responsible for this collapse. Our belief
is reinforced by the following facts: (a) Grand American, as
the major correspondent banker to Intra Bank, had one of the
smallest claims against the bank, an indication that they had
withdrawn their funds and assistance from Intra Bank prior*

to the bankruptcy. (b) Sheik Ben Said Al-Madir is known to have stated that he had seen a confidential report in Dubai that had been prepared by the Beirut branch of Grand American for its head office in New York. Our agents in Beirut and in New York never found evidence that such a report had been issued or received. (c) One Margie Phillips, secretary to Robertson in Dubai at the time, when interviewed a few months after she was fired by Robertson, remembered clearly typing a report about Intra Bank, but she refused to disclose its content. She did not appear to be very bright.

From Dubai, Robertson was transferred to Head Office in 1967 as Vice President in charge of International banking. He assumed the Presidency in 1969. Since 1974, the bank's assets have been growing at the rate of twenty billion dollars per year. Robertson claims full credit for this extraordinary growth. Sheik Al-Madir has remained a friend of Robertson who nurtures his friendship constantly. Al-Madir is the largest client of Grand American (see above).

It is our opinion that agent must concentrate on Robertson. He shows all signs of an ideal target. Any method can be used (except violence) whether moral or immoral. Agent must remember that what conditions the morality of her actions, are the benefits accruing to France, nothing else.

Simone stopped reading. "How come I can't hate you, Pierre Beauchamp? Are you suggesting that I should prostitute myself for the glory of France? I thought you loved me. How could you send me on such an assignment?" Tears came to her eyes.

"Rough, eh?" commented Georges, "but don't let it throw you. Beauchamp gives you all the rope you need, but then, he hopes you will only use part of it. It's your life, it's your conscience. It's your sense of values. How important is France to you?"

Simone lowered her head and read again. "Any method

can be used (except violence) whether moral or immoral". Then she remembered the murder of Antoine at My Lai and her oath to avenge that murder. She brushed the tears away and returned to her reading.

> _Sheik Ben Said Al-Madir_ – Male , Arab, age 50, 5'10, about 190 lb., black hair, black eyes, olive skin, three wives – names unknown and not important. Many children, names also unknown and not important. Numerous brothers and cousins. One brother in New York, Mohammed Ibn Al-Madir, is thought to handle part of his brother's affairs in the US. (Robertson lived in his house in Dubai from 1964 to 1967.) Exterior physical marks: Long scar below right ear to shoulder from knifing sometime in late 50's when his cooperation with CIA was discovered in Dubai (see below). Also three slight marks on right cheek, source unknown. He boasts he was bitten by former movie star, Rita Hayworth, when she was married to Ali Khan. Unconfirmed. Other signs: Not circumcised and for some unexplained reason he has reddish pubic hair.

"They must have inspected them intimately one by one", murmured Simone to herself. "I wonder who had that assignment?"

> _Religion: Islamic. Fervent believer. Is known to quote Quran frequently and to use such quotes to support his arguments. Does not drink nor gamble in his house or in front of his brothers and cousins but is known to play as hard as anyone else when away from home. He and Robertson have frequently thrown parties involving liquor, women and hashish. The casinos on the Côte d'Azur know him well. He gambles there heavily twice a year._

> _Sheik Al-Madir graduated from Harvard Business School during the war. He was and still is one of the few Arabs of his generation with a good university education. While_

at Harvard, he was contacted by the CIA and worked as an agent for them from 1945 to approximately 1958 or sometime after the knifing episode which involved also one Alexandre Stanoff, commercial attaché at Russian Embassy in Cairo. In payment for his cooperation, CIA obtained franchises for the Middle East or part of that territory from Coca Cola, Westinghouse, Shaeffer and a number of others. These franchises are at the source of his fortune, helped by his relationship with Grand American Bank and his friendship with Robertson who has been most generous in approving loans to Sheik Al-Madir before the oil discoveries in Dubai. Sheik Al-Madir no longer needs to borrow.

Today, Sheik Al-Madir is the financial advisor and investment manager of the United Arab Emirates. As such, he controls all the funds of the Emirates plus the personal fortunes of its Rulers, their families and their friends. It is impossible to know how much money is under his control. Possibly about one hundred and fifty billion dollars with half of it probably still not invested and kept in cash and gold.

The United Arab Emirates were established in 1968 when the British announced that they would withdraw their forces from the Trucial States by 1971. The Emirates includes Bahrain, Qatar, Abu Dhabi, Ajman, Dubai, Fujairah, Ras Al Khaimah, Sharjah and Umm Al Qaiwain. Sheik Al-Madir reports directly to the Supreme Council of the Emirates which is composed of the Rulers of the Emirates. The Council has explicit trust in the ability and experience of Sheik Al-Madir. His Harvard education, former work for the CIA and personal success in business had convinced them that their fortunes were in good, competent hands. In fact, he is a brilliant businessman. His Arab pride, however, will not let him forget, let alone forgive, that the Americans for years have spread an image of Arabs as camel drivers, filthy tribesmen, sex maniacs, belly dancer lovers, etc.

His big weakness: He sometimes lets his personal feelings and Arab pride take over his business judgment.

This is a weakness that agent must exploit. It is suggested that agent familiarize herself with the Quran. It would help her understand Sheik Al-Madir, for Allah has written: "Marry not idolatrous women till after they have believed, surely a believing bond woman would make a better wife than idolatress, however pleasing she may appear."

Simone's reading was interrupted by Georges. "What about some lunch? You have been reading for more than two hours"

"I would rather finish the main report."

"You are getting quite an education."

"I wish they had shown me this file in Paris", said Simone.

"Why? Would you have turned down the assignment? Too rough for you?"

"How well do you know Pierre Beauchamp?" asked Simone.

"He is the best intelligence director in the world!" stated Georges proudly.

"That's why I am here also," replied Simone. "Had I seen this file in Paris, I would have suggested that Beauchamp assign this job to a man. Not to a woman."

"How do you expect to plant a man in Hardrock's or Robertson's office?" queried Georges. "It's too late anyway. You have the job...and the honor, I hope. See you after lunch. Don't leave before I return. I must secure these files back in my safe."

Communications – Your contact in New York is Georges Monti. His title is Third Vice Consul at the French consulate in New York. He is one of our top agents. You can trust him entirely. Your messages will be relayed by diplomatic means quickly, without danger. In case of emergency you may cable. Address your cable to your "mother", P.O. Box H224 Paris. That is one of our confidential boxes. Disguise the real message by using normal family events such as births, marriages, deaths, etc. You will receive direct replies in the same disguise. You will never meet other agents or your superiors in the US other than Georges but meetings could easily be arranged in Montreal. For the time being, Montreal is a safe city. Canadian authorities no longer keep under surveillance the French embassy and consulates in Canada. If they did and it became known, there would be a terrible uproar in French Quebec. Canadian Intelligence Services do not spy on British installations either.

Other Information – This file contains financial reports published by Grand American Bank and information gathered by other agents on Hardrock, Robertson, Sheik Al-Madir, Judith Watson and a number of other persons. It contains also statements on the relation between gold and money made by bank officials, the US Government and the Chairman of the Federal Reserve Board. Study them. The more information you accumulate, the better your chances of success.

Plan of Action – We have none to offer. You are on your own inside the enemy camp. We have described to you the principal characters around you. You know your goal. Only you can decide what to do and when. Take your time. Keep in touch. Bonne chance et Vive La France!

Her reminiscences were roughly interrupted. "Excuse me, would you like another Dubonnet?"

Simone jumped, looked at her glass, at the planes moving on the tarmac, then at the waiter and nodded absentmindedly. But as soon as he left, she glanced at her watch. "Mon Dieu, quatorze heures vingt. How could it be? Garçon, my check please, forget the Dubonnet."

She had been daydreaming for more than two hours and had forgotten lunch. It was now too late. She would barely reach the cathedral in time for her three o'clock rendez-vous with Pierre. She stood, dropped the money on the table to pay for her Dubonnets and looked in the direction where she had first seen the blue, white and red French Concorde. It was long gone. It was already over the Atlantic on its way back to France, without her.

The taxi driver was surprisingly courteous. He took her luggage from the porter, placed it in the trunk of his car, opened the rear door and shut it carefully after she had sat comfortably. "What a difference with the attitude of New York's drivers. Even if you paid them, they would never leave their seat nor put out their sickening cigars." Her taxi picked up speed leading towards the exit to the city. "Où allez-vous, Madame?"

"A la cathédrale."

"Sur Dorchester?"

"La cathédrale Marie Reine du Monde."

The taxi turned right and after a long curve to the left, she saw a sign "Centre Ville – Downtown".

For a while she watched the cars whistle by and glanced at the rows of bungalows along the highway to her right. Soon, she was again heedless to the surroundings, imbued with her lassitude and lost in her memories. She remembered the frustration of her first eight months at Grand American Bank when nothing exciting ever happened. She had found Hardrock pleasant and proper, exactly as described in the report. Robertson remained unknown to her. She saw him from time to time when he came to Hardrock's office. He called her Simone from the day she was introduced to him. He called everyone by first name. Otherwise, he paid little attention to her and she was at a loss as to how to break into the life of the man without appearing to show interest.

She had studied carefully all the material that crossed her desk and was now most familiar with the activities of the bank, its major clients, its foreign operations. Every week, she arranged to meet Georges Monti and delivered to him her report for dispatching to Paris. She never received acknowledgments, she never received instructions.

Her first break came in early April 1977. She had been with the bank barely three months. Hardrock had dictated a memo suggesting to Robertson that in view of the importance of Arab deposits to the growth of the bank, it would be advisable that a daily report of all deposits in excess of ten million dollars be prepared for himself and Robertson. The memo asked Robertson to ensure that the Computer Division produce such a report at the end of each day, and that the report be filed by Simone de Rivoli under "Confidential Filing" in the President's office?

Within a week, the reports started to flow in. Hardrock would glance at them, initial them and give them to her for transfer to "Confidential Filing". Once a week, discreetly, Simone made a Xerox copy of the summary sheet of the computer print-out and attached it to her report to Paris. Georges had looked at the first one and had said, "excellent, you are getting there." She felt she was getting nowhere and she was bored, bored to the point of screaming, alone in this too busy for happiness city, away from her people, her friends, her culture, her Paris, her Pierre.

She shuddered as she remembered the American Bankers Association convention and her rape by Robertson. He had raped her not so much physically as morally. He had soiled her soul. He had tarnished her dignity. Suddenly, she had realized to her horror that her sex, her bed and no doubt the bed of others contained the key to her mission. The fate of the world rested on her faked orgasms.

Following their return to New York from the ABA convention, Robertson had started to invite her for after work cocktails and pressed her to visit his apartment for further drinks "before dinner". But dinner never came and she always found herself in his bed, hungry most of the time. "Let's have an early screw," he would bellow.

"Andrew, please not so loud."

"I don't give a shit if the whole world knows that I am screwing you. You are the best piece of ass I have ever encountered."

One day she had been unable to restrain herself and she had retorted, "better than Judith Watson?"

"My god, yes, even better than Judith Watson. Eh! How come you know about Judith Watson?"

"Rumors are circulating, Andrew. You should be more discreet. You don't want the same rumors to circulate about us, do you?"

He never came to her place. They always went to his. "I feel funny about sleeping in a woman's bed," he had explained. "Your pink sheets, laces, frills and all that crap."

She never spent the night in his bed. Always, after midnight, satisfied, he would say, "you must go home now. Here, take a taxi." And he would hand her a ten dollar bill. He made her feel like a whore. For the glory of France!

Then, early in December, three months after the ABA convention, she had received a cable from Paris. "Visiting grandmother Montreal for Christmas can you join me staying Chanteclerc in Ste Adele. Mother."

Pierre was coming to Montreal! Pierre had broken his silence after nearly one year. She had barely finished reading the cable when her phone had rung.

"Andrew here. How are you? What about dinner."

And a good screw, she could have added. She quickly pleaded a bad headache. "Come over", he had said, "I am sure you have a screwing headache and I have a perfect cure for it."

"Andrew, really, I can't. I feel so miserable. I am already in bed."

"I'll come over then."

"Please Andrew, not tonight. And remember, you don't like sleeping in a woman's bed."

"But I have this big hard on for you."

"Call Judith Watson!" She had slammed the phone down. It rang immediately.

"Never do that to me again, you understand!" he had hollered.

"I am sorry, Andrew, but I am really very sick. Please try to understand." She had remained sick for him until the twentieth of December when she had started a two-week holiday and flown to Canada. She wanted to go to Pierre, her body clean. Three weeks of washing, bathing and scrubbing did not even seem enough to remove Robertson's filth from her. She had sent a cable to Paris addressed to her "mother" but sent to the agency's confidential box. "Madame Germaine de Beauval, PO Box H224 Paris. Arriving Chanteclerc in Laurentians 20th December eager to see you have taken two week holiday. Love Simone."

Was it too much to hope that he could spend two weeks with her? She needed him so badly. She needed him to repair her broken soul and to soothe her damaged body. She needed him to lean against and to draw from his well of strength the courage to persist in her assignment. She needed him to borrow from his intelligence the inspiration that would permit her to find the key to her mission. She need him because she loved him.

He had arrived in the late afternoon on the twenty second, two days after her, the longest two days of her life. Her heart had contracted painfully when she had watched the airport limousine stop and Pierre assist an elegant woman step out. He had walked quickly in front of the stranger and extending his hand, "you must be Baroness de Rivoli. I had the pleasure of escorting your mother from the airport to here." He had winked. It had taken her a few seconds to understand the cover up and while her heart pushed her to the arms of Pierre, she had turned to the woman and embraced her, "Maman, comment vas-tu? Que je suis contente de te revoir."

The woman had answered, "I met Mr. Beauchamp on the plane. By coincidence he was also coming to Ste Adele to spend a white Christmas with some friends. He was kind enough to share the limousine with me."

Simone offered her hand to Pierre, "Mr. Beauchamp, your courtesy is much appreciated. Perhaps you would allow us to thank you by joining us for dinner. Should we meet for cocktails at seven? At the bar?"

"It will be my pleasure." He had let her hand go, warmed from the pressure of his, trembling from her desire for more.

"Mother, let me help you register." Then she had walked behind the bellboy arm in arm with her "mother". As soon as the door closed behind him, the other woman had offered her hand to Simone. "Permit me to introduce myself. Suzanne Laforet — alias Germaine de Beauval — I am attached to the French consulate in Montreal. I also work for Pierre Beauchamp."

"What are you doing here?"

"Pierre wanted to take all possible precautions in case you were being followed or your office checked on you. If someone has seen your cable to your mother, then your mother must show up. I am your mother."

"How long will you stay?" asked Simone, somewhat concerned about this intrusion in her holiday with Pierre.

"I will be leaving on Christmas, in the afternoon, on the pretext that friends have invited me to spend a few days with them in Montreal. Between now and then, Pierre will have become a friend and the two of you can proceed with your business."

"You know?" Simone had asked surprised.

"Everyone in the agency knows, my dear Simone. Permit me to call you Simone. We all know and we all sympathize with you. I would think that most women in the agency have at one time or another fallen in love with Pierre. But Pierre is still a bachelor and he will never marry. He is married to the agency!"

"We went to school together. I knew him before the agency", Simone said.

"Well, good luck to you."

Simone, somewhat sad, had returned to her room to dress for dinner. She wanted to call the operator and ask for Pierre's room number and run to him. But she knew she could not. She was at the bar fifteen minutes ahead of their rendez-vous. Pierre joined her a few minutes later and took her glass to a corner table away from the bar and indiscreet ears.

"I must apologize for all the precautions but I want to be sure we don't commit a faux-pas which could endanger your mission. Bear with me until Christmas. By then I should have established to my satisfaction whether or not we are safe here. I have asked Suzanne to leave on Christmas. Meanwhile, watch yourself. Don't forget to address her as your mother and when you use French, remember that you are in Quebec and here everyone speaks the language. So be discreet." Then he added in a lower voice, "I love you."

"I love you also. I want to touch you."

He looked around the room. "Not now. After dinner, excuse yourself and retire early. I have a suite next to yours. The connecting door is locked and must remain locked every time you leave your room or you expect hotel employees to enter your room. Here is the key." He handed her the key under the table.

"How did you manage that?" she had asked with a smile.

"This is Quebec, remember. This is still a French country. The front desk clerk was most comprehending."

She slid her foot against his under the table and felt the warmth of his leg. "Be careful", he said, "here is your mother."

"Maman, vous êtes splendide!" Simone rose and kissed her "mother" on both cheeks.

Pierre asked, "what are you drinking Madame de Beauval?" They ordered drinks and Pierre said loud enough to be heard, "I must congratulate you Madame de Beauval. Your daughter is even more beautiful than I had imagined. She is nearly as beautiful as you."

"You are flattering me", Suzanne had replied. "And you are making me blush," Simone had said.

It was evident that Pierre and Suzanne found the game amusing and soon Simone joined their laugher throughout dinner. Immediately after coffee, Suzanne had risen. "Mr. Beauchamp, please excuse me and my daughter. It has been a long trip and I am somewhat tired. I would like my daughter to help me finish unpacking. Thank you for an excellent dinner and the pleasure of your company. Good night."

As soon as they stepped out of the elevator Suzanne had said, "Good night, Simone."

Simone had rushed to her room, locked the door behind her after placing the "do not disturb" sign on the outside knob. She had taken the key to the connecting door and unlocked it, leaving the key in the lock. She had quickly undressed, taking care to hang her clothes to keep her room orderly and had bathed luxuriously.

She had been sitting less than three minutes at her dressing table slowly brushing her hair when through the mirror she had seen the connecting door opened. A feeling of ecstasy had enveloped her. A craving as she had never experienced before. She could not move as she stared at him in the mirror approaching her, barefooted, wearing only the blue dressing gown she had given him for his anniversary two years ago in Paris. He stood behind her, admiring her.

"You left your door unlocked Madame", he said happily.

"If you were a gentleman, you would not enter the room of a stranger", she had replied gravely, playing the game.

"By the end of this night, you shall no longer be a stranger, Madame."

He had removed the brush from her hand and his touch had set fire to all of her repressed emotions. She had brought his hands to her lips and kissed them, flooding them with tears of release. He had bent and kissed the top of her head, inhaling her perfume. Never would she forget the image of their profound desire for each other which the mirror had reflected when she had reopened her eyes.

She had turned, overflowing with passion, and putting her arms through the half opened dressing gown, had encircled his waist and buried her head against his stomach. The contact with his bare flesh had made her lose control. She had started to sob violently repeating ceaselessly, "Pierre, Pierre, Pierre...."

At lunch time on Christmas day, Suzanne had announced her desire to accept the invitation of her friends to spend a few days with them in Montreal and Simone had promised to visit her there later on during the week. Pierre was satisfied that they could now meet openly without her "mother".

"Do you really think that all these precautions were necessary?" Simone had asked him. "We have lost three days."

"You made up for them during the nights", he had whispered, "insatiable!"

On Saturday, he rented a horse-drawn sleigh and they left long before lunch following a deserted narrow road running through the pine forest behind the hotel over the mountains towards Val David. "I know a restaurant where the owner smokes his own hams after dipping them in maple syrup. We could have lunch there," he said.

"Sound delicious" and she had kissed him.

Bells were attached to the harness of the horse and they tinkled in the silent cold air as if advertising their arrival. But no one was waiting. They were alone in the forest with their happiness. They sat side by side, under a heavy bear rug, Pierre holding the reins carelessly. Although she was wearing a heavy sweater under her fur coat, felt comfortable under her fur hat and warm under the long white wool scarf around her neck, she suddenly shivered.

"Are you cold?" he asked.

"No, I am fine."

"You just shivered."

"I have something to tell you, but promise not to look at me until I finish. If you do, you will make me cry and I will not be able to finish. I must tell you. I can't hold it any longer."

She opened her purse and put her sun glasses on and stared at the two parallel tracks in the snow that preceded them and led them beyond the hill deeper into the forest. She told him about Robertson. From the start at the ABA convention until three weeks ago in New York. She told him calmly, coldly, while exerting a tremendous effort to control her emotions and to give her voice a quasi-business like quality. She was an agent reporting to her superior, alone with him in the forest, safe, away from indiscreet ears.

"When Robertson attacked me in Atlanta, I first resisted and then I realized that this was the only way to get to him. Your instructions had stressed that sex was one of his weaknesses but I had not paid sufficient attention. I must admit that it had never entered my mind to use such tactics. They were not implicit in your instructions although I now understand more clearly the meaning of your remarks, "any method can be used whether moral or immoral." I have been seeing him frequently in New York. Two or three times a week. I eat with him. I drink with him and I sleep with him. I can say that I know this man today better than anyone else. Better than his wife, because I know many things about him that she does not know. Including Judith Watson and me. I know how he thinks. I know when he pretends and when he is serious. I know how to make him mad and how to please him. I know now how to use him. Unknowingly, he is going to be my partner in my mission. What I don't know is when and with whom."

They were going downhill and the horse started to trot. She stopped talking, her soul empty. They listened to the bells which seem to ring louder as to celebrate a victory. Pierre raised his voice over the noise.

"Is that all?"

"That's all."

"You should have written this in your report."

"How could I?" she asked incredulously.

"You are an agent. Your duty is to report everything that is relevant to your mission." His tone was clinical.

"And let everyone from Georges Monti to your secretary to every clerk who has access to my reports follow the weekly chapters of the amorous New York adventures of the Baroness?" She had never been so mad at him.

"You were withholding vital information."

"I suppose I should have reported vital statistics such as the color of his pubic hair and the length of his erect penis so that you could have run to a mirror and compared it to yours."

He stopped the sleigh, removed his gloves and slapped her. "Never, you understand, never mix our relationship with your work. Your actions revolt me as much as they degrade you but I manage to leave my feelings out of my work. You did not have to accept this assignment. You did so freely. If you now find it is too big for you, say so."

She turned to him and hid her face in the warmth of his neck. "It's my love for you that is too big. I die every time another man touches me."

"You want to be replaced?" he asked.

"You know very well that is not possible, Pierre." She was praying, "Pierre, what assurance do I have that I am not losing you?"

"Once, I waited nine years for you when you went to Vietnam with Antoine. I can wait two years, if I need to."

"Two years? Do you think it will take that long? Pierre, I will not be able to stand it. I must move faster than that."

"Have you a plan?"

Allah has written 'He who follows the right way follows it to his own good'."

"Can you tell me the meaning of this riddle?"

"I shall sir, next time we meet, if by then you have not guessed or if I fail. End of report, sir. Let's go and eat."

She had kissed him, the cold sealing their lips.

The horse had continued his trot without further prodding and the tinkles of the bells matched the elation of her heart.

The taxi had stopped sharply. "You said the cathedral?" asked the driver.

For the second time today, Simone was rudely brought back to reality. She shook her head as if to chase away her memories and asked, "could you wait for me, I shall only be a few minutes."

The driver had watched her in his rear view mirror and said jokingly. "I have your luggage if you decide to flee to heaven. All right, but I can't wait here. I will be on the side street."

Simone had stepped out and had admired the cathedral, majestic in the afternoon sun. The Cathedral-Basilica of Mary, Queen of the World, is a miniature replica of St. Peter's in Rome. On its roof stand large statues of the twelve apostles overlooking a garden in which a monument has been erected to honor Bishop Bourget who conceived the idea of the cathedral in 1870.

It was also Bishop Bourget who in 1868 had sent five hundred intrepid soldiers to Rome to defend Pope Pius IX under attack from King Victor Emmanuel. The motto of these modern crusaders had been "Love God and go your way." The recollection amused Simone as she pulled the heavy bronze door and entered the portico. On her right, a clock marked two minutes to three. She opened the inside door and walked into the massive nave with its impressive gold decorated columns extending at infinity to the gothic arches supporting the cupola. For the second time today, she thought of France, of the beauty of its cathedrals and monuments.

The grandiosity and splendor of the church crushed her. She lowered her head, crossed herself and walked down the aisle until on her left by one of the columns she distinguished his form, kneeling. She kneeled silently next to him and in the darkness extended her hand over the prie-dieu. He pressed it.

"Is your taxi waiting?"

"Yes."

"Wait five minutes then go to the Ritz Carlton Hotel on Sherbrooke Street. Your mother is in room 123. Suzanne again. I am in suite 455. I'll call you in thirty minutes."

She could only say "I love you" and he was gone, using the side door to the north of the building. After a while she crossed herself again, rose and exited as she had entered, turning left around the corner and found her taxi waiting. "Take me to the Ritz Carlton Hotel, please."

Half an hour later, she was in his suite. After he had kissed her and looked at her longingly, she said, "order us some champagne, loads of champagne."

"What are we celebrating?"

"My victory."

"What do you mean?"

"Exactly what it means. V-I-C-T-O-R-Y. I bankrupted Grand American Bank yesterday morning at 8:30 am."

"You did? You should have cabled me immediately."

"I did. Why do you think you are here? I wanted to tell you face to face. I have not seen you since last Christmas."

Pierre phoned room service, ordered a Dom Perignon, opened his briefcase, took a file out and sat comfortably in one of the arm chairs as if prepared for a long session. "All right, agent de Rivoli, I am ready for your debriefing."

"Pierre, I am very excited but at the same time I feel terribly depressed. Exhausted. Like at the end of a race after you have crossed the finish line and you want to collapse. I even forgot lunch today, while I was daydreaming. Did you ever have that feeling?"

"It happens often," said Pierre, "when you reach your goal. Tell me what happened?" He now appeared just as eager to know as she was eager to tell.

"Will you bring me back to Paris?" she asked expectantly.

"Perhaps, if your mission is really accomplished. Let me hear the good news."

She told him what had happened since her return to New York following their two week holiday in the Laurentians. She told him the details which she had omitted from her regular reports. She described her actions, her methods, what she had said, what she had done. From time to time Pierre took notes or glanced at the files, at one of her reports, at press clippings. She reached the events of the last ten days.

"I knew, Pierre, that I had both the Sheik and Robertson ready for a set-up ten days ago. At the request of Robertson, I had been dating the Sheik assiduously for nearly five months. Robertson was thrilled by the information I gathered on the business activities of the Sheik. The Sheik and I were seen everywhere together. The best restaurants in New York, diplomatic receptions in Washington or at the United Nations, social gatherings in Newport. I was his escort, I was his woman. It was the consensus of everyone that I would become his fourth wife. That I was his favorite. He kept pressing me. Asking me over and over again to marry him. I had to buy time. I told him that I could not marry him as long as I was not ready to choose freely his religion, that he could not marry a non-believer. He said I had to convert to Islam to prove my love. I stalled by taking a long time to read the Quran, by discussing it with him, questioning him, showing my interest, my doubts. Ten days ago, he introduced me to his father who came to visit his brother in New York. It became evident that I could no longer say no. He was ready."

"What did you do?" asked Pierre intently.

"Oh, I set him up beautifully. He and his friend Robertson. You remember that I had moved to a small apartment on Fifth Avenue. A gift from the Sheik. He wanted me to live in the comfort he was accustomed to. I wrote all of this in one of my reports." She paused. "Pour me more champagne, we are moving into the clincher." They tipped their glasses; she sipped her champagne, her eyes sparkling. "Friday evening, a week ago, Robertson called me about seven o'clock. He sounded as if he had already been drinking. He wanted to invite me for dinner and the usual after dinner exercise."

She blushed, looked at him, sipped more champagne and continued. "Robertson had never been to my apartment. He still thought I was living on 56th street. I had the same phone number so he did not know the difference. I always went to his place. That's the way he operates with all his women." If the "his" hurt Pierre, he did not interrupt her.

"So Robertson asked me to come to his place. I declined. He insisted. I pleaded sickness. I was hoping for one reaction. Last December he had wanted to come to my place when I had refused to see him before the holidays. He reacted exactly the same way. "I'm coming over," he said. "Please don't. Please Andrew." The more I protested, the more he wanted to come. I had him hooked solid. Finally I said, "all right, pick up some Chinese food somewhere and come after eight. And Andrew, I have moved, let me give you my new address." He exclaimed, "eh! that's right around the corner from me." "I know", I replied, "I got tired of taking taxis three times a week." He came. Eager. Eager like this. And she extended her arm in front of her, her fist closed.

Pierre looked at her, shocked. "You can skip the vulgar gestures."

"I thought you wanted full details," she said laughingly and continued.

"I stalled him. He had a drink, then a second and a third. He tried to bring me to the bedroom. I said I was hungry. We ate the Chinese food. Rather, I did the eating and he watched, soaking up more gin and tonics. He really got impatient, tried to take me in the living room. I heard a key in my front door. I pushed Robertson away. He got mean, tore my dressing gown from me and, holding me down nude on the couch , with one arm, he dropped his pants with the other. He was standing between me and the entrance to the living room. Over his shoulder I saw the Sheik, his face contorted, the key to my apartment still in his hands, his eyes bulging from disbelief. I shouted "Andrew, leave me alone, you are hurting me!"

"I want you. I am going to fuck you here and now. I have waited long enough."

"I shouted again, 'Andrew, please' as he dropped on me, heavier than usual, letting out a long moan."

"There was glass all over us from a lamp broken on Robertson's head by the Sheik. When I felt the impact, I closed my eyes praying "God, protect my face." When I reopened them, the Sheik was rushing out of my apartment. Robertson never saw the blow coming. He could hardly believe it when I told him that his attacker had been his good friend the Sheik. He was furious. "Why, the no good fucking bastard. I will kill him. Who does he think he is? Does he think he owns you? I met you before he did. I introduced you to him. When I get my hands on him, I will make a eunuch out of him and it will serve him right."

"Robertson went home very unhappy. I tried to call the Sheik but he was always out or too busy to talk to me. A whole week went by. I started to worry. And then bang! Thursday the Sheik phone Hardrock and set up an appointment for 8:30 Friday morning. Just himself and Hardrock. No Robertson. No secretary. That's what he said. I knew then that I had succeeded."

"Friday morning came. I could hardly wait to get to the office. I was a bit early and met the Sheik wearing his formal attire as he was coming out of Hardrock's office. He was very cold to me. Very formal. What a day! I have written a final report for you on that victorious day. Friday, June 30, 1978. It's historical. Here it is." She handed Pierre a blue folder tied with a red ribbon.

"My gloom has disappeared. I want more champagne. Pierre, please order another bottle, this one is empty."

"How will I itemize that on my expense account?" he asked jokingly. He called room service once more.

Simone started to talk again. "But the biggest news, the unexpected development are yet to come. Do you have any idea how much money the Sheik has on deposit with Grand American Bank?"

"Sure", replied Pierre, "it shows in their weekly reports you have been sending me. Somewhat over twenty billion dollars."

"You won't believe me", she said excitedly. "I know you

won't believe me and it is not the champagne. Listen carefully. Sixty billion dollars! That's the amount of the cheque presented to Hardrock by the Sheik yesterday morning. Sixty billion beautiful worthless American dollars!"

"But that's half the assets of the bank!" exclaimed Pierre as he rose to open the door to the waiter.

Simone shouted after him. "That's also what Robertson said."

Pierre turned quickly placing his fingers over his lips and opened the door.

They slept together in her bed. She had insisted. "You are my visitor." Adding gaily, "I no longer want to be sent home at two in the morning."

"Perhaps I will leave you during the night."

She ran to the connecting door, grabbed the key and placed it under her pillow. "Just try! I'll let you escape in the morning only. I'll go with you and help you ruffle your bed to convince the maid you slept in it."

"You think of everything, don't you? You have become quite experienced, I must say." He was teasing her.

She bowed. "Only to love you better, master."

In the morning, while she was dressing, Pierre read carefully Simone's report in the blue folder. As he read it, his face seemed to harden. He was concentrating, trying to understand the true meaning of the confidences made by Robertson to Simone during their dinner at the El Morocco. He could sense that something was wrong, that the victory was not to be earned so quickly.

She entered his suite, happy, dressed in a cream cotton chemise, the high open collar framing her beautiful face alive with an enticing smile. "I am ready for breakfast and I am famished." She brushed his cheek with a kiss. He did not respond.

"What's wrong?"

"Sit down Simone. I have read your report carefully. We are in trouble."

"Trouble? What type of trouble?"

"I don't know what exactly but I feel it. Something is going wrong. It is in your report and we must find it. Breakfast will have to wait."

Simone sat, dejected. "Pierre, it is impossible for Grand American to pay sixty billion dollars. They don't have that much cash or readily marketable securities."

"Exactly," replied Pierre. "What would you do if you were Hardrock and faced this problem?"

"I would call the Federal Reserve Board and the FDIC."[3]

"Correct. You would report your liquidity problem to the Feds and ask FDIC for financial assistance. Did Hardrock or Robertson call them?"

"Hardrock did not. All his calls go through my phone. As to Robertson, I would not know."

"That's it. That's what's missing in your report. We have no evidence that they asked for assistance."

"Which means?" asked Simone.

"Which means that they have a way out of their dilemma. And that's why they are flying to Zurich at noon today. I could not understand why both of them would leave their office at the same time when confronted by such a massive withdrawal. They have made a deal with the Sheik. They will not honor his cheque until Wednesday. Tuesday is a holiday and nothing will happen on Monday. So they are off to Switzerland to borrow money."

"Surely not sixty billion dollars," said Simone.

"No, but probably fifteen to eighteen billion and on long term. That's what I would aim for if I knew where to find the missing forty-five. But Robertson is crafty. He can juggle with figures and balance sheets like a magician. He is an artist and he has found a way out of the trap that you set for him."

"Goddamn it!"

"Simone! You have been seeing so much of him, that you are even using his language."

She rose and went to the window overlooking Sherbrooke street. She watched the sparse Sunday morning traffic. The

---

3 Federal Deposit Insurance Corporation

morning sun enrobed her with a huge diamond of light. She turned to Pierre, looking like a Joan of Arc in anger. "I'll kill him." Her tone was so hard, so convincing that Pierre jumped from his chair and grabbed her wrists. He raised his voice, "Simone, we never use violence."

"Let me kill him," she pleaded desperately.

"What will that achieve?"

"There will be no one to tell Hardrock what to do. He can't run that bank without Robertson. "

Pierre took the evening flight to Paris. Simone accompanied him to Mirabel airport. "I have not seen you for six months and you are leaving me already." She was crying.

"I must be in Paris tomorrow morning and must alert our people in Zurich. Something is going to happen tomorrow and we must be on top of things. If we move rapidly and carefully, we might still salvage the operation".

"What do you want me to do?" she asked.

"Don't change anything in your plans. Report to Louise in New York tomorrow and let her know where you can be reached. You told Robertson that you would do so. I have asked Suzanne to stay at the Ritz with you until Tuesday night. You can now leave together. Suzanne will take you to the airport. When you return to New York, you must find out what is going on and inform me as soon as you do. Contact Georges once or twice a day if you need to. I'll advise him to use the consulate coded messages by exception." His flight was called. "One more thing", he said, "you must make peace with the Sheik. You must know what he is doing or planning to do."

"How do I do that?"

"The appearances are that Robertson raped you in your apartment. He was your aggressor. You must convince the Sheik that nothing really happened thanks to his smashing one of your lamps on Robertson's head. You could add that you had a most difficult time in convincing Robertson not to sue the Sheik for assault. It would have made a nice scandal.

I can see the headlines, "Bank President attacked by jealous Sheik in bedroom of French Baroness."

"It was my living room," she corrected, amused.

They walked to the gate, holding each other by the waist in a possessive manner and kissing like young lovers, unaware of the staring public around them.

On Monday morning she called Louise at the office and told her where she could be reached in Montreal.

"I am sorry about your grandmother," Louise said sympathetically.

"She was very old. It had to happen," replied Simone. "Any news from the Big Man?"

"He called half an hour ago. He said everything was going smoothly in Zurich. I expect him to call again around noon our time. Any message?"

"Yes. Ask him to tell Mr. Hardrock that I am returning Tuesday night and that I will be in the office early Wednesday morning, in case he needs me."

Louise had said, "Shall do. Have a good time," and hung up.

"Have a good time," she reflected. In Montreal, without Pierre, and with her "mother" who is not her mother.

She decided to go to the cinema in the afternoon and enjoy a French film. To her distress, it was an espionage film but she sat through it patiently, until near the end, it struck her. "I must have Robertson followed!"

A new dimension was added to her mission. She felt elated. She knew that his activities were bound to provide her with the solution to the enigma of the sixty billion dollars. She could easily follow his whereabouts during the day and naturally during those nights she spent with him. But what about the others, where did he go? Whom did he talk to? She had to know. Georges Monti would help her.

She walked back to her hotel eager to return to New York.

She phoned Suzanne. "Simone? Am I glad to hear from you! I wondered where you were. I received a call from Zurich. I'll come to your room if you want me to."

"Come right away," Simone said.

Within minutes, Suzanne was knocking at her door. Simone let her in, closed the door behind her and stated "Robertson called!"

Suzanne looked at her, "How did you guess?"

"I believe he is jealous."

"Or suspicious?" suggested Suzanne.

"Tell me everything he said, "Simone asked.

"I was preparing to go out for lunch at about twelve forty when the phone rang, "long distance", the operator said, "from Zurich." The Zurich operator came on "Is this Madame de Beauval?" I said, "yes." "Just a moment please, Mr. Robertson calling you." He came on, "Madame de Beauval, Andrew Robertson here, from Grand American Bank. Your daughter Simone works for me. I have been trying to reach her but her room does not answer. Is she with you by any chance?"

I said, "No. She is not. Do you wish her to call you back?"

He said, "Do you know where I can reach her?"

I replied, "She went shopping. I am sure she will be back sometime this afternoon. We are having dinner together. Could she call you then?"

"No, never mind. Tell her I may need to call her tomorrow. The funeral went well?"

"Yes."

"You have my sympathy, Madame de Beauval, good-bye." He hung up.

"Did he sound to you like a jealous lover or a suspicious boss?" asked Simone.

"Both", replied Suzanne. "What are you going to do now?"

"Go back to New York and screw him."

"Simone!"

CHAPTER THREE
THE CONTRACT

"America's banks are in trouble. Many of the largest and most powerful banks have been on a five-year expansion binge, spurred by bankers convinced that bigger is better. In their pursuit of growth, they have jeopardized the safety of your money, not to mention the survival of the entire banking system. Americans, accustomed to entrusting their money to banks without the slightest worry, should begin to worry — now."

(From Playboy, February 1975. "Banks on the Brink." by John B. Tipton)

Up above Zurich, in a large park bordering a golf club, stands the august Hotel Dolder. The hurried businessman might prefer the Baur-au-Lac, more central and more easily accessible, but for comfort and elegance, nothing surpasses the Dolder.

Hardrock and Robertson had just returned from their second meeting with Dr. Shermer, the Chairman of Swiss International Bank. Hardrock was furious.

"I am not going to do it. I can't. I just can't."

"Peter, you have no choice. Either we give the Swiss what they want or we don't get the twenty billion. You know what that would mean."

"But their demand is unfair. They are taking advantage of our situation. They want to use me. You don't do this in business. One must have some standards of ethic."

"Peter, in business, the Swiss have only one ethic: Money. In banking they have two: Money and Secrecy. In that order. I will admit it; they are holding us by the balls. I was right in telling you that they would not ask many questions. They did not. I was right also when I told you they would form a syndicate. They did. That was easy to assume. Twenty billion dollars was too much money for Swiss International. They had to call in the other big Swiss banks. I am surprised that they did not invite more banks. They still might. But when they threw that condition on the table! Whew! They are smart, Peter. They are a smart bunch of rats."

"Your invectives will not solve our problem."

"Fair enough, but it is good to know what type of people we are dealing with."

"You should have realized that before we walked in there."

"Who in the hell could imagine that these rats would set such a trap? We got caught stupidly, Peter. We can't get out of it. Call your brother."

"I am going to disgrace the family," moaned Hardrock.

"Your brother is a wise politician. He will find a way to put this through Congress."

"That's right! It would have to go to Congress. That makes it even worse."

"Come on Peter. You are exaggerating the problem. There is neither a senator nor a congressman who hasn't got a numbered bank account in Switzerland. How in the hell do you think those guys make money these days? They work hand in hand with the multinational companies and receive their rake off from an offshore source directly into their account here. That's why the FBI and the IRS have pressed every Administration to attack the Swiss bank secrecy. They know what's here but they can't prove it. At least they could not until 1973 when, under tremendous pressure from Washington, the Swiss finally gave in and signed a new agreement permitting the US government in certain cases to acquire from Swiss banks useful information. Remember the Irving-Howard Hughes case. And what about Sedona and Franklyn National Bank? But what Americans don't understand is that bank secrecy in Switzerland is not a law that can be amended by agreement, it is a way of life, and it is more sacred than religion. The Swiss have never forgiven the Americans for the 1973 agreement. Today we gave them the chance to get even. They did not miss it. Peter, call your brother. There is nothing else you can do."

"Put him on the line," said Hardrock resignedly. "Here, you have to use his private number. Don't tell the operator you are calling the President of the United States, she will take you for a crank. Just ask for this number. No names. He will know a member of the family is calling. No one else uses this number."

The two men sat in silence while the operator worked on the call. After fifteen minutes, Robertson rose, "I'm going to have a drink. You want one?"

"It's too early to drink. First, we have to get back to Shermer with our reply and we are invited for dinner."

"With his strait-laced German wife," added Robertson. "I can think of a hundred better ways of spending an evening. We should have brought Judith Watson with us. She is the best traveling secretary I have ever met." Robertson could not suppress a smile.

"Skip it", said Hardrock. "All we need now is a snoopy photographer to catch you in Zurich with Judith Watson, super call girl! Who needs the scandal?"

"No smoking, no drinking, no screwing. How do you manage to stay alive?" asked Robertson. The phone rang. He reached for it. "Hello?"

"Your number is ringing, sir," said the operator.

Robertson handed the phone over. Hardrock heard his brother's voice on the line. "Barry? Peter here. How are you? Sorry to disturb you in the middle of your morning work but an emergency has arisen here and I must talk to you. Can you talk?"

"I can talk Peter," said the President. "I had a number of Cabinet members for breakfast. They have just left."

"Any problems?" asked Peter.

"The usual. They all want more money for their pet projects. More handouts. They can't win votes on their own merits. They must buy them with giveaways. None of them has enough worth to get elected, so they dream up these stupid projects. You can't tell them they cost money. Sometimes I think they believe that I print it."

"Don't you?"

"Don't be funny. But surely you have not called to hear about my problems. What's yours?" asked the President.

"I have a bad one for you, Barry. For us. For everyone. I really don't know how or where to start."

"It's that bad?"

"It's worse. Listen carefully. I am in Zurich with Robertson. We came here to raise twenty billion dollars."

"For whom?"

"For us."

"For Grand American? Twenty billion? Why would you need twenty billion? I though you had billions coming out of your ears. Especially Arab billions."

"We did," Peter replied, "and that's the problem. Some of the Arab billions want out."

"Why?"

"We don't know. Yet. But it hurts."

"Are you in serious trouble?" asked the President.

"We could be if we don't get this loan."

"How long is the loan for?"

"Five years."

"The rate?"

"Seven and a quarter."

"Any points?"

"No."

"Where do I come in?" asked the President

"There is an essential condition. They want to reopen the 1973 Bank Secrecy Agreement."

"Only that!" exclaimed the President.

"Only that."

"And who is they?"

"The three big ones, Swiss International, Swiss Credit, Swiss Union."

"Always the same sons-of-bitches."

"Always."

"I can't do it," said the President.

"You must," pleaded Peter.

"It's beyond my personal powers. I would have to go to the House and the Senate. The Senators, individually, might go along but the press will get on their back. You know some two-bit little punk journalist who never saved enough money to own a foreign bank account and resents anyone else who has one. He will shoot for a Pulitzer prize by reopening the whole bank secrecy debate. It's a can of worms. The Senate will vote it down."

Peter looked at Robertson who punched his left hand with his right fist in a fighting gesture. He returned his attention to the phone. "Then we are dead."

"What do you mean?"

"My dear brother, my bank, the family bank, will close its doors and the scandal will sweep you right off your presidential seat."

"I assume you have told White and the FDIC about your problems?" suggested the President.

"Are you crazy?"

There was a long silence. "Barry! Barry, are you still there?"

"I am still here, Peter, and I am trying to think. There has to be a way out of this. Can't you borrow elsewhere?"

"No way. The only banks with money these days are the banks trusted by the Arabs. Us and the Swiss. That's why we are here."

"Are you sure this loan will pull you through."

"Positive," said Peter, not believing it. Another long silence.

"All right," said the President.

"What do I tell the Swiss?"

"Tell them I'll do it. I'll remove all pressures against their bank secrecy. I'll rewrite the 1973 Agreement."

"They won't believe me."

"Christ, you are my brother, after all!"

"That's not good enough for a Swiss banker."

"I'll have it in the press tomorrow!" barked the President. "And Peter, in future, with news like this, don't call me." The phone went dead. Hardrock turned to Robertson.

"Call Shermer."

He came on the line quickly. "Dr. Shermer? Peter Hardrock here. You have a deal."

"That's fine, Mr. Hardrock. I am very pleased, but how can we be sure?" asked the Swiss banker.

"I'm telling you," said Hardrock stonily.

"I understand that, but how can I reassure my confreres?"

The Swiss don't even trust each other, thought Hardrock.

"If they don't believe you," he said, "tell them to read the morning papers." He could not resist adding, "unless they want to spend the night watching the Dow Jones ticker."

The doctor missed the unpleasant remark. "This means that we could sign the loan agreement in the afternoon tomorrow. Shall we say four-thirty? My office?"

"Will you have everything ready?"

"I would hope so. And now that we have settled this little problem, at what time do you wish me to send the car for you? Martha would like to serve dinner at eight. Would seven thirty be convenient?"

"It would," replied Hardrock.

"A bientôt," said Shermer.

Hardrock turned to Robertson. "You were right. The rats have won. As usual. And we must eat with them."

"Congratulations!" Dr. Shermer was extending his hand warmly to Hardrock and Robertson.

"What for?" asked Robertson. "We have not signed yet."

"It's the Fourth of July. Your Independence Day."

How can we be independent when in a few minutes we are going to owe you, rats, twenty billion dollars? thought Robertson.

The other two bankers, Henry Stratti, Chairman of Swiss Union and Dr. Mario Schoenfeld from Swiss Credit rose and added their congratulations to those of Dr. Shermer. They all sat around the boardroom table at the headquarters of Swiss International Bank. Dr. Shermer took the presiding chair.

"First, let me tell you gentlemen, and I am speaking here on behalf of Mr. Stratti and Dr. Schoenfeld as much as in my name, that we are most pleased to demonstrate, once again, a proof of our cooperation to Grand American Bank and our friends the United States. This cooperation is well reciprocated. I received a call this morning from Herr Direktor of our National Bank who read to me the content of the statement made to the press late last night by President Hardrock. It came on their Dow Jones news service early this morning. I have copies for each of you." He distributed the photocopies around the table. Robertson quickly read his.

"Washington – July 3rd, 1978. In an unexpected move, the President of the United States announced tonight that he has decided to ask Congress to ratify a new constitutional amendment recognizing the right of citizens to the privacy of their banking affairs.

Immediately, the FBI and the IRS protested such action. The President explained that the Constitution, in guaranteeing the freedom of citizens, certainly meant to guarantee their freedom to trade and the freedom to manage their own affairs. In a modern economy, where less and less money was being used for trade and more and more transactions were being handled by bank computers, citizens had no choice but to deal with banks. But that freedom became endangered by the complete lack of discretion and secrecy found in the banking system. Under present practices, anyone, any merchant, retail credit association, any court, any government agency, at any time can have access to citizens' bank accounts, thereby infringing their privacy. Certainly this had never been the intent of the Constitution and the President, who as a Senator in 1975 had chaired the commission investigating the spying on private individuals by government agencies, thought the time had arrived to correct this injustice. The new Bill provides for heavy fines and imprisonment for breach of bank secrecy in the future. While the FBI and IRS will continue to claim that their means of investigating crime will be greatly curtailed, constitutional experts were of the opinion that the measure was well within the spirit of the Constitution and would be passed quickly by Congress and ratified by the Senate.

The President did not refer to the 1973 Agreement on Bank Secrecy between the US and Switzerland but it is evident that if the US Constitution is amended to clearly recognize the secrecy of bank transactions for its own citizens, the US can no longer ask other countries to open their records to US investigators and the US-Swiss agreement will no longer apply. It was too early to obtain comments from Swiss bankers but knowing how much importance the Swiss attach to the sanctity of their bank secrecy, it is expected that they will strongly support the action of the President. As a result, the relations between the two countries, strained since the 1973 Agreement imposed by the US on Switzerland, should improve considerably."

"I don't know how we are going to convince one million bank employees to keep their mouth shut," remarked Robertson.

"We have no difficulty with our employees," stated Dr. Shermer. "It's a tradition here, as you well know."

"Gossiping about a persons bank account is a national pastime in America," said Robertson sadly, "we are going to end up with half our staff in jail."

"That should greatly reduce your overhead," commented Dr. Schoenfeld, without smiling.

"Gentlemen," commanded Dr. Shermer, "should we go on with our business? I am distributing to you the loan agreement. It reflects clearly the terms and conditions agreed upon yesterday — term five years, rate seven and a quarter, penalty of three percent for prepayment starting the third year and diminishing one percent per year, etc., etc. I believe you will find everything in order. There is one slight change. The amount of the participation by each bank. I had to obtain the approval of my Board. So did Mr. Stratti and Dr. Schoenfeld. I must let you know Mr. Hardrock that our three Boards have had the same reaction. The amount of the loan is too large. There was also considerable surprise expressed regarding your need for this loan. After all you are the world's largest bank..."

"We can't take less than twenty billion," interrupted Hardrock.

"We assumed that. So we took upon ourselves to invite a fourth bank. It was not easy. We wanted only one more participant. Otherwise, there will be indiscretions and I am sure you don't want the banking "fraternity", if I can use that word, to know of your predicament."

"It's not a predicament," interjected Robertson sharply. "It's a perfectly reasonable conventional and rational transaction.

We wish to reduce the ratio of our short term liabilities. You would do the same thing if you were in our situation."

"Perhaps we would," said Shermer, "except that we are not in your situation nor do I think that we want to discuss your situation. You are the largest bank in the world. No doubt, you gentlemen know what you are doing."

"Then can we close this loan?" asked Hardrock.

"Unfortunately", said Shermer, "I have yet to receive the official agreement from the fourth partner, although their President has given me his verbal consent subject to his Board's approval. This is reasonable."

"Who are they?"

"Crédit Lyonnais from France. We maintain a very close business relationship with them. We can depend on their discretion. I understand that their President, Daniel Laberge, knows Mr. Robertson fairly well."

"Yes, we have met often," said Robertson.

"So I understand. I took the liberty of telling him where you were staying as he indicated that he wanted to telephone you."

"When do you expect to close this loan?" asked Hardrock again. "We hold reservations on the three ten flight to New York tomorrow. I told my office I would return no later than Thursday."

"I see no reason why we cannot finish this transaction and deliver our check to you at eleven tomorrow. I should hear from Crédit Lyonnais later today or early tomorrow." Shermer rose. "Gentlemen, that's it for today. Have a good evening."

Once in the privacy of the taxi taking them back to the Dolder Hotel, Hardrock turned to Robertson. "What do you think?"

"I don't like the participation of Crédit Lyonnais in this transaction. You cannot trust French banks. The Swiss are schemers but they take their own decisions. French banks run to their government as soon as a transaction is large or unusual. We certainly don't want the French government involved in this affair."

"Can you talk to, what's his name, Laberge about it?"

"I certainly will," Robertson said, "but he is only a super civil servant. If there is a danger to his ass, he is bound to say: Vive La France et Merde aux Américains."

"I hope you are wrong."

As they entered the lobby of their hotel, Robertson heard his name called. The page boy with his bell and blackboard was walking in front of them. Robertson snapped his fingers. "Here boy!" The page boy turned and looked at him defiantly.

"There is a gentleman waiting for you in the reading room, sir."

They went down the hallway to the right of the main entrance. Robertson walked in first. "Laberge!"

"Monsieur Robertson," replied the French banker.

"What are you doing here? I though you were in Paris. We were just talking about you."

"I intended to phone you, but certain transactions are better negotiated face to face. Air France had a convenient flight which brought me here an hour ago. I am returning to Paris in two hours." He looked around. "Where can we talk?"

"Let's go to my suite," suggested Hardrock. He shook hands with Laberge. "Good to see you again, Mr. Laberge. I am glad you came so we can finish this little business quickly."

"I don't think of it as a little business," said the French banker ominously.

Hardrock and Robertson looked at each other, Hardrock appearing the more concerned of the two. Once they were seated in Hardrock's suite, each with a drink, Robertson addressed the French banker. "If you wish to take the seven fifteen flight, we don't have much time to lose. Shoot. Give us the good and the bad news."

The French banker looked at the two men quietly and opened his briefcase. "I have here a copy of the loan agreement that Dr. Shermer, no doubt, distributed to you this afternoon. The only difference is that our name does not appear in your copies. It does in this one. We have approved the loan. The syndicate is now complete. The twenty billion dollar loan will be shared as follows: Swiss International Bank – nine billion. Credit Lyonnais – five billion. Swiss Credit – three billion. Swiss Union – three billion. Total – twenty billion. Gentlemen, it is a very large loan, a loan that is draining most of the surplus cash from our bank and the three big Swiss banks."

"Daniel," interrupted Robertson, "I am sure you did not fly from Paris to Zurich to discuss the size of this transaction. So come out with it. What do you want?"

"Gentlemen, my Board has authorized me to sign this loan agreement provided we are given some collateral."

"Never!" exclaimed Robertson.

"Please, hear me out," said Laberge. "We want very specific collateral." He paused. Hardrock and Robertson waited for the punch. "We want gold."

"But we don't have any gold," protested Hardrock. "You know that. American banks are prohibited from buying gold for their own account. They can only trade on behalf of clients."

"If that is the case, I have wasted my time in coming here to help you. I can't sign this loan agreement." The French banker rose.

"Wait a minute," said Robertson. He scrutinized the face of the impassive Frenchman. *He knows*, thought Robertson, *the bastard knows and he is here to squeeze me.*

"Peter, can I talk to you alone? Excuse me, Daniel."

They walked to the adjoining room. "What's going on?" Hardrock asked. "It does not make sense. How can he ask for something which we have not got? Gold? If we had gold, we would sell it and we would not need their darn money."

Robertson took a hard look at Hardrock. There was no way out. He would have to tell him. "Peter, you are wrong on three counts. First, it makes sense to ask for security. He is no fool. He can read our balance sheet and he is probably closer to the Arabs than we are except that the Arabs don't trust the French franc. Second, if we had gold, we would not be able to sell it in such a large quantity without depressing the market. Christ, five billion dollars is equal to half the reserves of the US. Thirdly, listen to me good. We have gold!"

Hardrock was speechless. "Where?"

"In Dubai," answered Robertson.

"How much?"

"At todays price about six and a half billion dollars. We bought it at thirty-five dollars. It closed today at two hundred and forty-five dollars. We bought about one billion dollars worth. It's worth seven times more. Nearly six and half billion."

"When did we do that?"

"In '64."

"When you were in Dubai?"

"Yes, after the bankruptcy of Intra Bank. The Sheiks came to me with their deposits but in return they asked me to buy their gold discreetly. They could not sell it on the market. The proceeds were to be used to buy arms for their war against Israel. Everything had to be handled quietly."

"You never told me."

"You would not have approved and I would have lost the deposits."

"I never saw the gold in our books."

"It's not there."

"What do you mean, it's not there?"

"The books of Dubai have been falsified for the last fourteen years."

"By whom?"

"By me."

"You are fired!"

Robertson looked at the dejected Hardrock; a smile of victory came to his lips. "Fine, Peter, I leave you to negotiate with Laberge. Without gold, he won't sign the loan agreement. You won't get your loan. If Laberge does not sign, the Swiss will worry. They will think that he knows something detrimental about our situation. Being prudent, they'll cancel the loan. So go back to Sheik Al-Madir in New York, empty handed. Back to square one."

"You are a crook, Andrew Robertson, and I am an honest man. You are still fired." Hardrock averted his eyes.

"And what will you tell the Board?" asked Robertson, sarcastically. "That you fired me because I falsified the books of our Dubai branch? For the last seven years, you and I have signed every balance sheet issued by the Bank. You are an accessory. Hiding the gold. Hiding the profits. Not paying the income tax. IRS will soon get involved. You know how they would love to get your skin and that of every member of your family. Even your brother the President won't be able to save you."

Hardrock placed his head in his hands. "God, he moaned, "what am I going to do?"

"Let me handle the Frenchman," said Robertson, sure of himself. "Let's find out how much he knows and how much he wants." Without waiting for a reply, Robertson walked back into the living room. Hardrock followed silently.

"My dear Daniel, your request shocked Peter and me."

"I don't believe you have any reason to be shocked Mr. Robertson, Dubai is a small community. So is the Arab world. Such a large quantity of gold is difficult to hide. I can understand, however, Mr. Hardrock's surprise if he had not been told previously," the Frenchman intimated.

"Mr. Hardrock is chairman of our bank and as such..."

"Very interesting," interrupted the Frenchman. "So we are in agreement."

"I'll let you have one billion," tried Robertson.

"I want all of it."

"That's all we have."

Laberge looked at the file on his knees. "At today's price, you have five billion two hundred million dollars worth of gold in your vaults in Dubai. I want all of it."

"You are a goddamn snoop."

"I still want your gold," said the French banker, coldly ignoring the insult.

There was a prolonged silence. The Frenchman's figures were wrong. He was not asking for all the gold. Perhaps his information was incomplete.

"How long will it take to move the gold? inquired Hardrock feebly.

"Depends where they want it."

"We want it in our vaults in Paris," the Frenchman stated flatly.

"Who pays for transport?" asked Hardrock.

"You do, naturally."

Robertson rose and started to walk up and down the room. How to get out of this one. Could he fail to deliver after the loan was consummated? "It will take time and we wish to close the loan tomorrow," he said.

"I am ready to sign now," replied the French banker. "As soon as the two of you complete this pledge of security form."

"Are you not taking a risk? What if we don't deliver?" He was testing his opponent.

"Then we shall mail a coy of this assignment form to your Government."

"You bastard!" shouted Robertson. "Let's sign, Peter, we have no choice. But one day we will get even. I swear it."

They both signed the form pledging 21,500,000 ounces of gold to Crédit Lyonnais and returned it to Laberge who read it, folded it carefully and placed it in his briefcase. "Gentlemen, everything seems to be in order. Here is the loan agreement properly signed and sealed by our Bank. Dr. Shermer already has our instructions to disburse the five billion dollars."

"You mean to tell us that you had already signed this loan agreement and had already authorized the release of your funds?" inquired Hardrock incredulously. "How did you know that we would sign?"

"Did you have a choice?"

The French banker rose, avoided shaking their hands and

bowed discreetly, "Messieurs, it was a pleasure doing business with you. Je vous souhaite une bonne soirée."

After he left, Robertson looked at Hardrock. He could not contain his rage any longer but there was no one to pass his rage upon. He seized his empty glass and hurled it at the door. "Merde! A thousand merdes to you, Frenchman!"

Outside the Dolder Hotel a black Citroen was parked across the courtyard upon which the main entrance opened. As soon as Daniel Laberge emerged from the revolving doors, the Citroen lights blinked and the black limousine approached. The hotel doorman rushed to open the back door of the car. Laberge slid into the back seat and the car rolled away immediately.

Pierre Beauchamp leaned forward and said to the chauffeur. "Take us to the airport slowly. We have more than an hour." He turned to Laberge. "How did it go, Daniel?"

"It's signed, sealed and will soon be delivered."

"All of it?"

"The whole twenty one million ounces."

"Any trouble?"

"As you expected, Robertson barked, raged, and called me a snoop and a bastard, but he signed. So did Hardrock. What's going to happen now?"

Beauchamp looked at the banker. "It's entre nous?"

"Naturellement."

"Go short on gold for the next few days."

"Why?"

"Because Robertson has another five million ounces in Dubai."

"But you told me he had exactly twenty one million, five hundred thousand ounces! That's what I told him. He accepted that figure as correct."

Beauchamp was really enjoying himself. He had analyzed Robertson to perfection. He smiled. "I want Robertson to keep enough gold to cover his position in his books and make a slight profit. He has been falsifying his books in Dubai for fourteen years. Now he must balance his books again. He is going to drop the five million ounces on the market. At two hundred and forty-five dollars per once, that's worth about one billion two hundred million dollars. His cost is about one billion. He will show a profit and the gold is out of his books."

"But if he sells that much gold, he will depress the market."

"That's why I told you to go short. Sell the gold that you don't have tomorrow. When Robertson's gold hits the market, you can cover yourself at a depressed price and make a substantial profit for your bank. You deserve it. You have rendered a great service to France."

For years, Pierre Beauchamp had been working closely with French banks and corporations. His agency spied for them abroad. They assisted him by divulging to him otherwise confidential information. As soon as Dr. Shermer had called Daniel Laberge inviting Crédit Lyonnais to join a small syndicate to advance twenty billion dollars to Grand American Bank, Laberge had phone Pierre Beauchamp who had just returned from Montreal. "Why are you telling me," Beauchamp had asked.

"Because I find it unusual for Grand American Bank to borrow such a huge sum of money. I have looked at their most recent balance sheet. Their ratio of short-term liabilities is inching towards the eighty percent mark. Most unhealthy and their twenty billion dollar annual growth does not make sense. It has to have come from Arab deposits. I don't believe they have ever respected the bank's thirty billion dollar limit. Perhaps one of their Arab friends wants his money back."

"You are a smart banker, Daniel Laberge," Pierre Beauchamp mused. "You would probably be shocked if you knew that their Arab deposits are in excess of twice the limit." His guess had been right. Hardrock and Robertson had gone to Zurich to borrow. He had estimated fifteen to eighteen billion dollars. The figure was now confirmed. Twenty billion dollars. That meant they had found a way to cover the other forty billion.

"What is the size of your participation?" Beauchamp asked.

"Five billion dollars."

"Any security?"

"None."

"You can't do it without security. Let me come over to explain."

Beauchamp had rushed to the office of Laberge. He was formulating a plan in his head. Fantastic! he exclaimed to himself. Five months ago, by one of those lucky coincidences that happen only to honest agents, his Dubai man had concluded his regular report by a most interesting disclosure:

> "I have met one Ahmed Assouf who recently resigned from the local branch of Grand American Bank. Under heavy influence of hashish, Assouf started to curse a certain Robertson, surely the same Robertson who used to manage the branch here in the early sixties. Andrew Robertson. Assouf was accusing Robertson of not having kept his word, of not having taken care of him as he had promised. Assouf claimed that he had resigned from Grand American to avenge himself. Intrigued, I befriended the man who soon took me to his home and showed me a gold bar buried under a loose tile in his kitchen. He wanted to sell it to me at half price. He swore the bar was authentic. "Robertson let me down, I took care of myself," he said. I asked him if he could get more at that price. He said no, but if I bought his bar, he would tell me where I could find many more. I returned the next day with cash and bought his bar at half price. (I used money from this agency so the profit is yours.) He then produced photocopies of ledger sheets bearing the name of Grand American Bank and indicating that they had in their vaults in Dubai over twenty six million ounces of gold.

These documents are attached for your information. I am awaiting your instructions."

Once again, Beauchamp had scrutinized these documents before visiting Daniel Laberge. He had quickly obtained Laberge's cooperation. The two of them had flown to Zurich: Laberge to obtain secretly sufficient security to guarantee the repayment of his loan, Beauchamp to make sure that his scheme would work and to advise Simone in New York of this interesting turn of events in Zurich.

Simone had been at her desk less than fifteen minutes on Thursday morning when Hardrock walked in. "Good morning, Mr. Hardrock."

"Good morning, Madame de Rivoli."

"You had a good trip, sir?"

"Yes, very good and very successful."

Simone scrutinized his face. He looked haggard and tired. She knew why. The day before, Georges Monti had called her late in the afternoon asking to see her urgently. After work she had rushed to the French consulate. A message from Pierre awaited her. Georges had already decoded it:

"With great difficulty, Grand American Bank has borrowed twenty billion dollars from a syndicate consisting of Swiss International – nine billion, Crédit Lyonnais – five billion, Swiss Credit – three billion and Swiss Union – three billion. Term – five years. Rate – seven and a quarter. No security. You must find out where the other forty billion to repay the Sheik is coming from. As of now, your mission is back to square one. Sorry, but Grand American appears to have been saved. Good luck."

"Bad news, eh?"

"It does not make sense. They cannot have raised forty billion from their own assets. I have looked at their balance sheet ten times since my return from Montreal. It is just not there."

"What are you planning to do now?"

"I need to have Robertson followed. I need to find out what he is doing."

"That's not easy and that's dangerous. You are a woman and he knows you."

"But he does not know you." Simone pleaded. "Listen Georges, I know pretty well what Robertson does most of the time. At the office, it is easy. The nights I go out with him," she hesitated and blushed, "we can skip. But the other nights, particularly when he is whoring around or on a trip, we must follow him. You must do it for me, Georges."

"Let's ask Beauchamp."

In the morning they had received his approval. She felt better. While Georges followed Robertson, she would concentrate on the Sheik.

Between the two, she was sure she would find out what had gone wrong with her well prepared and perfectly executed plan to bankrupt Grand American Bank.

She heard her buzzer. "Yes, Mr. Hardrock?"

"Bring me my appointment diary."

"Yes, sir."

She went into his office. He was emptying his briefcase and arranging his papers. He took a document from which he detached four checks. Suddenly, his face contorted and he went livid. Simone rushed to him. "What's wrong, sir? Are you sick?"

He pushed her away. "Jesus Christ!" She was shocked to hear him swear. "Get Robertson. Quick!" He slumped in his chair. "The double crossing bastard!"

"Can I get you something, sir?"

"Get me Robertson, as I told you to do. Didn't you hear me?"

Simone straightened up, "I have heard you, Mr. Hardrock, and I have already buzzed Mr. Robertson's office. He is on his way. I though that perhaps you would want a glass of water."

"Just leave me alone and get out of here!"

"What about your appointments, sir?"

"Appointments! Christ! I need appointments like I need a hole in the head. Cancel them all and get the hell out of here!"

Simone was really taken back. Never had he been rude to her. "Mr. Hardrock, I don't believe I deserve..."

"Just get out of here, please?"

As she did, Robertson was walking in. "Hi, Simone, had a good holiday?"

Hardrock growled at them. "Robertson! Stop the socializing and get in here!"

Simultaneously Robertson and Simone lifted their shoulders at each other, unable to understand the sudden outburst of Hardrock. Robertson entered and closed the door. "What's eating you so early in the morning? You look like you have seen a ghost."

"I have seen worst than a ghost, my dear Andrew Robertson. You and your good friend Dr. Shermer."

"Stop the sarcasm, Peter and tell me what's wrong."

"What's wrong? What's wrong? You are asking me what's wrong? Look!" He threw the four checks to Robertson. "Look. Then **you** tell me what's wrong!"

Robertson picked up the checks and started to examine them. When he reached the third one, he froze. "The double crossing bastard!"

"I have already said that," cried Hardrock.

"But he had promised to leave the funds with us on a seven day basis for as long as possible. That was only five days ago."

"Yes. He had and now he draws a check for nine billion dollars on the account. You know what that means?"

"I know. We are short nine billion dollars. We should not have trusted Shermer. He is a smart cookie. I am sure he figured we were in trouble. So he was not prepared to increase his risk and lend us more money. In fact, he is lending us our own money by drawing a check on his account with us where we had just deposited eighteen billion for the Sheik. Smart. Very Smart." Robertson raised his eyes and looked at Hardrock. "But you, my dear friend, you are a stupid fool! Did you not verify these checks when Shermer gave them to you?"

"No, I did not. We all signed the loan agreement and he told me "here is your twenty billion", as he handed me our copy of the agreement and the four checks. It never entered my mind...."

"It never entered your mind! Nothing seems to ever enter your mind, Peter. That's why we are in such a mess."

"Let me remind you", said Hardrock, flushed with anger,

"that you created this mess with your friends the Arabs to feed your ambitions and show how smart a bank President you were. So don't try to pin this mess on me. It's on your lap where it belongs."

"Shit! I give you the solutions and you can't even execute them properly. Imagine, closing a twenty billion dollar loan without even checking the disbursements. And you call yourself a banker."

"Andrew, we are fighting for nothing. This is the end. Let's save our energy for the Feds. I am going to call White."

"If you touch that phone, I am going to bust your nose in," menaced Robertson.

"Andrew, there is no way out of this one. Even if you find one of your usual crooked ways, I want no part of it."

"I'll remember that," said Robertson. "Meanwhile, just shut up for a moment and let me think."

He lifted the phone and dialed sixty one for the International Division. "Reeves? Robertson here. Listen. We credited the account of Swiss International Bank for eighteen billion last Friday. Remember?"

"Yes, I do."

"Did you not receive instructions from them to place these funds on seven day call?"

"Yes, we did on Monday but not for the whole amount."

"Why only on Monday and why not the whole amount?"

"Well, when you gave the instructions on Friday, Zurich was already closed, so I figured we might as well enjoy the funds and earn the interest for the weekend. I put the deal through first thing Monday morning and received an immediate acknowledgment. Their instructions were to place only eight billion on a seven day basis and to place ten billion on a two day call. They called nine billion yesterday."

"You should have told me," reproached Robertson.

"You were in Zurich at their office, your secretary told me. So I figured you knew. Is something wrong?"

"No, Reeves. Nothing is wrong. You have done as instructed. Thank you."

"What was that all about?" Inquired Hardrock, eagerly.

"If you want to know how much of a double-crosser Shermer is, listen to this. You and I were sitting in his office Monday when he gave instructions to place only eight billion on seven-day call. We were probably in his office again yesterday when he called nine billion to cover the check he gave you, and because you are such a big shot, you did not even bother to verify."

"Andrew, go to hell and take Shermer with you! I am calling the Feds."

"Just stay put, Peter. Did you not tell the Sheik you would pay him his cash in ten days from last Friday?

"I did."

"So what's the big panic? What's the rush?"

"You have a solution? Another scheme, I should say?"

"No, but I'll find one. I'm not going to throw in the towel and kiss good-bye to thirty years of sweat and blood for a lousy nine billion dollars. There has to be a way out of this again."

"And I want no part of it, I have told you before," repeated Hardrock.

"I have heard you, Peter. I have heard you more than very well. You want no part of the solution. For me that means you want no part of the future of this bank."

"I have not said..."

"Peter, you can't have both. Come to think of it, the time has come for you to retire."

"Retire?"

"Yes. I have been running this bank, anyway. Doing my job and yours. Because you are never here. You don't care. You are Chairman not because you are a good banker but because your grandpa was born before you. You are too busy with your Foundation and your arts. If, in fact, I am going to run this bank, I want the top title also."

Hardrock was panicking. "But Andrew, we have been together so long. We make such a good team. I have already agreed to go fifty-fifty on the bonus. What more do you want?"

"I want it all," said Robertson sharply. "I want all and right now. I am going to save this bank despite you. But I want all the credit. All the honors. All the power. All the money. You are going to resign and have the Board appoint me as Chairman and Chief Executive Officer. The post of President is abolished. We don't need two heads. I'll assume the two functions. I'll take the two salaries and the total bonus. You can stay on the Board and watch me go."

"What if you fail? What if you don't find the nine billion?"

"Don't worry, I will. But should I fail, your name is clean. The bank will go bankrupt under my chairmanship, not yours. You can save your precious family name. I am being most generous to you, Peter. We are so deep in this thing that we should sink together. But take the raft. Save yourself. I'm going to stick with the ship."

"What do I tell the Board?" worried Hardrock.

"Tell them that you are fifty-eight. That you wish to retire prematurely to devote yourself entirely to the Foundation. They will understand that. Tell them that you wish to retire at the top when the bank has experienced its greatest success. They will understand that also. Tell them you feel that I should run the bank from now on. After all, since '64, I have built the growth nearly single-handed. They know that. They will buy it. It will be a routine matter. You and your family control the board anyway. You have a board meeting tomorrow. The timing is perfect. We can release the news after the markets close. We will make all the Sunday papers. Big story. Your life, your career, your arts, the whole shebang. Monday morning, I take over. Peter, it's the thing to do."

Hardrock turned his chair towards the window as he often did when concentrating. It was now sunny in Manhattan. Life outside looked appealing. The river and the ocean beckoned him. *I'm rich. Why do I need this aggravation?* he thought, while he heard himself say aloud, "I'll let you know tomorrow morning."

On Friday morning, exactly one week after Sheik Al-

Madir had presented his sixty billion dollar check to Grand American Bank and set in motion, unknowingly, a series of irreversible events, Peter Hardrock resigned as chairman of the bank. When the board meeting ended, shortly before noon, Andrew Robertson, praised by many directors for his past accomplishments, his loyalty and his leadership, had been elected Chairman and Chief Executive officer. His salary was set at three hundred thousand dollars a year. Somewhat less than the previous combined salaries, but substantially more than he was earning as President. The performance bonus remained intact. All of it would now accrue to Robertson.

Robertson, his voice charged with emotion for the circumstance, thanked the Board members for their trust and promised to keep the bank on the path that had made it the largest bank in the world. He then impressed them by declining to join them for dinner. "There are a lot of important details to handle this afternoon. We must tell the Stock Exchange, advise the Feds, prepare press releases, and circularize our staff. I wish to look after these details personally. After that, with your permission, gentlemen, I would like to enjoy a two-day rest in Miami. I want to be in top form on Monday when I take over from Peter."

He returned to his office and talked at length with Charles Browning, the manager of the Public Relations Department of the Bank. He warned him. "No news before the markets close. No leaks. Ask Madame de Rivoli to do your typing. She is the only one to know.

"He lifted his private phone to call Judith Watson.

"Call me later," she said. "I'm still asleep."

"It's two o'clock."

"Jesus. That's the middle of the night for me."

"Wake up Judith. I want you to come to Miami with me for the weekend."

She was suddenly awake. "Why didn't you say so before?"

He lowered his voice. "I need to see Vic. Can you tell him we are coming?"

"I'll phone him right away. I know he is there. I talked to him two days ago. When do we leave?"

"We have seats on National at five."

"I'll never be ready."

"You have to. It's Friday. To beat the traffic, I need to pick you up at three thirty. I'll use a cab, don't keep me waiting."

"My hair is a mess."

"Bring your wigs."

"I hate you, Andrew Robertson!"

"Screw you, Judith Watson."

"Promise?"

At three p.m. Simone called Georges. "I must see you now and I can't leave."

"Can't you come over at five?"

"It can't wait that long."

"Can you talk over the phone?"

"Impossible."

"Where do we meet?"

"Call me from the bar at Delmonico's. I'll take a fifteen minute break and join you."

He called her at three fifteen. In less than five minutes, she was sitting next to him. "Big things have happened. Hardrock has resigned. Robertson is the new Chairman."

"I have not heard anything on the news or seen it on the tape."

"We are releasing the announcement at four o'clock only."

"How come you know?"

"I'm typing the material for Public Relations. They don't trust anyone else. You must cable Pierre immediately."

"OK, I will."

"Something else. Robertson is going to Miami for the weekend. He told Louise he was going for a well deserved rest. He is taking Judith Watson with him. Some rest!"

"Are you sure? Who told you?"

"Louise. She made the reservations on National. Today, five p.m. Can you make it?"

"Barely. I must return to the Consulate and code the message to Pierre, then try to reach La Guardia airport in time.

I can make it if I use the Consulate's limousine. What are you going to do?"

"I must rush back and finish the press releases by four o'clock. Good luck and keep in touch."

She was back at her office at three forty and completed her work for Public Relations. At four fifteen, Hardrock opened the door to his office, "could you come in, Madame de Rivoli?"

"Right away, sir."

He had emptied his desk drawers and sorted out his personal files from those of the bank. "Will you see to it that my personal files are sent to my office at the Foundation?"

"Yes, sir. What about the paintings?"

"They all belong to the bank except the "Departure of the Sheik". I am leaving it here. I wish to offer it to Mr. Robertson. He should appreciate it. He is so close to the Arabs."

Simone glanced at Hardrock. She could not help feeling sympathy for the man. "I am sorry you are leaving," she said.

"That's life, Madame de Rivoli."

She baited him. "I have typed the various press releases, this afternoon, am I supposed to believe them?"

He looked at her for a long time as if he wished to confide in her, but he swiveled his chair and watched a ship leave the harbor and sail towards the Atlantic. "Look at that ship", he said. "One day it left the harbor with a new captain on board. They told the retiring captain. 'You are too old now. Not in terms of age but in terms of technology. We are more audacious, we go faster, and we ignore storms. The old-fashioned ways of sailing are no longer satisfactory. You are too prudent. You spare your ship and crew. We don't make enough money with you! Madame de Rivoli, I am like that retired captain. I am an old-fashioned banker. The speed, rules and methods of today have overtaken me."

She thought he was crying.

"Younger men need to take over," he was continuing. "Different men with new methods, modern techniques. It is the age of the computer. There is no room left for your reason, your heart and your principles."

She could only say, "I'm sorry."

"So am I. This is our family bank. Our name has always been linked to it. We were always proud of it. Very protective of its reputation. Clients came to us because they believed in us. Now, we are a big graphic symbol. We are three letters on the New York Stock Exchange ticker. GAB. Like Bob Hope once told me, jokingly, Grand American Bullshit! He never knew how right he was."

"What are you going to do now?" she asked.

"I'm going to go out in the world and enjoy my freedom. What about you? Will you stay?"

She had not thought of it. Did she want to work for Robertson? She needed to. She had to stay until her mission was completed. What if Robertson did not want her? No doubt, he would want to keep Louise. If he did want her, how would she stand sleeping with him and working with him at the same time? She heard herself say, "Provided Mr. Robertson needs me; I am prepared to stay as long as necessary to ensure a smooth transition."

"He will need you all right. I'll talk to him. But enough sad things. Let's talk about a more pleasant subject. My wife will be entertaining a few friends, mostly clients and relatives, Sunday night to mark my retirement. Nothing elaborate. Very impromptu. She has also invited a few directors and officers. Would you be free to join us?"

"I don't know whether it would be appropriate."

"Why not? You have been a most loyal assistant for the past eighteen months. I owe a lot to your efficiency, discretion and savoir-faire. You would be most welcome."

"Thank you, Mr. Hardrock; I am touched by your invitation."

"That's settled then. I'll send my chauffeur for you at six. As our estate is a good distance from New York, some of our guests will be spending the night. So why don't you bring an overnight bag. The limousine can take you directly to the office Monday morning."

"That's very kind of you."

"See you Sunday, then. That's it for today. That's it for this year. That's it forever, I should say. Forever!" He paused. "Call my car, will you? I'll be downstairs in five minutes."

Georges Monti sat comfortably on an aisle seat in the first class compartment of the big National DC 10. He had reached the gate barely five minutes before the final boarding call. As usual on Friday afternoon, the Miami flight was oversold and he had had to use his Diplomatic Passport to obtain a seat. By sheer coincidence, he sat immediately behind Robertson and a magnificent, glamorous redhead, no doubt Judith Watson. *I'm going to like this mission,* he thought.

He had never met Andrew Robertson but he knew him well from the photos in the File at the Consulate and those frequently published in newspapers and magazines. A smile came to his lips as he remembered the File and Simone's reaction. *I wonder wether Judith Watson goes out with this big brute because of his right hanging balls.* Then he thought of Sheik Al-Madir's red pubic hair. *The diplomatic service really involves you in strange situations,* he mused.

"Honey, bring us more champagne!" Robertson called to the stewardess.

"No more for me," Judith had said. "You know how champagne makes me feel all strange."

"The stranger you feel, the better I like you. Give her some. She will drink it."

"Andrew, I'll never last until tonight."

"Just last until nine o'clock."

"What happens at nine?"

"That's when I carry you across the threshold of the hotel room and drop you on the bed."

She looked around, concerned. Her eyes met those of

Georges. He gave her his most engaging smile. She had to return it. "Not so loud Andrew. Everybody will hear you."

"Who are you smiling at?"

"Oh! At no one and everyone. I was only trying to cover up your loud comments."

"Baby, on this trip you keep your smiles for me. Not only your smiles, all of you. You are off duty. You are out to celebrate with Big Daddy. Your smart little friend here is now the biggest daddy of them all."

"You are?"

"Yes, as of eleven o'clock this morning. My dear Judith, you are now talking to the new Chairman of the Board of Grand American Bank who, tonight, is going to screw you. What do you think of that?"

Once again, panicking, she glanced around the compartment. Once again her eyes met those of Georges, amused. "Andrew, it's great! I can't believe it. You told me you would do it. And now you have. Is this why you wanted to see Vic?"

This time it was Robertson who looked around him, quickly. He seized her arm, violently, lowering his voice. "I have told you never to pronounce his name in public. Someone is bound to hear. We would all end up in a nice mess. So watch yourself."

She rubbed her wrist. "You hurt me."

"I had to remind you to be discreet."

"I don't like it, Andrew, when you are violent with me."

"Then watch your mouth."

"If I had known that it would start this way, I would not have come."

Robertson sneered. "You would still have. You like my screwing and my money too much."

"Let's talk about something else, shall we?"

While pretending to read, Georges Monti had been slumping forward behind them to grasp every word of their conversation. Eventually, he rose and walked to the toilets. When he returned, Judith Watson was leaning against her window, starring into space while Robertson was trading inanities with the stewardesses in the gallery. When Judith Watson turned, he smiled at her. She first looked at him rather stonily, then seemed to reconsider and returned his smile warmly.

It is an advantage to have that French touch, he told himself. He returned to his seat and was soon dozing while his brain invented a wild love affair in a luxurious Miami hotel between an elegant French diplomat and a gorgeous redhead named Judith Watson.

His taxi followed theirs to the Golden Bay Club on South Biscayne Avenue in Miami. Georges had never been to the Club. It had opened in early '75, launched with fireworks and a bevy of stars. But soon, rumors had circulated that some of the dubious characters of Miami, attracted by the luxury of this new condominium-hotel, had moved in from the Jockey Club on North Biscayne Boulevard. Their consorts had soon followed. Money brokers, wheeler-dealers, call girls, union leaders, lawyers, a few movie stars and a number of European visitors who believed that the Golden Bay Club was the new "in" place in Miami.

Georges waited until Robertson and Judith Watson had left the hotel lobby before approaching the front desk. "I would like a large double room for the weekend."

"Are you alone, sir?"

"My wife may join me." That was not true. Georges was not married and had no intention to spending the weekend alone in a hotel room. He remembered his dreams about Judith Watson.

"This is a private club, sir. Do you know any of our members?"

Georges had not expected this problem. He reached in his jacket and placed his Diplomatic Passport on the desk and took a chance, "Vic knows me." Those words seemed to break all resistance.

"We don't have a double room overlooking the Bay, sir, but I could let you have a nice two-bedroom apartment. You will find it most comfortable.

"That will do."

The clerk rang the bell. "Front desk. Apartment 2605 for Mr. Monti."

"Should I tell Mr. Ferrani that you have arrived?"

"No," answered Georges quickly. "I'll phone him from my room. I want to surprise him".

"As you wish, sir."

Saturday morning, the bright Miami sun rising over Biscayne Bay interrupted Georges' sleep. He checked his watch. "My God, nine thirty!" He slid open the door connecting his room to the large balcony and stretched luxuriously while admiring the scenery. In the distance, to the left, the Port of Miami, empty of its cruise ships gone to the Caribbean for the weekend. Behind it, the roof line of lower Miami Beach, pretty from a distance, but in fact a mass of grey cement ready for the demolition blast. On his right, across the bay, the island of Key Biscayne floating into the ocean like a Japanese garden.

He went back to his room and took his field glasses out of his briefcase and returned to the balcony. He sighted the helicopter pad in front of what used to be President Nixon's winter residence and, to the left of it, the stands where the boat races were held. He spotted a number of fishing yachts leaving the bay for the open ocean and, closer to the Golden Bay Club, a row of luxury vessels, floating palaces that seldom sailed, permanently anchored to their moorings, providing discreet rooms in their hulls for conducting business conferences that needed to be held far away from unwanted eyes and ears. More transactions, more deals, more schemes were conceived, discussed and agreed upon in the master quarters of these yachts than in the boardrooms of legitimate businesses in America. "Who said life was a floating crap game?"

Suddenly, Georges froze, his binoculars pointing to the terrace separating the swimming pool from the mooring area. Robertson stood there, in white slacks and navy blue T-shirt, speaking to Judith Watson. She wore the tiniest bikini, a challenge to the law of gravity. She turned and Robertson patted her bottom. She raised her fist in protest and ran away from the pool.

Robertson walked down the steps to the dock and climbed the gangway of the largest yacht moored at the Golden Bay Club. A black boy dressed in a white sailor uniform immediately removed the gangway and showed Robertson to the door of the main cabin. Georges focused his binoculars on the back of the yacht. In bold gold letters he read: "The Goddaughter, Fort Lauderdale, Florida". He smiled. His eyes went back to the swimming pool. Judith Watson lay on her back on a lounge chair offering herself to the sun. "Merde, alors!" He rushed to the phone. "Can I buy swim trunks in this hotel?"

Twenty minutes later, Georges approached the pool attendant.

"A lounge chair, sir?"

Georges slid a five dollar bill to the blond young man. "Yes. I wish the chair next to that redhead."

"Which one?" the boy asked innocently.

"You know the one. I have been watching you falling on your face every time you walk by her, your eyes popping out of their sockets."

"Oh! That one."

"Yes, that one."

"Taken."

"The girl or the chair?" He slid him another five dollars.

"I could always squeeze another chair on the left side of hers."

"Place it on the right."

"Why?"

"I'm left handed!"

Georges followed the blond boy, excusing himself as they passed between the sun bathers. They reached the girl. Georges stood between her and the sun.

She opened her eyes. "Do I know you?"

"Don't think so," he said.

"What do you want?"

"Nothing. My chair happens to be next to yours. "It's slightly crowded here today. Sorry to disturb you."

"Are you sure I don't know you."

"Positive."

"Then buy me a drink."

"Don't you think it's too early?"

"Oh shit! Don't tell me you are one of those. Preachers! Preachers and brutes! That's all I meet these days"

"All right! All right! I'll buy you a drink."

"Forget it. Eh? You have an accent."

"I'm French."

"Buy me champagne, alors!"

When the champagne arrived, Judith Watson sat and looked at her neighbor carefully. "I have met you before. And I know where. On the plane last night. What's your name?"

"Georges."

She offered her hand. "I'm Judith Watson. Call me Judith. What do you do?"

"I work at the French consulate in New York."

"Are you a spy?"

"Yes," he laughed.

"Whom are you spying on"?

Georges fixed his eyes on her magnificent breasts. "You!"

"Thanks for the compliment and the champagne. Say, would you mind rubbing some sun tan lotion on me?"

"Not if you turn around."

"Why? Are you shy or something?"

"Something."

She placed the champagne glass on the cement deck and rolled on her stomach on her chair. "Untie my top and rub me all over."

Georges' heart missed a beat, then resumed its beating. Fast. He placed his towel over his lap and poured some lotion on her back. "I though I saw your husband with you on the plane?"

"He is not my husband."

Georges started to spread the lotion on her shoulders moving down her back to the bikini bottom. His fingers touched it.

"Don't stain my bottom."

"Sorry. Is he coming back?"

"Who?"

"The man who is not your husband."

"He is here."

Georges stopped rubbing her. "Don't stop. You have such a gentle touch and, don't worry, he is only a good friend."

"How good?"

"I sleep in my own room."

"Before or after?"

"Funny, funny."

"I don't suppose I can invite you for dinner?"

"No. I'll be busy. But you can invite me for a nightcap."

"What time is nightcap time?"

"About three in the morning."

"Won't he find out?"

"He will be pleased to get rid of me. He likes to sleep alone."

"And you?"

"I have always craved for French company."

"How French?"

"As French as you care to be. What's your room number?"

"2605."

"Draw me a hot bath and leave your door open."

Georges wiped his hands on his towel and poured more champagne in their glasses. "You want me to leave before the man who is not your husband returns?"

"His name is Andrew. Andrew Robertson. I'll introduce you. Be more fun this way. He's a big shot. Big banker, you know."

"I'm only a third-grade diplomat. I have no need for bankers."

"Stay just the same. Maybe there will be a cocktail party on Vic's yacht."

"Which one is that?"

"The big one, naturally. Vic must always have the biggest."

"Is that the Goddaughter?"

"Yes. Don't you know Vic Ferrani? He's a big shot too.

Perhaps bigger than Andrew. When these two get together for a party, bang!"

"Is that what they are planning now?"

"Are you spying again?"

"Just curious."

"They are probably planning to hold up Grand American Bank." She laughed at her joke.

"Is that what Vic does for a living?" He laughed also.

"Who knows?"

"You know him well?"

"I christened his yacht."

"You did? With that name?"

"It was all a joke. Remember that Marlon Brando movie, The Godfather? Well everyone started saying that Vic was the biggest Godfather in America."

"Is he?""

"Stop spying! Anyway, Vic has always liked my sense of humor. He calls me his Bette Hope, you know after Bob Hope, so he asked me to christen his yacht. She is his refuge. His cove. His love. He cherishes that yacht like his own daughter. That's what gave me the idea of "The Goddaughter." At first, Vic protested but then he said, "if I am going to have the reputation, I might as well feed the rumors."

"So you work for Vic Ferrani?"

"Mister, Judith Watson works for nobody but for Judith Watson."

"What do you do?"

She opened her eyes, raised her head and turned to him. "I take care of big bankers and make love to prying little Frenchmen."

She had forgotten that her bra was unhooked. As she rose, she exhibited the most voluptuous breasts Georges had ever seen.

He could only stammer, "your bath will be ready at three o'clock."

Aboard the Goddaughter, Andrew Robertson and Vic Ferrani were having an early morning drink. The usual gin and tonic for Robertson. Vichy water with a spoonful of Remy Martin floating on top of it for Ferrani.

"How can you drink gin so early in the morning?" asked Ferrani.

"How can you drink cognac?" replied Robertson.

"This is called a "floater". He placed his glass in front of the table lamp. "You see, the cognac sits on top of the Vichy water. When you drink it, you sip a bit of one and some of the other. Nice drink. Never get drunk on it."

"Well, I get drunk on gin and tonic. That's why I drink it. What's the use of drinking if you don't get drunk? It's like fucking without coming."

"You are still at it, Andrew?"

"Vic, it's the thing that keeps me alive."

"How's Judith?"

"Judith is great, as usual."

"Where is she?"

"Sunbathing."

"You shouldn't leave her alone."

"No danger. She always comes back to Daddy."

"Just the same, you should have brought her aboard".

"I wanted no witnesses".

"She could have sunbathed on the deck."

"That's still too close."

Ferrani looked at Robertson knowingly. "You, my friend, have a big problem."

Vic Ferrani could read the thoughts of another man like nobody else. He had a sixth sense about it. He could perceive the electrical impulses of another person's brain as clearly as if his receptors were plugged into the other person's head. He had been only fourteen when he had discovered this phenomenon. In Camden, the sin city of New Jersey, where he was brought up by his grandmother, little Vic had soon organized the most ruthless gang in the Italian community. He was the leader. They called him "Vic the waves" because he used to say "my waves tell me..." and he was always right. He always knew what the enemy was plotting. He was always aware of his friends' thoughts. Because he knew more, he was more successful, more often victorious.

Today, at fifty, Vic Ferrani controlled the largest crime syndicate in America but most of its activities were now legitimate. By the late sixties, he had accumulated so much money that he had had to invest it in respectable companies. After Sheik Al-Madir, he was probably the largest client of Grand American Bank. Bigger than Standard or General Motors or ITT. He dealt with Grand American because he did not trust small banks and Robertson was his friend.

His forays on the stock exchange had bought him control of many large corporations and banks. There were few activities in America that did not come within his circle of influence. He and his friends at the Teamsters Union had even acquired a majority interest in Bankers Express. He controlled management. The Teamsters controlled the drivers. What a combination! Nobody in America but Vic knew that most funds transferred between banks were consigned to Vic Ferrani's Bankers Express. His was the only conglomerate which had survived the collapse of that industry in the early seventies because his was the only true conglomerate. Indeed he was Mr. Conglomerate himself.

Robertson leaned forward. "Vic, I have the biggest problem of my career."

"I know," said Vic. "You have managed to dislodge Hardrock from the Chairmanship and you are now the real big boss of the whole shebang. The most important banker in the world. But you are the big boss over a sleeping volcano."

"How do you know that?"

"Vic knows everything."

"I have a deal for you, Vic. A big one. The biggest of your career. After this one, you can retire."

"Who wants to retire? Do you?"

"I would if I had one billion dollars."

Vic whistled. "In one deal?"

"One only."

"Any risks?"

"None whatsoever."

"No shooting?"

"No shooting. No publicity. No police. No nothing. Fast, clean, neat. One cool billion dollars in cash."

"Good cash?"

"Real cash."

"When?"

"Monday."

"Too soon."

"Must be Monday."

"Where?"

"New York."

"I'll have to leave today."

"Yes."

All cycles were flashing in Ferrani's computer brain. "No party?"

"Only after."

Ferrani's eyes X-rayed Robertson's forehead. "We will have one before also. Right now. Go and get Judith." Vic Ferrani rose. "But before you go, let's have another drink."

Robertson knew he had a deal."

There were already four passengers in Hardrock's limousine when Simone walked out of her apartment. Patrick White, Chairman of the Federal Reserve Board and his wife, Sadie. René Mathieu, the President of Companie de Suez and his wife, Madeleine. Mathieu stepped out to let Simone sit with the other women in the back and the two men rode the folding seats. Within an hour they arrived at Hardrock's estate, a rambling property — the largest in the State of New York — overlooking the Hudson river. A number of other limousines were already parked in front of the garages.

Inside, thirty guests were milling around, drinks in their hands. Pamela Hardrock greeted them enthusiastically. "Mr. Mathieu! Mr. White! It's so nice to see you again. Oh! Simone, you look magnificent. Sadie! Madeleine! Nice of you to come on such short notice. We are keeping everything informal. We had to improvise this party. Peter always does these things to me. He came home Thursday night saying, 'what would you say if I resigned from the Bank and spent all my time at the Foundation?' 'Fine with me,' I said. Bingo! Friday morning he called me and said, 'if you want to throw a party tomorrow, I am a free man.' There was no way I could have done it yesterday with the catering and all that, but I got on the phone and managed to reach all of you in time for tonight. How nice. Please come in. The bar is wide open." Pamela Hardrock walked to the bar with Simone. "It must have been a shock to you, dear, his resignation."

"I'm very sad Mr. Hardrock is leaving," said Simone sincerely.

ɪ going to work for the Big Man?"

ɪmiled. Even Pamela Hardrock knew the nickname

ɪn. "I have agreed to stay at least during the ɪeriod."

ᴗ... ɪat's so much like you. You are so loyal."

"I try my best."

"What will you have to drink?"

"I'll have champagne, thank you."

"Naturally. Oh! Excuse me, Simone, other guests are arriving."

Simone's eyes followed Pamela to the entrance hall. There stood Sheik Al-Madir, impassive in his official attire. His eyes met hers, blinked, and then continued to survey the room. He accepted the greetings of Pamela Hardrock, "Sheik Al-Madir, I am so thrilled that you could make it. Peter will be so pleased." She took his arm through his robe. "And I have a surprise for you. Simone is here." She directed him to the bar where Simone stood, undecided as to what attitude she should adopt. Pamela was beaming. "Simone, look whom I found. I thought the two of you had had a lovers spat. We have not seen your names in the papers for at least two weeks."

Sheik Al-Madir bowed and took the hand that Simone presented and brought it to his lips politely. "Madame de Rivoli, I did not expect to find you here."

"Don't look so disconcerted," said Pamela.

"I am only surprised," replied the Sheik.

"Simone has been so close to Peter during the last eighteen months, I felt that she deserved to be invited to this little gathering. Peter is really going to miss her. He once told me he owed to Simone most of his recent accomplishments as Chairman. As a matter of fact, I started to get jealous. Are you drinking champagne also, Sheik Al-Madir? Simone, be a darling and get a glass of champagne for the Sheik."

Pamela walked away. Simone offered the glass of champagne to the Sheik and glanced at him hoping he would not reject her. "I have a toast to propose," she murmured.

"I'm listening."

"To our reconciliation."

"I am not prepared to celebrate, yet."

"Although I am not guilty, I am begging for your forgiveness."

"It is said: 'Do not take outsiders as your intimate friends, they will not fail to cause you injury.'

"It is also said: 'Allah is the Most Forgiving, Ever Merciful.' Why do you want to be harsher than Allah?" she pleaded.

"I'll think about it. And now, if you will please excuse me."

Simone watched him walk away, her mind fast at work devising ways of getting back into his good graces. She knew that her Quran quote had shaken him. His "I shall think about it" left the door ajar. She had to take advantage of it. He was now her last hope of salvaging her mission.

Georges had telephone her from Miami late Sunday morning to report on his activities. "I have not learned much," he had said. "Robertson is here with Judith Watson. Yesterday, he attended a meeting on board a yacht called "The Goddaughter." Yes. Don't laugh. That's the name. It belongs to some shady character called Vic Ferrani. I was unable to obtain from my source any information on the nature of the meeting."

"Who is your source, may I ask?"

"None of your business, Simone."

"Is she still in your bed?"

"I'm more discreet than that!"

"Ferrani, Ferrani. I know that name. Is he not connected with the Trans Ocean Grain Company? You said shady character. My God!"

"Do you know him?"

"I know of him. You are sure that Robertson and Ferrani met?"

"I saw Robertson board his yacht."

"Are you positive Ferrani was on board?"

"I am."

"Georges, come back to New York immediately. We know enough."

In fact, she did not know anything that might help her immediately but the information that Robertson and Ferrani had met in Miami on the Goddaughter might prove useful. Judith Watson. That name kept coming back to her mind. Perhaps she should have paid more attention to that call girl. Perhaps she was a missing link in her chain. She met Robertson often and now it transpired that she was connected to Ferrani.

"Encore du champagne, Madame la Baroness?" Simone came out of her state of concentration. The handsome Sergei Moroyneff stood in front of her, his hand extended. She gave him her glass. Moroyneff was the director of the International Museum of Arts, a pet project of Pamela and Peter Hardrock. She had seen him often at the bank. "What's your latest acquisition, Mr. Moroyneff?"

"We have not acquired a painting or a sculpture in months. You can't find masterpieces anymore. Either they are protected and you can't export them such as in France and Italy or the Arabs have emptied the market. In the last two years, particularly, they have been buying everything. Not satisfied with having all the money, all the gold and all the diamonds, now they have all the good artworks."

"Surely there must be some artworks left at the Louvre," said Simone. "I always understood that there were thousands of paintings that remained crated in the basement of the Louvre for lack of space to exhibit them."

"You are right, Baroness, but the French government refuses to open those crates. The only artworks that have left France in the last four years were shipped to the Middle East. Probably bartered for oil. Imagine sacrificing your heritage for a few drops of fuel."

"I thinks it's a real shame that they are permitted to take over the world," interjected Candice Turner who had just joined them with the Chairman of the Joint Chiefs of Staff of the U.S. Army, General Max Atterson. Candice Turner had inherited the real estate fortune of her father, Kenneth Turner, who had sold most of his Manhattan real estate to Saudi Arabia, just before his death. She had been married four times and divorced as often. She was now "in between" as she said. Wealthy, thanks to the Arabs, with nothing to do, she kept busy as President of the Hudson River & Country Club where Wall Street bankers and financiers met weekends to exchange their sorrows about the state of the world's economy.

"If the President had listened to me," said General Atterson," we would have solved the Arab problem a long time ago."

"Violence has never solved anything, General," said Moroyneff.

"It solved World War II and it would have solved Vietnam if you liberals had not undermined the authority of the President of the United States and sapped the courage of the Pentagon."

"I agree with the General," said Candice Turner. "If you go to war, you must win it. You can't win with half a gun, half a bullet and half a plane. You must go all out or nothing."

"Including murders, I suppose," suggested Simone, coldly.

"Baroness, in war there are no such things as murders. Soldiers kill or get killed. Period."

"There are no such things as ethics and morals either would you say?" questioned Moroyneff.

"Our ethics and morals are well defined in the Geneva Convention. Those are our rules of war," stated the General.

"It's a game then?" asked Moroyneff.

"You could define war as a game," said the General, "and as in all games some lose and some win."

"And who is the referee?" asked Simone. "Don't answer me. I'll tell you. It's death! If you kill more than the other side, then you win, don't you General? You get judged by the number of bodies left on the battlefield. Be they soldiers, children, women or old people."

"We don't shoot at children..." he tried to interrupt.

"You don't? How many files like the My Lai one have you hidden in your safes and vaults, General?"

"Baroness, surely you are not attacking the integrity of General Atterson," protested Candice Turner.

"I am attacking the integrity of the whole United States Army of which he happens to be the head commander."

"I don't think you have a right to an opinion about a thing you don't know anything about," pronounced the General primly. "After all, what do you know about My Lai?"

"My husband was murdered there!"

She walked away leaving them with consternation on their face.

The butler broke their shock. "Ladies and gentlemen, dinner is served".

Simone sat near the head of the table, presided over by Peter Hardrock. Opposite her were Sheik Al-Madir, Patrick White, from the Federal Reserve Board and René Mathieu from Compagnie de Suez. On her immediate left was Senator Edward Clark, Chairman of the US Senate Banking Committee and on her right, Bob Wintack, a senior editor with the Wall Street Journal. At the table also were Senor Antonio Lopez, Mexican Ambassador to Washington, Jack Reeves, Vice President, International Division of Grand American Bank, Joe Simmons, President of Standard Oil of Maine, Sergei Moroyneff, Candice Turner and General Atterson. The men were all accompanied by their wives except Moroyneff who was a bachelor and Sheik Al-Madir, but in his case everyone assumed that he was escorting Simone.

Bob Wintack stood and raised his glass. "Dear friends, I believe this occasion calls for a very special toast. Peter Hardrock has retired from Grand American Bank. What few people remember is that on the second of July of this year, he completed thirty-five years of service with the bank. He was only twenty-three when in July 1943 he joined Grand American Bank as a junior clerk because his father wanted him to learn the business from the bottom up. During his stay at the Bank, he saw it reach — I should say, he led it to

— the peaks of international finance. There is no bigger nor stronger financial institution in the world and our dear Peter is the man responsible. "Hear, hear," they all shouted, except Al-Madir and Simone de Rivoli. Bob Wintack raised his glass again. "I propose a toast to honor Peter Hardrock, the Banker of the Century."

They all rose. "To Peter Hardrock!" They all drank their champagne except Sheik Al-Madir and Simone. Their glasses were empty.

At the other end of the table, Sergei Moroyneff pushed his chair back and tapped the rim of his glass with a spoon to attract the attention of the guests. "Friends, the toast proposed by Bob Wintack honored the past of Peter Hardrock. He talked about his success as a banker. We should not forget his accomplishments as a Patron of the Arts, past, present and now future as I understand that he has decided to devote all of his time to the family Foundation and the Arts."

"Don't forget me," put forth Pamela Hardrock.

"We shall consider lending him to you in between exhibitions," he retorted. He picked up his glass. "To Peter Hardrock, Patron of the Arts." They all rose again. "To Peter." This time Sheik Al-Madir and Simone joined them.

"A speech, a speech," scanted Candice Turner.

Hardrock smiled, slightly embarrassed. He had never liked public speeches or ceremonies. "Friends, thank you. Thank you for being here. Thank you for your help and trust in the past that made Grand American Bank possible. Thank you particularly to you Sheik Al-Madir and you René Mathieu and Joe Simmons, your trust was most important to us. Thank you to you Senator Clark and you Patrick White, government understanding of free enterprise helped us considerably. Thank you, Bob Wintack, for your fair criticism in the Journal. It kept us on the straight and narrow. Thank you, Jack Reeves who represents here all members of our staff. Your dedication, hard work and support contributed to a very large extent to our success. Thank you to all of you, good friends and collaborators, your sacrifices and friendship reduced greatly the loneliness of my office."

He addressed himself more directly to Simone. "Finally, to you Baroness de Rivoli, a very special thank you. In recent months, your elegance and your class set the style of the Chairman's office. I owe you a special debt of gratitude for your dedication to me and your loyalty to the Bank. Madame de Rivoli has informed me that she might be leaving after the transition. If she does, it will be a great loss to Grand American. In front of all our friends here, I am asking you to stay."

"It would be most difficult for me to work for any other Chairman than you." She was not entirely lying. She thought of Robertson and she shivered. Her eyes met those of René Mathieu. She blushed.

"You don't have to blush," said Pamela Hardrock. "I understand your feelings toward Peter and I want you to know that I have eliminated from my head all thoughts of jealousy."

General Max Atterson broke the sudden silence. "A toast to all our charming ladies. Life would not be worth living if it was not for them." They drank once again.

"I did not know that generals could get sentimental," remarked Simone.

The food arrived and the conversation died while everyone helped themselves from the series of dishes presented by the butler and his assistants. Even an informal dinner at the Hardrock's was an elaborate affair.

Bob Wintack broke the long silence. "Now that the management of money is no longer your profession, Peter, I guess we can talk about money during dinner. It's no longer talking about business."

"There are better subjects," replied Hardrock. "I remember when at one time it was forbidden at this table to discuss religion, politics, sex and money. Imagine the four subjects that rule and condition our lives."

"What happened?" asked Candice Turner.

"We all stopped practicing religion," replied Wintack, "so the subject ceased to be controversial."

"I still go to church," said Angela Atterson.

"What for?" queried the General.

"To pray for you. You should thank God that you are still alive."

"I prefer to thank my gun."

"What about politics?" risked Senor Antonio Lopez. "In my country we always talk politics at dinner."

"That's understandable in a dictatorship," remarked Senator Clark. "When you only have one party and everyone belongs to that party, you can never say anything wrong."

"Permit me to object to your term "dictatorship," replied the Ambassador. "We have elections in Mexico. Our President is elected by popular vote."

"I though he was designated by his predecessor."

"He may be, but he still has to campaign to explain his program to the people. At the end of his campaign, we vote."

"You vote but you have no choice. Let's say that you have a democratic dictatorship."

"I still resent your term put permit me to state that our system works while yours..."

Hardrock intervened. "Gentlemen, if we try to solve the problems of the US here tonight..."

"They are insoluble," interrupted René Mathieu.

"Well, well," said Wintack. "All this to say that politics at one time was banished from conversation around this table and while politicians will always be with us — they are one of those necessary nuisances — as long as the brother of Peter is President of the United States, as a matter of courtesy, we should keep this subject on the taboo list. Which leaves us sex and money."

"Sex at our age," complained Ethel Simmons. "Anyway it's too early to talk about it."

"Speak for yourself," declared Candice Turner.

"That's leaves us with money," announced Bob Wintack.

"Unfortunately, all the money in the world now belongs to Sheik Al-Madir and his cousins, so we have nothing to talk about."

"Let's go back to sex," insisted Candice Turner.

The Sheik addressed her. "It is written: 'Everyone has a goal which dominates him.'"

"Sheik Al-Madir, don't bring your religion into this discussion," said Senator Clark. "Let's stay on the subject of money."

"Money is the source of all evils," said Evelyn Reeves, stupidly. They all looked at her.

"Only those who are poor and the communists say that, my dear," said Jean Clark. "What do you think Sheik Al-Madir?"

"I have learned in your schools that money was a mean of payment to facilitate trade. I don't understand how that can be evil."

"I have learned that also," said Patrick White. "Unfortunately, most people have forgotten this elementary lesson and wish to use money as a store of value."

"Those who do," said the Sheik, "are storing nothing."

Simone looked at him. "I agree with Sheik Al-Madir. In order to be used as a store of value, money must be worth something."

"But surely money is worth what is written on it," said Candice Turner. "A ten dollar bill for me is always worth ten dollars."

"Exactly," said Sheik Al-Madir, "but how much is ten dollars worth, Madame Turner? I have many of your ten dollars. What can I get for them? If I went to your Government in Washington and asked them to reimburse me for my ten dollar bills, what will they give me?"

"They will give you butter, wheat, soup, meat, steel, plastic, cars, planes and guns," proclaimed Senator Clark. "They will give you whatever you want."

"And after that, if I still have ten dollar bills, what will you give me?"

"What more do you want?" asked the Senator. "Our blood?"

"I want money."

"But you have money, more than you can ever hope to spend."

"It's only paper. It's nothing. At one time, on your bills, one could read 'The US Government promises to pay...' That promise is gone. Since President Nixon closed the gold window, you promise to pay me nothing. As a matter of fact, you don't even promise anything anymore. The phrase has been removed from your money."

"I have never paid attention to our money. What does it say now?" asked Candice Turner.

"It only says 'In God we trust!' replied the Sheik, "but I for one, believe in Allah."

"Our money is backed by the full credit of the United States," affirmed Senator Clark.

"That's certainly not worth more than your faith in God, or is it, Senator?" asked the Sheik sarcastically."

"Who knows the solution to this riddle?" questioned Bob Wintack.

"Gold!" declared simultaneously Patrick White, Sheik Al-Madir, René Mathieu and Simone. They all laughed.

"Well, we seem to have unanimity here," guffawed Senator Clark. "Don't tell me you want to reopen the gold file. I though we had buried gold definitely in 1971. What was the expression used then? Bob, you should remember."

"You demonetized gold, Senator," said Wintack.

"You always forget my testimonies, Senator," explained White. "Time and time again, I've told you and your Banking Committee and I've told the President also, that by removing the backing of gold from the dollar, by eliminating gold as the tool of settlement of international trade, it is not gold that you demonetized, it is the dollar itself. From a piece of paper convertible into gold at any time at the choice of the holder, you have made our dollar a piece of paper convertible into nothing, forever."

"I disagree," said the Senator. "The US will always honor its obligations."

"You missed the point," said White. "Our money is no longer an obligation to pay. Therefore, you have no obligation to meet."

"How come everyone is most happy to accept our money?"

"We are not happy," said the Sheik. "As a matter of fact, we are most unhappy, but for the time being we have no choice. But I must warn you that the time will soon come when we will have completed all of our purchases from you, satisfied our needs for factories, trained our own technicians, and developed our own know-how. When that day comes, and it is not very far away, we shall have no further use for your paper money. We shall then insist on real money."

"Gold!" Patrick White, René Mathieu and Simone said again in unison.

"But we have very little gold," protested Senator Clark, "less than ten billion dollars."

"Senator," said Hardrock, "you are still counting at the old fixed and artificial set price of forty-two dollars per ounce. Today, gold is trading at roughly two hundred and fifty dollars per ounce. The gold reserves of the US are in fact worth some sixty billion dollars, not ten billion."

The Sheik smiled. "Even at that price, I must agree with the Senator, that's very little gold."

"Which means, ladies and gentlemen," pronounced Patrick White, "that our country is broke. If we wanted to honor our obligations, as Senator Clark claims, we would not have enough gold to redeem all the paper money that we have printed in the last thirty years to finance our deficits, to pay our trade bills and in the case of Sheik Al-Madir, to purchase his oil. That's why President Nixon closed the window. We had no more true money."

"What's going to happen to us?" Candice Turner wanted to know.

"Madame," said René Mathieu, "in France when one is

broke, one must 'déposer son bilan'. Being broke, the United States should file for bankruptcy. But once you do, you will lose all of your wealth and your power. You will have to adjust your standard of living to your new condition of a poor nation. It is not a very pleasant prospect."

"The American people will go to war first," roared the general.

They soon retired to the living room. Outside, on the terrace overlooking the Hudson River, a five-piece band played dance music, and a few couples started to move to the appealing rhythm.

Simone walked toward the Sheik who stood at one end of the terrace, sipping a glass of cognac, lost in meditation. "I've never danced with you when you were dressed in your official attire."

"You know that I don't like to dance. That's for others to do for my enjoyment."

"If you don't dance with me, people will start talking. Already some were surprised that I had not arrived with you."

"How much longer do you intend to play this game, Baroness? How much longer do I need to pretend that I still want you?"

She moved closer to him until her perfume surrounded him. "That is not a pretense. That is still a fact. Come, dance with me, mon beau Sheik."

He could not push her away. They danced slowly, his robe enveloping her, his right hand trembling from the contact of her bare back.

"I admired your argument in favor of gold," she flattered him. "You pleaded like an economist."

"You forget that I attended Harvard."

"They don't teach gold theory at Harvard."

"I also took a post graduate course at la Sorbonne."

"I thought that your arguments matched those of a French economist, I went to the Sorbonne also."

"You never told me."

"You never asked me. In your country women are not expected to be educated. If you want to know, I hold a Doctorate in Economics."

"Perhaps I should call you doctor from now on."

"Perhaps you should elect me to your board of advisers. I'm an expert on banking matters. I worked at the Bank of France at one time."

"That's very interesting. Now I understand why Hardrock praised you so highly. I was surprised. I though it was Robertson who..."

"You don't have to bring him into this conversation."

"I must. He is the one who stands between us."

"He attacked me. He forced me. He tried to rape me. He would have without your intervention. I have tried to explain it to you before, but you will not listen. You are judging me without hearing my side."

"What was he doing in your apartment?"

"We had been working late and he drove me home."

"I can't believe that!"

"Would I have telephoned you and invited you to my apartment, knowing that Robertson would be there? Forget your anger for a moment and try to remember. You came that night because I telephoned you. You did not surprise me. I am the one who wanted to see you."

He kept dancing silently, hurting from the memory of Robertson lunging at her. Then he remembered her protests: "Andrew leave me alone. You are hurting me." Perhaps she was telling the truth. He promised himself to avenge her. "Perhaps I was unfair to you."

"You were."

"May I apologize?"

"Just dance with me. Closer."

On Monday morning confusion reigned at Grand American Bank. The "Big Man" was moving to Hardrock's suite. Four building maintenance men were rearranging the furniture in the office. Boxes of files, books and documents waited to be unpacked. Robertson's numerous honorary degrees, granted to him in return for gifts from the Bank to various universities, all framed in mahogany, lay on the floor awaiting a place on the walls that only Robertson could assign. The telephone service men were installing a new private line in the office and a more complex intercom system between Robertson's desk, Simone's, Louise's and senior officers of the bank.

At eleven, Sheik Al-Madir walked into this confusion. As soon as Simone saw him stepping out of the elevator, she went quickly to meet him. "Good morning, Sheik Al-Madir. I must apologize for the disorder. I did not know you had an appointment."

"I have an appointment with Mr. Hardrock."

"Oh! But he is not coming back. I thought you would have assumed that from the party, Sunday night. Not only has he retired, but he is already gone. Would you care to see Mr. Robertson?"

"Are you sure Mr. Hardrock is not coming in this morning?"

"I'm positive. Should I ask Mr. Robertson whether he can see you?"

"Don't ask him; just tell him that he must see me. Now."

She lowered her voice. "Be careful, Ben."

"Why?"

"Not only do I hate the man as much as you do but I don't trust him either. I know about your withdrawal."

"Who told you?"

"He did. He is so mad at you he wants to kill you."

"I don't fear him."

"Nevertheless, don't let him fool you."

"He can't fool me with cash."

Simone went to Robertson's office.

"Yes, I'll see Sheik Al-Madir. Ask him to wait," Robertson said brusquely.

"I'd better not."

"What's wrong?"

"He is not in his best disposition."

"The fucking camel driver!"

"That will not solve the problem. Should I show him in?"

"Bring the bastard in."

Sheik Al-Madir walked in, refused the hand offered by Robertson, and took a seat.

"If you want it that way," muttered Robertson.

"I want it that way. Forever."

"Ben, I think you are being most unreasonable. Christ! We have been whoring and drinking together for more than fifteen years. Suddenly you see me screwing a girl you like and you bash me on the head and try to bankrupt my bank. I have screwed your girl friends before..."

"But not my wives."

"She is not your wife."

"I have asked her. It's the same. Everyone knew this. So did you. You have betrayed our friendship. I don't want to talk to you nor see you ever again. So give me my money and I shall quickly be on my way. As to you, it is written: 'Everyone shall suffer death, and you shall be paid your full recompense on the Day of Judgment.' I leave your chastisement to Allah. Allah who is All Knowing and Wise".

"Leave your God out of this."

"Where is my money?"

"You only get part of it today. Eleven billion."

"Why's that?"

"That's all we could assemble without alerting Patrick White and his cronies."

"That's not good enough. I have retained a whole fleet of Bankers Express trucks and my Concorde is waiting at Kennedy."

"They will have to make two trips. I can let you have the other nine billion on Wednesday. Take it or leave it."

"You are not tricking me?"

"I wonder who is trying to trick whom here. You want to go in my vaults and count it?"

"Where do I sign?"

"Right here. But read it before you do in case you still think that I am tricking you."

> "Received from Grand American Bank, New York, the sum of US$11,000,000,000 (eleven billion United States dollars) in cash as part payment of funds withdrawn from account no. 002- 10447-9 in the name of Sheik Ben Said Al-Madir in Trust.
>
> New York, July 10, 1978
>
> x_____"
> Signature of Client

Sheik Al-Madir signed the receipt. "Where is the money?"

"We will load your Bankers Express trucks right away." Robertson reached for his intercom. "Baxter? You may release the eleven billion to Bankers. I have a signed receipt from the client in my office. I'll send it to you right away."

The Sheik rose. "Wednesday, same time?"

"Same time."

"No tricks?"

"You should know me better."

"I know you well enough to want to kill you."

"If you did, you would never get your other nine billion."

As soon as Sheik Al-Madir had left, Robertson buzzed Simone. "Take this receipt to Baxter at Cash Clearing Department, right away. Take it yourself. I don't want anyone else to se it."

When Simone reached the second basement level, a guard stopped her. "I am looking for Mr. Baxter." She showed him her identification. He pressed a button and a large grille unbolted. She walked into a waiting room. Soon a door opened at the end of the room and a clerk, dressed in blue coveralls, came towards her.

"Are you looking for Mr. Baxter?"

"Yes, please. I have a document for him from Mr. Robertson."

"Which one? The "Big Man?""

"Himself."

"Show me your identification."

She did. He glanced at it. "You look better in person. Follow me."

They entered a huge vault. There were carts covered with cash everywhere and more clerks in blue coveralls handling canvas bags. Next to each clerk, a guard stood, revolver drawn. They reached a steel door. He pressed a bell. She saw an eye appear through the peep hole and heard a voice. "Code please."

"534 Strangelove."

She heard a metallic click and the door opened. "I am Baxter," said the new man. "You have the receipt?"

"May I see your identification first?" she asked.

He looked startled. "What for? Down here, everybody knows I'm Baxter."

"I don't."

He reached for his wallet. Across from where she stood, bullet proof glass windows ran from wall to wall and through them Simone counted four Bankers Express trucks. Baxter finally produced his card.

She gave him the receipt. "I just wanted to be sure. This is

Mr. Robertson's first day as Chairman. I guess no one wants to make the first mistake."

"Well, he seems to be starting his reign by emptying my vaults," Baxter said.

Simone pretended she did not know what he was taking about. "You mean all this cash is leaving? Somebody broke the bank?"

"After we complete this load we won't have much left, I can assure you of that. It's a good thing we are getting more this afternoon."

"You are?"

"Did Mr. Robertson not tell you? One of his Sheik friends is making a ten billion cash deposit this afternoon. Cash! Well, you win some and lose some, I always say. That's our game down here."

"Thank you Mr. Baxter. I need to rush back to Mr. Robertson's office."

"I'll help you get out of here, because right now you are a prisoner. We don't mind, because we don't often see women in our vault. It's kind of lonely here."

They reached the last grille, which the same guard opened.

"Hope to see you again," Baxter said.

Simone left under the approving eyes of the two men.

Baxter turned to the guard. "Jim, I have been buried here a long time. Thirty years. But I have never seen anything like it. Imagine! One Sheik just took out eleven billion dollars in cash."

"Eleven billion!"

"Yes, sir. But that's not all. This afternoon another Sheik is bringing us ten billion, also in cash."

"That goes to show you that cash is not worth anything anymore."

Sheik Al-Madir's private Concorde, its nose lowered for taxiing, was parked in the Pan Am cargo hangar at Kennedy airport. The Captain had filed his flight plan, estimating his time of arrival in Dubai at nine fourteen the next day. It was perfect timing. His cargo would be unloaded and brought to the vaults of the Al-Madir Trading Company before noon.

The Bankers trucks had left Manhattan forty minutes before and were expected at Kennedy within minutes. Someone shouted, "here they are." Immediately ten Arabs, machine guns ready, disembarked from the plane and took their position at the four corners of the hangar. The four trucks drove in. Their guards jumped from the front seat, their guns drawn, checked the surroundings and unlocked the back doors. The Bankers men started to load the plane. The captain stood by the conveyor belt, counting the bags. It took close to one hour to load the two thousand one hundred and eighty sealed bags.

"There it is," said the Bankers supervisor. "Sign here captain, where it says two thousand one hundred and eighty bags. Eleven billion dollars."

"Here you go."

"Thanks captain. And don't crash now. It would be a shame to drop this load in the ocean. It's the largest I have ever handled.

"Don't worry."

A limousine appeared. Everyone stood at attention as Sheik Al-Madir boarded his plane.

"Are we all set captain?"

"Yes, sir."

"Good weather?"

"We should be flying over any turbulence."

"At what time tomorrow do you expect to bring me back to New York from Dubai?"

"I expect to land in Dubai at nine fourteen a.m. If we left around noon, I would have you in New York in time for a late dinner."

"Let's go."

Simone had barely returned from lunch when the phone rang. "Mr. Robertson's office. No he has not. I don't expect him before three. Would you care to leave a message? Hello? Hello? Who is calling him please? To say what? I can't hear you well. 'Vic has left for Miami'? Is that all? Hello? Hello?" Simone looked at the dead phone with surprise. She wrote down the message. – At two forty-three p.m. some unidentified person called you. Left a message 'Vic has left for Miami'. Said you would understand.

When Robertson returned, he picked up his messages, selected this strange one from amongst the others, crumbled it slowly and dropped it in his waste paper basket. He then sat in his swivel chair and turned it towards the river and the harbor in a gesture that reminded Simone of Hardrock.

"Simone, my first day has been a good day. A very good day. Tonight you and I must celebrate. Call the El Morocco."

"I would prefer that we stayed home."

"Oh no! To get my head bashed again by your Sheik!"

"He is away. He went to Dubai."

"I know but he will be back."

"How do you know?"

"He has an appointment with me on Wednesday."

"You did not tell me. Should I note it in your diary?"

"Not necessary. There is no way I can forget it. In any event, the Sheik will see to it that I don't".

"Why?"

"I just screwed him good."

When Pierre Beauchamp reached his office in Paris the following morning, he found the cable from Simone. He read it at least ten times and he was as perplexed after the last reading as he was after the first.

> "Using Bankers Express, Sheik Al-Madir withdrew eleven billion dollars in cash this morning from GAB and flew on his private Concorde to Dubai. I suspect that he delivered the cash there but have no assurance. I have learned that GAB is expecting a cash deposit of ten billion this afternoon from another Sheik. Unable to identify. Robertson elated, claims quote: I have screwed Sheik good unquote. I am again on speaking terms with Sheik Al-Madir. Additional information: Sunday night, during a private dinner at Hardrock's residence, Patrick White defended gold against Senator Clark's paper money stand. Robertson during weekend in Miami with Judith Watson met Vic Ferrani known to be top man of Syndicate. You have file, no doubt. Monday afternoon I received an anonymous message for Robertson. Quote: Vic has left for Miami unquote. Georges and I unable to draw conclusions from the above. Solicit your suggestions.

Beauchamp called in two of his assistants. "Paul, I want you to contact Interpol and run down everything they have on Vic Ferrani, the alleged leader of the U.S. Syndicate. I want it today. Great urgency. Daniel, Sheik Al-Madir flew from New York to Dubai, yesterday. Find out who was his pilot. If it was Jacques Bruneau, contact him. I want a copy of his manifest for both passengers and cargo."

At exactly noon, on Tuesday, New York time, Simone walked into Delmonicos' bar and quickly sighted Georges seated behind a small table along the wall. He placed a message in front of her:

"Al-Madir's plane carried crew of eight, twelve guards, the Sheik and cargo of eleven billion US dollar bills in two thousand one hundred and eighty bags. Arrived in Dubai nine twenty-two. Left same day for New York via Zurich at eleven thirty-four a.m. Crew of five, two guards, the Sheik, no cargo. ETA New York seven ten p.m. today. Vic Ferrani confirmed leader of Syndicate. Very wealthy. Believed to own secretly large blocks of shares in many US corporations. Uses Trans Ocean Grain Company as a cover. Uses same to move vast sums of money around the world. Trans Ocean known to bank with GAB. This might explain relationship Robertson-Ferrani. Can't help you otherwise. Can only suggest you check daily report on Arab deposits ten million and over. Withdrawal by Al-Madir and new deposit of ten billion by other unidentified Sheik should appear. Pierre."

Simone placed her head in her hands. "How stupid of me! Of course I should have checked the reports"

"You did not?" asked Georges.

"I only do it on Friday when I photocopy them and deliver a copy to you."

"Is it too late?"

"They are gone to Confidential Filing. I was showing Louise how to handle them just before I left to join you."

"Can you retrieve them?"

"It would look suspicious. How very stupid of me! Now

we have to wait until tomorrow for the next report. Order me a drink. Double vodka martini. Very dry, with an olive."

"Simone!"

When Simone stepped out of the elevator into the executive floor shortly before nine on Wednesday, Sheik Al-Madir was sitting erect in one of the armchairs in the waiting area, a lonely king in wrath, his eyes full of cruelty.

"Where is he?"

"You mean Mr. Robertson?"

"I mean that thief."

"You look furious and you are shouting. That's not like you. Why don't you wait in his office?"

"I'll wait here. I want to tell him to his face in front of everyone."

"That will not serve any purpose."

"I want the whole world to know. He belongs with the scum of the earth." He hesitated. "And you do also if you work for him."

"Please follow me," she begged.

They entered Robertson's office. "What happened?" she asked.

"He tricked me. He is worse than the lowest of horse thieves. He robbed me. I shall have his hands cut off like we do to thieves in my country. May Allah bring his wrath upon him!"

"You still have not told me what he has done?"

"The bags were empty."

"What bags?"

"Bankers Express. Not empty, stuffed with paper. Newspapers, all nicely cut up and stacked like bundles of cash."

"I don't understand a word of what you are trying to tell me."

"Last Monday, I withdrew eleven billion dollars from my account. In cash. Robertson paid me with cut up newspapers. That's all I found in the bags."

"Whose bags?"

"Bankers Express. I hired them to take the bags from here to my Concorde at Kennedy."

"Grand American Bank would not do this to you."

"They have."

"I can't believe it. Could your money have been stolen along the way?"

"Out of Bankers Express armored cars? That's not possible."

"What do you plan to do now?"

"First, I plan to recover my money. Right now! As soon as that vulgar thief walks in. Second, when I walk out of here this morning, you are coming with me."

"I can't."

"You must. You can't stay here working for crooks. A person of your reputation and class does not fit in with these thieves."

"I can't leave just like that."

"You will or I will have to assume that you are part of this scheme."

"Ben!"

"And that would be the end of us. Forever this time. I don't want to lose you. I thought I had. I would not be able to stand the suffering again. The void in my life. Get your things ready, you are leaving with me."

"But Ben..."

The door opened noisily.

Sheik Al-Madir jumped from his seat. "Oh! There you are!"

Robertson froze at the door. "Eh! What is this? What are you doing in my office?"

The Sheik turned to Simone. "Please leave us alone, Madame de Rivoli, and thank you for your kindness."

"I see that the lovers have made up," remarked Robertson.

Simone stopped, turned around and glared at the "Big Man."

"I don't have to listen to your sarcasm or stand for your prying into my private life."

"May I remind you that you are talking to your superior," Robertson said sharply.

"Superior, you never were. Employer, yes." She paused. "But no longer."

"What's that supposed to mean?"

"I quit. Now. Right now!" She walked out and slammed the door.

Louise looked at her, shocked. "I could not help hearing you. What's going on?"

"If you heard it, you know. I have quit, resigned, I am finished. You can have your "Big Man", all of him. With his bad manners, his dirty jokes, his crooked friends... and his right hanging balls!"

"Simone!"

She had gone too far. This was not the time to resign. She knew she was close to the end of her mission. She remembered her orders: "You can't resign. Don't get fired." Perhaps her uncontrolled reactions had now jeopardized her whole mission. But who was the most important player to help her reach her goal. Robertson or Sheik Al-Madir? What other use could she make of Robertson? The Sheik appeared to her a better instrument to accomplish her aim. After all, he controlled that sixty billion deposit. Not Robertson. Pierre will have to understand that. The name of Pierre reminded her of his last instructions. 'Check daily report on Arab deposits.'

"Louise, have you received today's report on Arab deposits?"

"Just came in."

"Could I see it please?"

Simone read the names and amounts listed first by order of branches and then by strict alphabetical order. She scrutinized the dollar column looking for the ten billion dollar figure.

She found it in the Head Office listing, under A. She gasped, stunned and paralyzed with fear:

"N° 002-11211-8, Al-Madir, Begum Simone de Rivoli, maturity 7/10/80, rate 6%, US$10,000,000,000."

Sheik Al-Madir was glowering at Robertson. "Where is my money?"

Robertson seemed amused. "What money? Your nine billion? It's here in our vaults waiting for your trucks."

"You know exactly what I mean, you thief! Where are my eleven billion dollars?"

"How should I know? You withdrew your funds Monday. We delivered them to Bankers Express as you instructed. We have their receipt and yours. If you have lost your money, don't ask me. Ask Bankers."

"Your bags were full of newspapers."

"That's a lie! That's a complete lie. It took at least twenty employees to count and deposit your cash in more than two thousand bags. Each bag was checked by two employees. When Bankers arrived, they double-checked the content of each bag and then sealed it. We delivered cash. So I don't know what you are talking about."

"Andrew Robertson, you are a filthy liar. You are also a thief. Either you find my eleven billion right now or I shall go to the authorities."

"If you do, you will be hanging yourself."

The angry stare of the Sheik did not leave Robertson's face. Robertson rose from his chair, walked around the desk and stood, towering, over the Sheik.

"You thought of me as a stupid ass, didn't you? You thought you could befriend me, entertain me, flatter me and use me for your own ends, didn't you? You told yourself that Robertson is a big moron, all muscles and no brains. Leave him to me and I know what to do with him, didn't you? You told your camel riding Rulers that you were going after the biggest plum in the Western world, the ownership of Grand American Bank. To achieve your aim you connived and plotted and lied and cheated, didn't you?"

The Sheik moved.

"Sit down and hear me out. Well, your not-very-bright Robertson saw through you from the first day. You never cared about me, about my bank, about Simone, about anybody. You cared about yourself, your ambitions, and your greed. My friend, you aimed too high. Ben Al-Madir, we have no room here for your type. Go back to your camels and take Simone with you, that's where she belongs also."

"Leave her out of this!"

"Oh no, I won't. Because she is very much a part of all this and I soon discovered that also. You may have fooled her but you did not fool me. Not for one minute. You used her to spy on me. To find out information about the bank. To set-up the trap for your take over. Smart. Ben. Very smart. I introduced her to you. I am the one who asked her to spy on you. You converted her into a double agent. You turned her against me. And you did it beautifully. Waltzing her through the social register, taking her on fancy trips, making her believe you would take her as your favorite wife. Planning to catch me in her bed in her apartment — I should say your apartment — playing the offended lover and bashing me on the head. What a set up! What a production!"

"I didn't even..."

"Don't protest! It's useless. I know all the facts. I somewhat pity the woman for being associated with camel dung like you, but she betrayed me, betrayed her loyalty to this bank. It's only fair that she be punished and that the punishment be equal to her sins. I was going to forgive her. To sack her, now that I am Chairman. To tell her to go back to France and never come back here. But when she had me followed to Miami by her crony, Georges Monti, that was the end."

"I know nothing about that."

"Don't make me laugh. It was all planned between the two of you. But what you two forgot is that we have our own security system here. Every senior officer and every employee who occupies a sensitive position is checked regularly. More, they are investigated, followed and the confidential reports come right to my desk. I instituted the system. I control it. So I know what I am talking about. At first, I could not understand why she would deliver photocopies of our Arab deposit reports to the French consulate instead of to you. It did not make sense, until I had your boy there, that Georges Monti, followed. Every time she met you, the next day she saw Monti at the consulate, and they had lunch at Delmonico's. And when you had him follow me to Miami, when nobody knew I was going to Miami, and when, for hours, he grilled Judith Watson about me, about Vic Ferrani, I knew then that you were all working together against the bank. Against me."

"I don't even know Georges Monti."

"You are a liar, Ben Al-Madir. But that's not important. I don't care if you are the King of England or the worst bum in the world. I have got you. I have got you by the balls and what I should do is pull hard and send you back to Dubai to join your bunch of eunuchs. But I am a civilized man and I am going to teach you a lesson in elegant revenge. Listen to me. Listen to me carefully. What I have to say, I will say only once. What I am going to do, you can't stop. So don't protest. Don't try to negotiate. Just do as I tell you. You have no choice. I'm wrong. On the contrary, you have. Your alternative is to go to your Rulers and disclose to them that not only have you failed to take control of Grand American Bank, but in the process, you have lost eleven billion dollars. Within an hour, they will tie your arms and legs to the backs of four camels and whip them to the four winds until your bones break apart and your guts are dragged about in the desert sand and left there for the vultures. They will then parade your head on a spike through the streets of Dubai and the story will be known that you lost the fortune of the Rulers and your balls for the cunt of a French baroness."

A tremendous laugh, more like a thundering roar escaped from Robertson. "Listen to my deal, Ben Al-Madir. It's genial. First I have found part of your eleven billion dollars. I understand that two groups of Bankers Express trucks got their signals confused and your four made a detour and came right back to this bank. But a billion dollars was missing. They only returned ten billion. As to the four trucks that made the delivery to your Concorde, I don't know where they came from. A prudent man would have checked the content of the bags before accepting delivery. You did not. Your captain signed the receipt. Therefore, you have no claim. As to the missing billion, I understand that our friend Ferrani would know of its whereabouts but I don't suggest that you contact him. He might be less generous than I am".

"So we have recovered your ten billion and I have here a Certificate of Deposit evidencing that the funds are still with our bank. We have lengthened the maturity date to July '80 to give us some breathing space, but in return we have agreed to pay a good rate of interest."

Robertson handed the certificate to the Sheik. "Note that the certificate is in the name of Begum Simone de Rivoli Al-Madir. I though it would make a nice wedding present. After all, you were going to marry her, weren't you, Ben?"

"You bastard!"

"The bastard is you, Ben. Pretending that you loved her. That you wanted to marry her. Buying her an apartment on Fifth Avenue. Introducing her to your family. Asking her to study the Quran. To convert to your religion. In reality, you only wanted to use her to spy on us. Well, you have hooked yourself to your own trap, my dear Ben. If you want to recover your funds, you must now marry the Baroness, for real. She is the only one who can sign to withdraw your ten billion dollars from this bank and she must legally sign: Begum Simone de Rivoli Al-Madir."

"As to the missing billion, you shall recover it quickly. We have agreed to pay you six percent interest on this deposit instead of the customary one percent applicable to other Arab deposits. Consider yourselves lucky that we don't do like the Swiss and the Germans and apply a negative interest rate to your deposit. So you will receive five percent more than you are normally entitled to and, in two years, that amounts to one billion dollars. Nice and clean. I am starting to think that we are over-generous. But that settles your eleven billion.

"As to your nine billion dollar withdrawal today, the funds are ready. As soon as you sign this receipt, I'll call Baxter, the officer in charge of our cash operation. But this time, may I suggest that you check the content of the bags before they are loaded aboard your plane. Elementary, my dear Ben. With money, never trust your neighbor even if he is your brother because we have a saying in America: 'You feed a dog and it shits on your front porch.' That's how I feel about you. Therefore, make sure that you never come again to this office or to this Bank. And now get the hell out of here and take your baroness with you!"

Glowering, Robertson watched the Sheik in his white robe walk unsteadily to the door but before it closed, he could not resist adding, "Eh! Don't forget to invite me to the wedding!"

They were riding up Park Avenue in the Sheik's limousine. "You are coming with me to Dubai."

"Ben, I am not going anywhere."

"Simone, you have no choice. I have to go to Dubai now. My plane is waiting at Kennedy. You have to come with me."

"Why?"

"There are too many things I don't understand. I want to talk to you."

"You can talk now."

"I don't have time."

"How long will we stay there?"

"A few days."

"I need to pack."

"Let us stop at your place. I'll give you ten minutes."

The chauffeur took them to her Fifth Avenue apartment. She rushed upstairs while the Sheik waited in the air-conditioned limousine, lost in his thoughts, unaware of the heavy and noisy traffic.

What treachery was he being subjected to? The disclosure by Robertson of the involvement of Georges Monti and Vic Ferrani was a revelation. What role had Simone really played in all the events of the last ten days? Why didn't Grand American collapsed after his initial withdrawals? No doubt, he had softened the blow by accepting twenty-two billion dollars in Treasury Bills, but the other eighteen billion transferred to Swiss International should have hurt them. It had to hurt. Their balance sheet did not show sufficient liquid assets to meet his demands. That bastard Robertson! He had saved ten billion dollars of the bank's cash by rerouting his eleven billion withdrawal back to the bank...in the name of Simone! Talk about swindling!

He would now have to marry her, without letting her suspect the real reason. Then he would tell her that he has deposited money in her name as a wedding gift and ask her to give him a power of attorney in case of emergency or death. That should not be a problem, but to marry her? But to marry an infidel, an idolatress? His father and brothers would dishonor him. The Rulers would never allow him. Meanwhile, he had to find out from her how Robertson had maneuvered to save the Bank. There had to be a way of taking advantage of the situation. Hardrock and his fellow shareholders had to be brought to their knees. He, Sheik Ben Al-Madir, future Chairman of the United Arab Emirates, had also decided to become the Chairman of the largest bank in the world, the Grand American Bank.

He would then be free to open the bank to the deposits of his Arab brothers. He would solicit and welcome their deposits, without limits. The bank's assets would rise to three, four, perhaps five hundred billion dollars. It would control America. It would control the world.

Peter Hardrock did not believe that the laws of the US could be changed to accommodate his ambitions. Hardrock did not know his own people. No American was rich enough or sufficiently honest to resist the money of Sheik Al-Madir. He would pay as much as one billion dollars, if necessary, to change the laws restricting the ownership of banks. Every man in the world has a price. Even your brother, Peter Hardrock!

He looked at his watch. "Amah," he called to his chauffeur, "go and ask the doorman to inform Madame de Rivoli that we can't wait any longer."

When the phone-a-door rang, Simone had just finished briefing Georges on the events of the morning.

"Don't worry Simone. I had already awakened Beauchamp when you called me earlier to tell me that you had had to resign. I also reported your story about the Sheik accusing Robertson of having stolen eleven billion dollars from him. It did not make sense at the time but I believe that Beauchamp has taken immediate steps to protect you. So go to Dubai in peace. Beauchamp knows what he is doing. Meanwhile, I'll contact him with the good news that you have traced the missing ten billion...to your own bank account. Have a good trip Baroness Al-Madir." He laughed and hung up.

She rushed to the intercom. "I'm coming right down," she shouted.

Within an hour they reached Kennedy airport and were escorted to the door of the Pan Am Terminal. Inside, the Concorde was being loaded. Captain Jacques Bruneau was unsealing each bag to ensure that it contained dollar bills. He had never seen so much money in his life. *Perhaps I could crash this plane off the coast of Africa. I could bail out with an inflatable raft and two of these bags. I would be set for life.* He was still toying with this pleasant idea when Sheik Al-Madir and Simone approached the plane.

"This is Captain Jacques Bruneau. Captain Bruneau is one of your compatriots. I purchased this plane two years ago and Captain Bruneau came with it. He and this Concorde are inseparable."

"Madame la Barone, bienvenue à bord," said the captain.

"Will you soon be loaded?" asked the Sheik.

"The last bags are going up. We checked everyone of them. They all contain cash. One thousand seven hundred and eighty bags. Nine billion dollars. That's a lot of money."

"I hope you are not getting ideas, captain?"

"Can't help it, sir. But what would I do with all that money. You can't even spend it in a lifetime."

"You can buy a lot with it."

"Like what?"

"Like the world."

"The world? That's a very poor buy. You can have it!"

They were soon airborne and flying east, sixty thousand feet above the Atlantic, at twice the speed of sound. The

Concorde was a floating palace with three bedrooms, a dining room and living area, an office for the Sheik and quarters for the bodyguards.

There were three stewards, two stewardesses and a flying crew of three. Simone had flown on a regular Concorde before but never in such luxury.

"You like it?" asked the Sheik, proudly. "This is the type of life that I am offering you."

"I must admit that it is difficult to resist such an offer. I am both flattered and sad."

"Why sad?"

"Because I can't accept it. First, for the reason that I have already mentioned to you. You can't marry an infidel and I can't accept Islam as my religion. But foremost in my mind, is revenge against Robertson for you and me. I never told you before because I thought it would reflect on the reputation of the bank and perhaps endanger the business it enjoyed from you. But after you told me this morning that you suspected Robertson of stealing from you..."

"I don't suspect him. I know," interjected the Sheik.

"I still can't believe it. Why would Robertson do a thing like that? Why would he want me to inform on you? I always thought you were great friends."

He could not decide whether she was telling the truth or trying to fool him. But why would she turn against him? What would it achieve? What reward was she expecting? Apparently she did not know about the ten billion dollars in the name of Begum Simone Al-Madir, otherwise, she would not refuse the marriage. How else could she collect this money? How could he be sure of her? How far could he trust her? How could he convince her to marry him? He needed that power of attorney to retrieve quickly the ten billion before the Rulers found out that such a vast sum was missing.

"Who is Georges Monti?"

She did not seem surprised. "A friend," she said simply.

"Only a friend?"

"Ben, I know you were jealous of Andrew Robertson but

surely not of Georges Monti. He is a compatriot who works at the French consulate in New York. I have known him for years."

"Why did you see him so often?"

"Why all the questions? Who told you about Georges?"

"Just answer my questions."

"It is true that I have been seeing Georges. Two or three times a week. Sometimes for lunch. Sometimes for drinks. He is French, a widower and lonely in New York. So am I, especially when you are away. So we saw each other as often as we could, as good friends do, and talked about France. What's wrong with that?"

"What was he doing in Miami last weekend?"

"I didn't know he was in Miami."

"He was there with Judith Watson."

"Judith Watson? But she is a friend of Robertson! God! I never thought Georges was that lonely! She is a well known call girl! It should prove that there is nothing serious between Georges and myself."

"What about Vic Ferrani?"

"I have never met Vic Ferrani."

"I did not ask you whether you had."

"So what's your question?"

"Is Georges Monti a friend of Vic Ferrani?"

"How would I know?"

"All this is very strange."

"Ben, you have me all confused. What have Georges Monti, and Judith Watson and Vic what's his name, Ferrani to do with us and my decision to avenge myself upon Robertson?"

"Ferrani stole my money."

"Your eleven billion dollars?"

"Yes."

"Are you sure?"

"Robertson told me."

"Robertson knew?"

"I am sure he planned it."

"But why?"

"His bank was broke. He could not repay my deposit."

"But surely Grand American could find some twenty odd billion dollars."

"My deposit was much larger."

"It was?"

"Sixty billion dollars."

"My God!"

"You did not know?"

"How could I know? Did Mr. Hardrock know that you had so much money on deposit?"

He shook his head.

"Robertson?"

"Partly."

"You withdrew all of it?"

"Yes."

"But that was enough to bankrupt the bank."

"It was."

"But why?"

"I want to control it."

"Why bankrupt it if you wish to control it? It does not make sense to me."

"I did not expect it to go bankrupt. I thought that facing their difficulties, they would negotiate with me immediately. That they would offer me a block of shares. A controlling block, and a number of seats on their board of directors. They did not. They maneuvered me. They tricked me. They stole from me. I hate them more than ever. Now I'll destroy them for good."

The voice of captain Bruneau came over the intercom. "Please fasten your seat belts. We are starting our descent for an unscheduled landing. We have discovered a slight mechanical problem. Nothing serious, but I would rather have it corrected. We are now approaching Bordeaux in France and I have alerted the ground technicians. I don't expect we'll need to stay here more than one hour. Sorry about the inconvenience."

Sheik Al-Madir picked up the phone on the table beside him. "Captain, what is this all about?"

"One of our fuel gage lamps is flickering. Could be a faulty circuit, or some obstruction in the line. I don't think it's serious. The fuel seems to reach the engine under proper pressure but I want this light checked".

"All right. Can we get off the plane?"

"If you want. I'll tell the tower to send a car for you."

"Do that. The guards can stay on board, and so do you captain. It's your plane and you are responsible for its precious cargo."

"You don't have to remind me, sir."

He put the phone down. "These Frenchmen are so insolent sometimes." He looked at Simone. They both laughed.

"Insolent, innocent, indecent, which do you prefer, Ben?" She placed her hand on his lap.

"Madame la Baronne! Really!

A long black Citroen was waiting for them. Sheik Al-Madir was first to reach the bottom of the ramp. The door of the limousine opened and a man stepped out, offering his hand. "Welcome to Bordeaux, Sheik Al-Madir. I am Pierre Beauchamp."

The Sheik shook the extended hand then turned to help Simone. She stood frozen on the last step of the ramp. "This is Baroness Simone de Rivoli, a compatriot, Mr. Beauchamp."

Pierre reached for her hand. It was icy. He raised it to his lips.

"Come, Simone," said Sheik Al-Madir impatiently. "Let's get in the car." They rode to the end of the terminal and stopped in front of an entrance marked 'Entrée interdite. Administration'.

"I have already cleared you with immigration," said Pierre. "Permit me to invite you to our VIP lounge. We will be more comfortable there."

They climbed to the second floor and walked down a long hallway to a mahogany door. Pierre unlocked it and they stepped into a well appointed lounge, dimly lit. A number of large comfortable chairs were disposed along the walls and against the far corner, a small bar. "Drinks?" asked Pierre.

"We were drinking champagne on board," Simone said. She accepted a glass. "I would like to freshen up. Could you indicate where I can find the ladies room?"

"Let me show you."

As soon as they were out in the hallway, Pierre took her hand and led her into a private office next to the lounge. He locked the door behind them and she threw herself at him and kissed him fiercely. "Pierre! My Pierre! I never thought I would see you again." She kissed him again and again.

"What's happening?" they both asked the question simultaneously.

"You start," she said.

"Captain Bruneau is one of our men. As soon as Georges reached me and told me that Sheik Al-Madir had made you resign from the Bank, and somehow forced you to accompany him on this trip, I alerted Bruneau and we worked out a plan to bring the Concorde down here, if you were aboard. So here you are. As to my plan, I want to wait until you brief me on what you found out on board, it anything."

"I found out plenty."

Within five minutes Pierre had returned to the lounge. He had barely sat and taken a sip of champagne when Simone knocked at the door. She chose a seat next to the Sheik and Pierre took a chair facing them.

"Sheik Al-Madir, I have introduced myself as Pierre Beauchamp but I have not told you what I am doing here. I am a very old acquaintance of Baroness de Rivoli. We went to school together. I knew her before and after her marriage to Baron Antoine de Rivoli. I was a friend of the family. I am still, I hope, a friend of Simone. With your permission, I shall call her Simone. I always have."

"That's quite a coincidence to find you in Bordeaux greeting us. My plane was not scheduled to land here."

"It is not exactly a coincidence. Simone always consults me before she does anything. Mostly because I am the executor of the estate of her late husband," he lied, "and as such, I need to know what she is doing or planning to do. Naturally, when you asked her to resign from the Bank, which she did, and when you invited her to accompany you to Dubai, she telephoned me."

Sheik Al-Madir turned to Simone. "When did you do that?"

"From my apartment."

"That's why it took you so long?"

"Forgive me, but I could not leave New York without letting Pierre know."

"Continue" said Sheik Al-Madir.

"Simone told me she did not want to go to Dubai but that

you were insisting, so my immediate reaction was to alert our consulate in New York."

"Georges Monti, no doubt," said Sheik Al-Madir.

"Georges Monti, who is also a friend of Simone, was instructed to order Captain Bruneau to land in France."

"But that's my captain."

"He is first a Frenchman. So here you are and we must now decide what we do. Simone has asked me to advise her. I understand you wish to marry her."

"That's correct. But this is not a business transaction and, therefore, should not concern you. Surely in such personal matters she should be able to make her own decisions."

"On the contrary, I believe this marriage proposal is very much a business transaction."

"You are not impudent enough to imply that I wish to marry her for her money?"

"I am the executor, remember? Baroness de Rivoli has assets of her own."

"And I am Sheik Al-Madir, must I remind you? I can buy the Baroness' assets a thousand times."

"Should we say only fifteen?"

"What do you mean?"

"As of yesterday, I estimate the fortune of Simone at slightly more than ten billion dollars."

There was a tense silence in the lounge. The Sheik looked at Pierre and then at Simone. He walked to the window and pulled the drapes back. His Concorde sat, five hundred feet away, glistening under the lights of the airport, ready to take him to Dubai. He faced them. "So you know?"

"We know."

"What's your proposal?"

Pierre was expecting the question. "I believe that you and Simone have common goals, to avenge yourselves upon Robertson. He lied to both of you. He has used you and then betrayed you. I leave aside the stealing and everything else."

"I'll have him killed," pronounced the Sheik.

"I could kill him myself," added Simone, playing her part perfectly.

Pierre stopped them. "That would not avenge you. He would not suffer. Let's think for a moment. What has been the greatest ambition of Robertson? The chairman-ship of the bank. He has it. He must lose it. How did he get there? What has been his foremost achievement? The growth of Grand American Bank. Thanks mostly to your money, Sheik Al-Madir, Grand American is now the largest bank in the world. We must now destroy the bank for good."

"I would rather take it over," stated the Sheik.

"What for?"

"The power it would give me."

"There is no real power in owing Grand American Bank because it does not deal with true wealth. It handles only paper money. Printed money. Computer money. Book entries. There is no power there."

"Then, where is the power?"

"In gold."

"I have plenty of gold."

"How much?"

"Two, perhaps three billion dollars."

"That's not much. There is a least three times as much gold under the mattresses of France. Listen to me carefully, Sheik Al-Madir. The world will belong to those who own the world's gold. All of it."

"Why?"

"Because there is no other way out of the present international monetary mess. You can't pay for trade with paper. You can't pay for oil with paper. You can't store paper. Paper money has no value when it is printed at will by governments, without real backing, without something precious behind it, without a true store of value to support it. And what is real? What is precious? What is true? Gold. Only gold. You can own all the banks in the world, you can accumulate all the paper money on earth but as long as I have gold, I will always be richer than you, more powerful than you. How powerful do you wish to be Sheik Al-Madir?"

"I swore to my father that one day I would become more powerful than the Shah of Iran and the King of Saudi Arabia, that I would control more assets than the chairman of A.T&T, General Motors and Grand American Bank combined, that I would rule more territory with more influence than the President of the United States. I have accumulated more money that a man can wish for in this world. Now I want the power it can buy. How do I do that?"

"I have a plan", Pierre said.

"I'm listening."

Pierre went behind the bar, retrieved a briefcase from which he extracted a number of documents. "Sheik Al-Madir I want you to sign this petition."

"What is it?"

"A petition for your divorce from Baroness Simone de Rivoli. Simone, you also need to sign it. Under French law, a voluntary petition for divorce, freely signed by both spouses, leads to a quick decision by the court. I'll take care of that. I'll sign as a witness."

"We are not married yet," protested the Sheik.

"That's where you are wrong. You are. You are as of this afternoon, about six, two hours before you arrived here, by proxies in front of a "friendly" magistrate. I have here a properly signed and authenticated marriage certificate in the names of Sheik Ben Said Al-Madir, from Dubai and Baroness Simone de Rivoli, from Paris. You now have a new name Simone. Begum Simone de Rivoli Al-Madir. Too bad it will last only a few hours. It suits you well. You know, it's the first time that I see two people solicit a divorce before they knew they were married. If not for the circumstances, it's rather comic."

"I don't understand what this farce will accomplish."

"It is not a farce, Sheik Al-Madir. This marriage certificate, accompanied by a power of attorney that Simone will sign, will permit you to recover your ten billion dollars from Grand American Bank. This divorce petition will empower us to reclaim Simone from you . I am sure she does not wish to convert to Islam and we know that your regligion forbids you to marry an infidel. So this is really a marriage of convenience. The secret shall remain entre-nous."

"What do you expect from me in return?"

"Revenge. We want the head of Robertson. When you deliver it, we will give you the power of attorney and the marriage certificate. In other words, we are prepared to pay you ten billion dollars for the head of Robertson."

"But it's my own money."

"Perhaps, but it is currently in Simone's name."

"If I agree, will you assist me with my purchase of gold."

"By all means. Here is the Plan."

CHAPTER FOUR
THE PLAN

"No longer is it possible to ignore the attacks: the Devil must be cross-checked."

(Translated from l'Express (Paris), February 3, 1975. "Scénario pour gagner" by Jean-Jacques Servan Schreiber)

Robertson sat across the desk from Patric White at the headquarters of the Federal Reserve Board. "You know why you are here."

"I have read the papers," answered Robertson glumly.

"Where does it come from?" asked White.

"I don't know."

"Somebody knows a lot and that somebody is after you, viciously."

"That's the only way journalists win Pulitzer prizes."

"They are after your head," stated White.

"I can take care of myself."

"It's more than yourself, Andrew; you forget that you run the largest bank in America."

"In the world!"

"If you want. But our immediate concern is America. Today, a newspaper, as respected as the Wall Street Journal, reports from 'unimpeachable sources' that your bank is facing a serious liquidity crisis, that large Arab deposits have been withdrawn, that Swiss banks, aware of your difficulties, have moved their correspondent bank balances elsewhere."

"I know all that. I can read."

"Do you know Harry Stern, the journalist who wrote this?"

"I have talked to him on a number of occasions. He called me this morning."

"What did you tell him?"

"I told him to stick his paper up his ass!"

"Now he knows that the story is true!" White relit his pipe, puffed at it in long draws and blew the smoke in front of him.

Through the rising smoke screen, Robertson felt White's eyes reading his mind. "Andrew, you remember a year ago, after the ABA convention? I warned you. I knew then."

"We had no problems a year ago!" Robertson immediately corrected himself. "And we don't have problems today. These are lies invented to sell newspapers."

"Then you are going to deny them? Press conference or press release?"

"I don't take it that seriously."

"I do." The cloud of smoke was so dense that Robertson could hardly see White. He only heard his voice as if coming from outer space. "Andrew, this morning, I placed your bank on our critical list. As soon as you leave here, our inspectors will walk in for a surprise audit."

"I must object, very strongly."

"Have you looked at your recent returns?"

"I signed them."

"Then you should know that I know. Because I read them."

"They are only statistics. In a bank of our size, there are bound to be large fluctuations."

"Andrew, stop lying to me and stop lying to yourself. We are not talking about fluctuations. We are looking at a substantial decrease in your assets. Your best assets, not your loans, but your cash and your US securities. On the other side, your short-term liabilities have also decreased substantially."

"That should bring you satisfaction. You have always complained that they were too large."

"Andrew, I regret it, but at this stage I must believe the story of the Wall Street Journal. The short-term deposits that you lost were either Arab deposits or deposits from other banks. You have nearly no US securities left and a good portion of your cash is gone."

"I thought you were a friend."

"I am. But I am also the Chairman of the Federal Reserve Board. As such, I could order you to tell me what is happening. I would prefer that you volunteer the information to a friend."

"Could you put your pipe away for a minute? I can't see you." Robertson rose and walked to a window. He saw only dirty buildings, gray and black. Sad. Depressing. He kept facing the window. "If I talk to you openly, will you call off your inspectors? Having them walk into my bank hours after this story in the Journal could kill us. It would indicate that you believe the story. You can't keep the presence of your inspectors secret. Too many employees are involved."

"I'm not prepared to do that, Andrew. Look at it another way. If it is true that you have no problems, then, following our inspection, I shall be able to issue a public statement denying the allegations of the Journal. Otherwise, you'll have a run on your bank."

"On Grand American Bank? You must be kidding."

"Andrew, the words you just pronounced are exactly the same words that Gleason, the Chairman of Franklyn National Bank, used in this office when his bank was on the verge of collapsing in 1974. Remember what happened? In a matter of days, we had to pump one billion dollars into their coffers to answer the thousands of requests for withdrawals by their depositors. Within four weeks, it was one billion seven hundred million. How much money will I need to advance to your bank to save it and where do I get it from? I need that information if I am going to help you. So stop thinking that your bank is beyond a depositors' run. No bank is. The whole financial world is falling apart, and you know it as well as I do."

Robertson had lost most of his cockiness. He wanted to be harsh and arrogant but his brain was failing him. He had at last reached the top of the world but the world was slipping away underneath him. In a flash, he reviewed his career. The hard work, the rough bargaining, the discreet scheming, the sometime brutal stepping on toes as he climbed the ladder of success. The brilliant coup against Intra Bank in Beirut in '66, the vicious kick to The International Bank in the Cayman Islands in '74, when it became a pest, too big for its breeches, trying to teach Grand American and other large banks how to humanize their banking. Then, the more recent events. The unfair advantage he had taken of their situation to unseat Hardrock, the ballyhoo created by his own Public Relations Department about his accession to the chairmanship. He saw again the impassive face of Vic Ferrani in Miami when he had asked him to intercept the eleven billion dollars of Sheik Al-Madir. He shivered, but the cleverness of the coup brought a smile of satisfaction to his face. It had been so simple. On its way to Kennedy airport, the four Bankers Express trucks convoy of the Sheik had taken a wrong turn 'by mistake' while four other trucks were moving up the ramp to take the thruway to Kennedy and deliver to the Sheik's plane bags filled with bundles of newspaper. The real convoy had delivered one billion dollars to Vic Ferrani's plane at La Guardia airport and returned the remaining ten billion to Grand American Bank as a deposit in the name of Begum Simone de Rivoli Al-Madir. Let the Sheik figure a way out of this one!

"I see a smile," remarked White. "Have you found a happy solution?"

"Something rather amusing crossed my mind. If Grand American went under, God forbid, the FDIC would have to come up with their guarantee money and reimburse our depositors. Right?"

"Yes. Up to a maximum of fifty thousand dollars for each depositor. That's the limit of the insurance today, as you well know."

"How large are the reserves of the FDIC? Seven, perhaps eight billion, right?"

"About eight, yes."

"Do you know, Patrick, that nearly two billion dollars of those reserves are on deposit with us?"

"My God!" exclaimed White.

"And do you realize that the balance is mostly invested in Treasury Bills and other Government securities? FDIC would have to sell them to raise the cash to repay our depositors. To whom? There are neither enough reserves in the hands of FDIC nor enough cash in the banking system to cover our losses. Isn't that interesting?"

"Andrew, are you trying to blackmail me and the Government into bailing you out?"

"The idea is just starting to enter my mind that you would have no other choice...if we were in trouble, which I have yet to admit."

"Let me tell you something, Andrew Robertson. After we rescued Franklyn National Bank, we declared to the world that our actions were proof that the Government stood behind all our financial institutions. We had to make that statement to reassure both American and foreign depositors. But that case went all the way to the President's office and a formal decision was taken never to repeat the Franklyn mistake. It is neither the function nor the duty of Government to rescue private enterprises and their clients, in your case the depositors. Either you have a free enterprise system or a socialist one. It would be too easy for any entrepreneur to launch a business, be it banking, manage it imprudently or speculatively, and then run to government shouting: 'Bail me out. They are your electors.' If Government is expected to stand behind every free enterprise as the investor of last resort, Government might as well launch and own all businesses in the first place."

"It's a nice speech, Patrick, but policies, particularly presidential policies, are made to be adapted to the needs of the day."

"Andrew, this is more than a policy, it is the philosophy of our Constitution. The freedom to trade, the freedom to pursue happiness. Freedom can't subsist without financial independence. To think otherwise is to sell out to communism."

"You talk about happiness. I believe that the President of the United States would be a very unhappy President if he were to learn that his family bank is going under," suggested Robertson. "Perhaps sufficiently unhappy to reconsider his constitutional philosophy," he added.

White's intercom buzzed. "I have an urgent call for Mr.

Robertson, sir. I tried to take a message but the caller insisted. It's a Mr. Reeves from Grand American." White looked at Robertson who nodded. "Put him on."

"Andrew, I did not want to disturb you but I have a bad problem," said the Senior officer of Grand American Bank.

"Can't it wait?"

"I thought it could, but it is worsening by the minute. I have received numerous transfer orders from a number of foreign correspondents. At first, this morning, it was only a trickle, but now it's a deluge. Our foreign deposits are moving to other banks. I believe the story in the Journal is hurting us badly."

"The Journal does not circulate abroad. Or so little and so late."

"I know, but this was an AP-Dow Jones story. It went on their wire. It's being picked up by newspapers and radio stations all over."

"How much do we hurt?"

"Already over three billion."

"You should be able to take care of that."

"Not if I pay Swiss International."

"I can't talk now. I'll have to call you back."

"Andrew, I can't wait. Some of them want telex confirmation that we have executed their instructions. Others want us to effect transfers by phone."

"Do it."

"We haven't got the money!"

"All these transfers are one day settlements, and they are all subject to recall. So execute the orders. I'll find you the funds before tomorrow. As usual!"

Robertson turned to White. "You were not supposed to hear this conversation."

"But I have."

"Any ideas?" asked Robertson.

"Yes. You have given me a good one. I have decided to inform the President."

Harry Stern faced the senior editor of the Wall Street Journal. "I want you to release my story."

"I can't yet. We are checking with our legal department. Could be libelous."

"There is nothing libelous in my story. I am reporting facts, only facts supported by photos. Nothing else. I am implying nothing. I am making no accusations. Let the bastard explain his conduct."

"Grand American are friends of ours. We can't attack Robertson."

"We did, this morning, in that story about their liquidity problem."

"That story came out of Zurich on the news wire. We did not originate it here. It was news. Whether we had ran it or not, it would have appeared elsewhere."

"So will my story."

"How's that?"

"My source said: 'Unless you print it this week, I shall give it to somebody else.' And there is more to come."

"Who is your source?"

"You must be joking!"

"Reliable?"

"Top. Respectable. And immune to any investigation or prosecution, at least on this side of the ocean. I know that I have been given a good story. A real one. A real big one. The biggest in a long time. I urge you to release it."

The editor picked up the story and the photo of Robertson stepping aboard the Goddaughter at the Golden Bay Club in

Miami. He looked at Stern. "Can you take the Watson girl out of the story? It would diminish the blow?"

"What for? She is a well-known call girl. She is also an important link in the chain. Robertson knows that Watson girl intimately. Now we find that she works for Ferrani. Robertson visits Ferrani. Sleeps with Watson. I tell you, they are all in bed together. It's a great story. It has all the elements. Big money, sex, Mafia. What else do you want?"

The editor released the file to Harry Stern. "If our legal department says it's OK, go ahead."

The front-page story appeared in the next day's edition of the Wall Street Journal under the heading: "Grand American Bank goes sailing with Mafia." Below, a photo of Robertson with a caption "Chairman of GAB climbing aboard Goddaughter" and then a photo of Judith Watson in a bikini, raising a glass of champagne to her lips: "Girlfriend of Robertson, well known call girl Judith Watson, lives it up at posh Miami Club."

At the French consulate, on upper Fifth Avenue in New York, Georges Monti, satisfied, dropped the newspaper on his desk, reached for his telephone and dialed the Journal. "Stern? Good story. You can pick up your fifty thousand dollars."

At the White House, the door leading from the oval office to the cabinet room opened. "Gentlemen, the President of the United States." They all rose.

"Gentlemen, please be seated," said the President. "I have called this extraordinary joint meeting of the Cabinet and the Council for Economic and Financial Planning because we face the gravest of emergencies. Only one hour ago, I finished reviewing this critical situation with Patrick White from Federal Reserve and Arthur Caldwell from FDIC. Grand American Bank is in danger. Serious danger. You have seen the newspaper stories on Monday suggesting a liquidity problem and, today, the Mafia connections, sex scandals, etc."

"Now, before I ask White and Caldwell to brief you, I wish to make a statement. My grandfather founded Grand American Bank. Both my father and my brother, Peter, were at one time Chairman of the bank. The name Grand American Bank has always been part of the heritage of the Hardrock family. To my knowledge, the family is still the largest shareholder of the bank. But these considerations have to be pushed aside. It is not the life of Grand American Bank that is at stake; it is the future of our Nation. Therefore, you must forget, gentlemen, that the name of your President is associated with our emergency today."

"Mr. President," said Bob Campbell, Secretary of Agriculture, "we appreciate your honesty and we sympathize with your anguish. I am sure I can speak on behalf of my colleagues around this table in stating that we will rise above personalities and we will forget the name Hardrock in our discussions." He was lying. They all knew it, but they all nodded in assent. How could they forget? Their appointment was contingent on the goodwill of the President.

"Thank you, Bob," said the President, "I knew I could depend upon your sense of statesmanship. All right, where do we start? Perhaps Patrick White wishes to summarize the situation."

White placed his pipe on an ashtray, an ominous sign. "Gentlemen, I first want to remind the members of the Cabinet of their pledge of solidarity and the members of the Council of their oath of secrecy. Please do not take this reminder as an insult to your integrity, but the situation that I will expose to you today oversteps the borders of our national security. The fate of the world might be at stake."

They all nodded; again knowing very well that before the end of the day one of them will have leaked the news of the meeting and the topic of the discussion. In the name of the freedom of the press. In fact, in exchange for future press favours.

White knocked his pipe against the ashtray. "We completed, yesterday, a preliminary audit of the affairs of Grand American Bank. All of you are by now conversant with the newspapers report on their liquidity problem. I shall discuss this subject and this one subject only. I am sure that the Justice Department is looking into the allegations that Andrew Robertson may have maintained Mafia connections."

A number of them shifted in their chairs. They felt uneasy. They also had connections.

"The liquidity problem of Grand American is serious," continued White. "So serious that I had to alert the President. More than sixty billion dollars."

"Sixty billion!" a number of them exclaimed.

"Yes, more than sixty billion dollars, or more than half the assets of the Bank, have been withdrawn from the Bank during the past three weeks."

"Why?"

"By whom?"

"Where did it go?"

They were all asking questions at the same time.

"Gentlemen, please!" reminded the President. "Patrick White has a number of answers. Let him proceed."

"Substantial withdrawals were made by Arab clients. Many of us know that because of the close relationship of Andrew Robertson with the Arab world, the bank has attracted to itself — and to America — substantial funds from the Middle East. It helped the bank grow. It also helped America diminish its balance of payment deficits. In order to cover these withdrawals, the bank has borrowed large sums, twenty billion dollars to be exact, from Swiss and French banks. While the loans were apparently readily granted, these banks also suspected the extent of the troubles of Grand American.

Last Friday, one of them, Swiss International, called in most of its deposits totaling twelve billion dollars. They claimed that some of their own large Arab deposits had been withdrawn. We don't know if it is true, but what we know is that the dollars that they withdrew from Grand American were immediately converted into Swiss francs, German marks, some Canadian dollars and some French francs. At first, the Central Banks of those countries and our own Treasury Department intervened on the market to prevent a collapse of our dollar. But it soon became evident that the sums involved exceeded the capacity or the willingness to intervene of those Central Banks that are our friends. Unsupported, the value of our dollar has dropped by more than ten percent since last Friday."

"That should be good for our exports," rejoiced the Secretary of Commerce.

"But not for the imports," commented the Secretary of Energy. "I can hardly pay for our oil imports with the present value of our dollar. How do you expect me to pay after this further devaluation? The Arabs have told me bluntly that they would insist on another form of payment, if we did not stop the deterioration of the value of our dollar. As a matter of fact, I have expressed to the President, no later than yesterday, my great concern about this de facto further devaluation of our dollar. This is as grave a crisis as that of Grand American."

"We understand your problem," stated the President. "But as of now, we don't believe that the two problems can be treated separately. The liquidity of Grand American and paying for our oil imports are both money problems. Continue Patrick."

"When the AP-Dow Jones liquidity story came out Monday, it triggered a series of withdrawals from Grand American by foreign banks. By noon, the volume exceeded three billion. By four it was close to five."

"Who sold the story to the bastards?" someone asked.

"It would appear that it came out of their Zurich office," said the President. "Undivulged sources, but claimed to be reliable, as usual."

"The sacred Swiss bank secrecy! Tell the secret but don't tell who told it! Naturally, because it came from Switzerland, it had to be the truth. The Swiss never lie! We should never have revised the 1973 Secrecy Agreement."

The President ignored the remarks from the Attorney General and turned to White. "Go on Patrick."

"As I said before, I immediately dispatched my senior inspectors to the bank and I met personally with Andrew Robertson."

"Before or after the Mafia story?" asked the Attorney General.

"Before. I have not talked to Robertson since that story. It is a rather difficult subject to discuss between friends."

"Let's come back to the facts," requested the President.

"The facts are, gentlemen, that these last withdrawals by Swiss International, and by the other foreign banks, have broken the back of Grand American Bank. Its liquidity is gone. It is technically bankrupt."

"Oh no!"

"Impossible!"

"Christ, it's the largest bank in the world!"

"I can't believe it!"

"Goddamn foreigners!"

"We must do something!"

"Let's sue them!"

They were all deeply perturbed. Incensed. Shocked. Patrick White retrieved his pipe, lit it and watched the chain of smoke rise towards the ceiling and the ventilator. "The chain of tragedies," he recalled, talking to himself. "Gone with the wind. Corny, but point blank."

"How much do they need?" asked the Secretary of Commerce.

"Gentlemen," said the President, "that question was first asked when Franklyn National Bank went into default in 1974 and we decided at that time never to ask it again."

"How can we help if we don't know how much is involved?"

"How much does not change the principle. Government is not going to bail out private enterprise. It's not our function. I am adamant about this," said the President. "Otherwise, let's be honest with ourselves and let's come right out with socialism and government controlled industries. Look what it did to Britain. It bankrupted them."

"I believe we are bankrupt also," added Patrick White flatly. Again he deposited his pipe in the ashtray and waited for the storm. It did not come. They were speechless.

After a while, Arthur Caldwell the head of the FDIC moved on his chair. "Gentlemen, let me add to the shocking disclosures by Patrick. As you now, one of our functions at FDIC is to monitor the security of the banking system for the depositors. We have an "under observation list" and a "critical list" of banks. So has Patrick at the Federal Reserve but he uses different criteria. Banks normally appear on our lists when they or we discover a liquidity problem. We have presently slightly fewer than two thousand banks on our lists. Patrick has about the same number. Mostly the same names. Despite our efforts, some of these banks go under. We then have to make good their obligations to their depositors, up to fifty thousand dollars for each account.

In other words, we provide some form of insurance to the depositors. In return, we collect premiums from banks. By 1974, we had accumulated a fund of nearly seven billion dollars. Following the fiascoes of US National Bank of San Diego and of Franklyn National Bank in New York, we raised our premiums substantially and at one time during 1977, our reserves reached ten billion dollars. Following recent bank failures, they stand now at eight billion. If Grand American goes under, as it will if we don't find a solution, it will take twelve billion dollars to repay their depositors who are covered by us. That's four billion dollars more than what we have available. Remember also that there are still two thousand other banks on our surveillance list. Some of them will no doubt require our intervention in the very near future."

"Could you not borrow funds from the Treasury Department until your premiums replenish your reserves?" asked the Secretary of Housing. He only dealt with borrowed money.

"No way," said the Secretary of the Treasury. "Our coffers are empty. We are having a hard time selling our weekly Treasury Bills. We have had to reduce our offerings to a maximum of two billion dollars at a time. Government borrowings keep increasing as you people keep overspending. White has told you repeatedly and my voice is hoarse from shouting it. You can't run a country on continuous budget deficits. Nor a business. Nor your personal affairs. Something is bound to give. There is a limit to what we can borrow. Gentlemen, we have reached that limit."

"Oh, you are such a pessimist," said the Secretary of Social Welfare. "I'm sure White will find a way of creating some money for you. Print a few more bills. What is stopping him?"

"Credibility," said White. "Remember, you abolished gold as the backing to our money and replaced it by trust in the Government. Since 1971, we have been printing paper money backed only by our politicians' promises and used mostly to cover your budget deficits. Our foreign friends have been warning us since 1960. Today, they have stopped trusting us and our paper money. But that is not all. Tell them the worst, Bob."

Campbell bowed his head and closed his eyes. He said in a funeral tone. "Two billion dollars of the reserves of FDIC are on deposit with Grand American Bank."

"That's stupid," blurted a voice.

"It's not stupid!" replied Campbell. "We have to keep our funds somewhere. Certificates of Deposits of Grand American, our largest bank, were certainly the safest depository we could find. As to the balance of our money, it has been loaned to the Treasury Department."

"What do you mean?"

"We have bought nearly six billion dollars worth of Treasury Bills and don't you tell me that's stupid. If you don't have faith in the Treasury Bills of our own country..."

"Exactly," said White, "but Treasury does not have the money to redeem these Bills and would have to raise it by reselling them to the banking system. But, and listen to this, the largest purchaser up to now of Treasury Bills has been Grand American. There you have it, gentlemen. The perfect monetary circle. The most vicious. The day of reckoning has arrived!"

"Who can come up with a solution?" asked the President.

The Secretary of State banged his fist on the table. "We should have gone to war against those goddamn Arabs five years ago and taken their oil fields..."

The President stopped him. "And if they had destroyed them? Blown them out of production as they were quite capable of doing, what then? Are you suggesting that we should have gone to war also against Mexico? Nigeria? Venezuela? Norway? Britain? Canada? Come on now, we can no longer solve problems through wars."

The Chairman of the Chiefs of Staff also banged his fist on the table. "We did in the past and it worked."

"You can't sacrifice humanity for money," declared the President.

"Oh! Oh! and without money you can't feed your humanity. What comes first Mr. President? The chicken or the egg? Oil or money?" asked the Secretary of State, arrogantly.

"That will do for today, Mr. Secretary of State," said the President harshly. "May I hear a more intelligent proposal?"

Silence.

Finally, White spoke. "You know my proposal."

"Patrick, we buried gold five years ago."

"You forget that gold does not rot, does not tarnish, and does not corrode. It was a mistake to bury it. Let's dig up the coffin. I am sure the body is still healthy."

"We will not reopen the gold file," decided the President.

"You may well have to," retorted White.

"I resent your insistence."

"Mr. President, with all due respect, why don't you face the truth?"

"Mr. White, as long as I am the President, I will not tolerate this type of accusation around this table. And now gentlemen, as you don't appear, amongst your thirty brains, to be capable of devising a solution to our problem, I shall have to decide for you. In view of the gravity of the situation however, and after I tell you my decision, you will all be confined to this meeting room until seven o'clock tonight. I will address the nation at that time."

There were murmurs around the table.

"Shall we take a one hour break to permit you to contact your offices and rearrange your schedules of work for this afternoon? And may I remind all of you that no statements to the press are permitted. White, Caldwell, Justice and Treasury will please remain."

"How long shall we be?" asked White.

"Long enough to lick this problem," replied the President.

"**V**ic? Robertson here."

"Are you calling from a public phone?"

"Yes."

"What's that shit in the paper?" Vic's tone was icy.

"It's shit all right."

"Who is this guy Stern?"

"A punk!"

"What has he got against you?"

"I don't know."

"Bad, Andrew, very bad. 'Know thy enemies,' my dad always said. Have you talked to him?"

"I can't find him. The Journal can't find him. He has disappeared."

"How did he get this dope on you and me and Judith?"

"Don't know."

"And the photos?"

"Have no idea."

"You want me to find him for you?" The tone became ominous.

"I wish you would. But that's not why I called."

"Don't tell me you have more problems."

"We both have."

"How's that?"

"I have a deal for you."

"Another one?"

"A simpler one." Robertson was choosing his words carefully. "Vic, you are a friend. You have been for a long time. I want to help you."

"Cut the crap!"

"I'm very serious. I have a simple trade to offer you."

"What do I lose?"

"You lose nothing. That's the point. If you don't trade, you lose a lot."

"I have your word?"

"You have my word." Robertson knew that if he ever failed, he had just placed his head in the noose.

"All right, shoot."

"I want you to withdraw all your money and the deposits of all your companies from my bank before two thirty today."

"Why?"

"Don't ask. Just do it."

"Christ, Andrew, it's already eleven here while on the West Coast, some of my boys are still in bed."

"Wake them up. Do anything. But do it. Just do it. Today. Now!"

"What's your side? What do you want from me?"

"Two things. First, the Presidency of your company, Trans Ocean Grain Ltd."

Vic Ferrani answered him without hesitation. What a catch! "You've got it."

"Second, as your new President, I propose that we move the headquarters of the company to Grand Cayman."

"Why?"

"No taxes. No FBI. No IRS. No Wall Street Journal."

"Interpol is there."

"I have done nothing criminal."

"I want you to take Judith Watson with you."

"Why?"

"She needs to get out of New York. It's getting a little hot for her here."

"But she can't type."

"You don't want her to type, do you?"

"What about her reputation?"

"What about yours?"

Robertson did not answer. He could hear Ferrani's brain working, assessing the risks and rewards.

In fact, Ferrani's brain was assessing the usefulness of Judith Watson. Now that Robertson was no longer running Grand American, he did not need Judith Watson in New York to watch him. But he had no one in Grand Cayman to report to him on the activities of his new President. Dear Judith. Surely she will not object to the beautiful beaches and the sun.

Robertson kept holding his breath. He needed the job with or without Judith Watson. He had to get out of New York, remove himself from the rat race, and cut his ties definitively from his 'you'll miss your train' wife. She had served her purpose. He had no further need for her. His mind raced back to Judith Watson, to her frequent 'fuck me again.' Better than 'hurry up; you'll miss your train.' Definitely!

Ferrani's computer brain stopped. "Andrew, you have got yourself a partner, a beautiful secretary and new headquarters."

"Thanks Vic. You won't regret it."

At three o'clock, on July, 18, 1978, Andrew Robertson resigned as Chairman of Grand American Bank.

At four o'clock, that same day, press releases were dispatched by the bank. The Board would meet Wednesday morning to appoint a successor.

Robertson's reign had lasted nine days.

Sheik Al-Madir pressed the bell at the door of Simone's apartment. Three short rings and a long one. A large Arab opened the door. "Where is Madame?" asked the Sheik.

"Upstairs in her bedroom."

"Ask her to come down."

Ever since they had returned from Bordeaux, Simone had been held a prisoner, locked up by Sheik Al-Madir in her apartment. She had protested violently. "You have no right to keep me here as your prisoner. Get out of my apartment."

"Remember, it's my apartment. I offered it to you, but it is in my name."

"Then let me move to a hotel."

"Simone, you are staying here and I'm staying with you. These two guards also. We are all going to live together happily until you sign that power of attorney."

"I'm not signing it until you bring me Robertson's head."

"I have already done what you asked me to do. I have instructed Swiss International Bank to convert my eighteen billion US dollar deposit into Swiss francs, German marks, Canadian dollars and French francs. They told me it would take a few days. I don't understand, however, how this is getting back at Robertson and I don't like the negative interest which I will have to pay on my new Swiss franc deposit."

"My dear Sheik, in order to convert your US dollars into other currencies, you know very well that Swiss International will have to sell dollars on the open market. In order to do this, they will have to draw upon their account at Grand American Bank. That's where your deposit ended up anyway. It never left Grand American. It just moved from your account to the account of Swiss International through a book entry. But this time it's going to move for good. Mostly all of it. As to the negative interest, you should recoup it quickly. Just watch the drop in value of the dollar within the next few days."

"Then why won't you sign the power of attorney?"

"Because Robertson is a crafty bastard who previously fought his way out of more difficult situations. You should know. We are both here because we are the victims of his intrigues."

"So when will you sign?"

"When he resigns, or he is fired, or his bank collapses or somebody kills him."

"You forget my ten billion dollars."

"Your ten billion dollars are safe. If Grand American collapses, the Government will take over."

"How do you know that?"

"Have they any choice? It's their largest bank. The largest in the world."

"You don't believe they would let it go bankrupt?"

"It would bankrupt the country and the world, if they did."

"Simone, sometimes you are so smart. Perhaps I should consider hiring you as my permanent financial adviser."

"You can't afford me."

"You forget how much money I control."

"Worthless paper!"

"I'll pay you in gold."

"How much?"

"Name your price."

"I'll think about it."

Simone came out of the bedroom. "I should not admit it Ben, but I am pleased that you are back. I need to get out of here."

"Not tonight."

"I'm going to go mad."

"You can't leave."

"Take me out for dinner then."

"We can eat here."

"Why?"

"Look." He threw her the final edition of the New York Times.

She read: 'Nine day reign ended. Andrew Robertson resigns as chairman of Grand American Bank.'

They stared at each other for a long time. He then withdrew a document from the folds of his robe and presented it to her. It was the power of attorney authorizing Sheik Al-Madir to sign at Grand American Bank on account 002-11211-8 in the name of Begum Simone de Rivoli Al-Madir. "Sign it. I have delivered Robertson's head to you."

She looked at him and asked mockingly, "Is that your only command, my master?"

"Allah has said: "Women are as a garment for you and you are as a garment for them." Tonight, I want you to be my garment, to enrobe me in the folds of your charms and to bring your exquisite love to me. For it is said again: 'Those who believe will have as companions maidens with lovely black eyes, pure as pearls well guarded, a recompense for what they did.' So, my maiden with lovely eyes, make ready and bring me my recompense."

"Go to hell!" She walked away from him.

"If you refuse, I shall return my money to Grand American Bank."

She stopped, stunned. "You can't do that. We have a deal."

"And I have completed my share of it. You have Robertson's head. I want that power of attorney. That's the deal."

"Not exactly. You still own twenty two billion dollars of US Treasury Bills. You have agreed to present to the Treasury Department those that have matured and to drop the others on the market."

"Not until you have signed the power of attorney."

"You double-crosser!"

"Watch you language, woman."

"I'll get even with you."

"How? You are now my prisoner. More. You are my legal wife until I let you notify Beauchamp that he may file the divorce petition."

"What do you want me to do?"

"Disrobe!"

She endured his look for a long time then glanced around the room. The two guards stood by the door, immobile, seemingly indifferent. "At least send the guards away."

"They won't talk and they are inoffensive. Even you should know that."

"When will you deal with the Treasury Bills?"

"I have already. I removed them from my safety deposit box today. They'll be in Washington tomorrow."

She thought of Pierre. She remembered the plan they had elaborated in Bordeaux. Simone would return to New York with Sheik Al-Madir and deliver to him the marriage certificate and the power of attorney as soon as she received conclusive evidence that Robertson had been fired and that the bank had been forced to request Government assistance. Now the Sheik wanted her to sign the power of attorney.

But what about the bank? What about the balance of her mission? She knew that she was on the verge of victory. The sudden resignation of Robertson meant that Grand American Bank was in deep trouble. It had to be. Or had Georges released the Mafia information too early? Pierre had wanted to wait but both her and Georges had favored the one-two punch. They had told him: "If you give time to Robertson, he will recover from the new withdrawal by Swiss International and the rumors that our Zurich man will leak to the AP correspondent." It was her definite opinion. She knew Robertson. Pierre had listened. "All right, we shall hit him in Zurich and New York within twenty-four hours." They had, and now Robertson had resigned. But his bank still stood.

There were numerous rumors on the streets of America. Thousands of depositors were rushing to recover their savings before the rumor that all the banks were failing proved to be true. Early yesterday, numerous small banks had closed their doors. A large one in Chicago had asked for Federal help. But Washington had remained silent.

The rush soon became a stampede as banks started to run out of cash. Billions of dollars had frantically been withdrawn by nervous depositors but no reassurance had come from the Federal Deposit Insurance Corporation.

Depositors became angry. Their life savings entrusted to private banks, because of their trust in the supervision by their Government, were evidently endangered. The epidemic of withdrawals forced more banks to announce they would not reopen today. Was there really a danger that all the banks could fail? No denial had been issued by the Federal Reserve Board.

Even Grand American Bank had not replied to the story from Zurich or the Wall Street Journal's Mafia exposé. No denial. Nothing, nothing but an ominous silence.

She found it strange, frightening, and at the same time exhilarating. She could not touch it but she could smell her victory. Perhaps it needed another thrust, another push, another stab for the gates of destruction to open and the wave of her disastrous actions to sweep the mountain of "nothing" dollars out of circulation. She looked at the Sheik. He was still her best instrument.

She dropped her robe.

"Come to me," he ordered. He clapped his hands and the two guards walked around the living room, turning off all the lights and plunging the room into darkness, broken only by the incandescence of the television screen.

"Come to me," he repeated.

"Will you do as I wish?"

"About the Treasury Bills?"

"Yes. And my freedom?"

"Yes."

"Swear by Allah."

"I do."

The Sheik clapped his hands again. The guards rushed to him and started to undress him, removing his Djellaba but not the short Aba he wore underneath, woven of the finest hair of rare black camels. He also kept his headgear. The guards helped him sit on the pile of cushions. As he did, they raised the Aba so that he could enjoy the softness of the cushion on his bare bottom.

Slowly, she started to walk towards him but stopped suddenly, as the television screen went blank and the gravest of voices announced "Ladies and Gentlemen, the President of the United States."

"Turn that off," ordered the Sheik.

"No. Listen!"

"My fellow Americans. I am addressing you tonight to report an emergency that has necessitated my personal intervention. This emergency affects every one of you, every citizen of the

United States, in fact, it also affects the world. I don't intend to deceive you by diminishing the seriousness of the crisis. Nor do I wish to disappoint you by remaining weak and hesitant in front of the danger that menaces all of us. I am your President and, as such, I intend to lead this country out of the predicament into which some unknown enemies have thrown us."

"Turn that off," repeated the Sheik.

Simone ignored him. Now she could see the face of Barry Hardrock, President of the United States, his eyes showing deep concern, trying to reach the eyes of two hundred million other Americans.

"Since 1970, two hundred and forty-six banks have closed their doors in our country. Their losses have cost our Federal Deposit Insurance Corporation three point five billion dollars. It has cost you, fellow Americans, this amount to make good the mistakes, the errors, the imprudence, if not the follies, of a small group of entrepreneurs and financial managers. **We must put a stop to that."**

"Ben, we have made it!" exclaimed Simone.
"What?"

"Rumors about our largest bank, Grand American Bank, have emanated from foreign countries, hitting right at the top of the United States financial structure, endangering our capitalist system, discrediting our regulatory Boards and Commissions, insulting the integrity of the United States Government. **We must put a stop to that."**

Simone reached for the closest chair. "I can't believe it!"
"What you talking about?"

"Those rumors, irresponsible rumors, have started a run on our banks. We had two thousand banks in difficulty last

week. After two days of rumors and withdrawals, another three hundred had to request our assistance. They can't ask the larger banks to help because the latter are also under attack. Panic has set into our banking community."

"Because the financial structure of the United States has been endangered by these vicious maneuverings, the credibility of our Government abroad has been crumbling. Our partners no longer listen to us. No longer respect us. No longer believe us. **We must put a stop to that."**

Simone raised her hands to her face and breathed heavily.

"Come and sit with me," the Sheik insisted.

"Our dollar, which is floating against other currencies, has floated downward by more than twelve percent in the last five days. That's an effective devaluation of more than thirty-eight percent since 1971. We have reached a situation where some of our trade partners are refusing to accept our dollars in payment for our imports of oil and other essential commodities. Soon, we won't be able to pay at all with dollars. We won't be able to trade. **We must put a stop to that."**

"Ben, don't you realize what is happening?
"Yes, another political speech."

"In the last decade, banking has become the most profitable industry in America. Year after year, banks have been braking records. Record assets, record loans, record deposits and record earnings. Their shareholders received higher rates of dividends than the rates of interest paid to depositors. In addition, they doubled and tripled the value of their investments through sales and mergers. Banking licenses have become licenses to print money, without risks. **We must put a stop to that."**

"Political! He is attacking private banking!"

"So what?"

"Foreign depositors, unnerved by unfounded rumors, worried about the stability of our dollar, confused by the multiplicity of our financial institutions, have started to shy away from our banks. Close to five billion dollars have been withdrawn from New York city banks alone in the last five days. Foreign depositors don't trust our banks any longer. **We must put a stop to that.**"

"So, our plan worked!"
"Then, sign the Power of Attorney."

"Even you, my Fellow Americans, concerned about what you read and what you heard, started to have doubts about your own country's ability to solve its financial problems and you started to exchange your dollars for gold, thus creating an unprecedented rush to gold in the last week. More than four point two billion dollars left the United States to pay for the import of this metal. **We must put a stop to that.**"

"I'll sign only after you collect the payment for your Treasury Bills."
"That may be never!"

"In trying to raise money to finance the needs of your Government, in fact your needs for unemployment benefits, old age pensions, child care centers, needy mother allowances, farmers price support payments, veterans pensions, small business loans, free hospitalization, in trying to finance all these very legitimate needs to which you, as Americans, have a right by birth, the Treasury Department has stumbled. Stumbled upon the refusal of big banks to buy more Treasury Bills, stumbled upon their inability to finance their own Government. **We must put a stop to that.**"

"I knew it! I knew it!" exclaimed Simone.

"If you know so much, tell me how I can collect the payment for my Treasury Bills?"

*"Evidence has been produced of the infiltration of unsavory elements within our banking system, even in our largest institutions, bringing the vast resources of some of our banks under the evil control of the already too powerful underworld elements in this country. **We must put a stop to that.**"*

"You'll collect in gold!" she shouted.
"It had crossed my mind," he whispered, a conniving smile on his face, his arms extended towards her.

*"Yesterday, a French bank — I shall not mention the name — taking advantage of the fine print in a loan agreement, taking advantage, I should say, of the disarray created by the recent international monetary disorders, has foreclosed on a five billion dollar loan granted less than two weeks ago to one of our largest banks and seized its collateral security: more than five billion dollars worth of gold. This was done without respect for elementary ethics between bankers and without the courtesy of at least a discussion of possible measures to correct the default. **We must put a stop to that.**"*

Simone remained enthralled by the television screen. "I have won." She started to laugh hysterically. "It's all over. I know it. I know it." To her own surprise, she added "Allah is the Mighty, the Lord of Power."

"Fellow Americans, as your President, I have the powers to put a stop to that. Consequently, I have today called an extraordinary joint meeting of the Cabinet and the Council for Economic and Financial planning. At this meeting, I made recommendations, that have been accepted, I am proud to say, without dissensions. Unanimously.

A few minutes ago, I signed an Emergency Presidential Decree ordering all banks in the United States and all US controlled banks and branches abroad to close their doors tonight and to remain closed until next Monday morning.

Simultaneously, I have tonight signed another Emergency Presidential Decree nationalizing all banks in the United States and all banks abroad controlled by US citizens.

*In signing these two Presidential Decrees, I have placed the full credit of the United States Government behind all banking transactions in the United States. I have reestablished trust and order. When banks reopen on Monday morning, we shall no longer have fourteen thousand assorted, competitive, wasteful, divided, different, private banks. We shall only have one bank, your bank. **'The United States Federal Bank.**"*

The drums of victory reverberated in Simone's ears. A symphony of elation exploded over her, showering her body with notes of exalted delights. She drowned in a state of emotion so intense that her self-control abandoned her.

Suddenly, breathless, half clothed by her recovered robe, untouched by man, she wailed from exaltation, enraptured in the frenzy of an orgasm exceeding in intensity the trances of the love delirium, which until now, she had only experienced with Pierre.

The world was shocked. When radio and television stations abroad repeated the speech of the President of the United States, and when the implications of the nationalization of all the American banks started to be understood, other Governments quickly met in a series of emergency meetings, the press massed at their doors awaiting statements.

At noon, on Wednesday, Canada announced the take-over of all Canadian banks, "in order to adapt our banking institutions to the new reality in America," they said. From now on, there shall be only one bank in Canada, the Bank of Canada. Uproar rose from the Canadian provinces about this new centralization of power in the hands of the Federal government. They were ignored. The Confederation Pact granted the supervision of money to Ottawa.

In the afternoon, the Bank of Japan revealed it had absorbed all Japanese banks. The Bank of West Germany, the Bank of Italy, the Bank of Belgium, the Bank of Luxembourg followed suit and took over those banks that were still owned by the public or by private investors.

The world came to a stand-still as government after government ordered all banks to close their doors until the following Monday, in order to guarantee the safety of their depositors funds and especially to retain foreign deposits that might otherwise have moved to the United States Federal Bank. All local banks were nationalized.

In Moscow, Pravda commented dryly that the banks in communist countries had always belonged to the people. "It was inevitable," they wrote, "that the capitalist system would one day recognize this elementary principle of justice because all wealth, by definition, belongs to the State, as trustee for the People."

Tax havens such as the Cayman Islands, where more than three hundred and twenty-five foreign owned banks operated, were hit particularly hard. Within twenty-four hours, the number of banks had been reduced to forty-eight, those of the forty-eight countries that had nationalized their banks abroad. By Monday morning it was expected that most of these banks would remain closed forever. Only the Bank of England would remain. They had to provide banking facilities to a British Colony.

The banks in the Cayman Islands closed because no tax avoider would want to bank with a state owned bank, where secrecy would no longer be respected. Under international tax treaties, information would flow freely from one national bank to another. It was the end of all tax havens. To replace the loss of income, in an emergency session, the Assembly of the Cayman Islands quickly voted personal and corporate income tax bills, ending nearly three hundred years of freedom from all taxes. The church bells tolled to mark the tragedy.

The banks in France closed on Wednesday with a government announcement that there were no reasons to panic, as the three largest banks in France were already state-owned. The Council of the Ministers would meet Thursday and the President would talk to his fellow Frenchmen on television on Friday night.

Throughout the world, from Wednesday to Monday, for five interminable days, all bank accounts were frozen. Trade stopped. Payments by check were refused. Credit card associations suspended all their facilities. Charge account privileges were halted. Some cash changed hands, but only a few speculators were prepared to exchange goods for paper. Nobody trusted their paper money. Those who held gold double-checked their caches and cocked their guns ready to defend their only true wealth.

The world, facing the definite truth of its bankruptcy,

ceased breathing, and stopped walking. After ten thousand years of existence, private banking had disappeared from the surface of the Earth.

On Thursday afternoon, in Paris, the President of France summoned Pierre Beauchamp to the Elysée Palace. Sitting in the back of a black chauffeur-driven Citroen, Pierre watched the display windows of the couturiers and perfumers of Rue du Faubourg St Honoré, the Cardins, St Laurents, Hermès and Chanels. He remembered the pun about the 'sweet smell of money' related to him by Simone. Soon, the world would rediscover the infinite perfume of gold: strong, priceless, eternal.

His fingers tapped the briefcase on the seat next to him. It contained the latest report from Simone received early this morning by coded cable from the French consulate in New York. Simone and Georges must have been working late into the previous night. The cable had ended, "Mission accomplished. Request recall to Paris. Sheik's Concorde at my disposal Friday. Would like to spend weekend in Mougins." He had replied. "Will meet Concorde Nice airport Friday no later six p.m. in order to catch President's speech on television at eight. Inform Georges and other friends that the speech of the President of France will be transmitted around the world by satellite. Congratulations."

The Citroen stopped at the golden gate, Pierre identified himself and the car entered the large courtyard of the Palace.

The President greeted him warmly. "Mon cher Beauchamp, c'est un grand jour! Je suis heureux de vous revoir."

"Tout le plaisir est pour moi, Monsieur le President. It is indeed a great day."

"Have a seat Beauchamp, and repeat to me what you briefly explained in your telephone call this morning."

"Have you informed the Council of Ministers?"

"I have. The proposals have been approved. A vote of gratitude to you and your agency was endorsed by all the Ministers except, as usual, the two socialists and the communist."

"They can't be sincere. They know we are right. Our man in Moscow reports that the Presidium is elated."

"They should be. Beauchamp, let me add my personal appreciation. One day I shall decorate you with the Légion d'Honneur. Too bad that for the time being you must remain anonymous and still keep a very low profile."

"Thank you, Mr. President."

"All right, back to Washington."

Pierre opened his briefcase and took out Simone's latest report. "With your permission, I shall read our agent's very explicit report:

"Wednesday morning Sheik Al-Madir flew to Washington and requested the Treasury Department to repay his twenty-two billion dollars of Treasury Bills. The Secretary of the Treasury had yet to recover from the shock of the collapse of Grand American Bank and the decision by the President to nationalize all US Banks. You should know that total assets of the United States Federal Bank after the take-over are expected to exceed nine hundred billion dollars. The acquisition will cost the US Treasury, approximately sixty billion dollars. The price has been set at the actual book value of the nationalized banks, after deduction of bad debts. No profit. Shareholders are being offered twenty-year Bank Acquisition Bonds bearing interest at three percent. The President has rushed a Bill to the House requesting an immediate increase in the borrowing limits of the Government by this amount plus another forty billion, which the Government estimates it will have to inject into the newly created Federal Bank to shore up its activities."

"Poor Americans," commented the President of France. "You may continue Beauchamp."

"While the Secretary of the Treasury was still in a state of shock, the visit of Sheik Al-Madir broke all the dams. The Sheik has to be congratulated. His performance was grand. The previous night, I had carefully rehearsed every one of his movements and he executed them to perfection. He triggered a series of panic consultations. There were calls to Patrick White and the President. There were threats to the Sheik. Talks of armed reprisals. Then cajolery, bribes and promises. The Sheik stood by his original request. He wanted to be paid. No payment today, no oil tomorrow. He went further. No payment today, a new war with Israel tomorrow. The prospects of a new energy crisis and a new Middle East war on top of the Grand American Bank catastrophe was all that was necessary to finally bring the Treasury Department to its knees. At that stage, the Sheik compromised. But that was not part of our original strategy.

For half of his Treasury Bills, the Sheik accepted payment in gold at three hundred dollars per ounce — the market had closed Tuesday at two ninety. The gold started to move out of Fort Knox in the afternoon and is being flown to Dubai on a Boeing 747 chartered from Iran Air by the Sheik.

Since gold was demonetized in 1971, the reserves held at Fort Knox no longer appear in the books of the Federal Reserve Board or in those of the Treasury Department. Therefore, I personally suspect that this unusual withdrawal of gold to satisfy the Sheik will not be recorded anywhere. The movements of trucks will no doubt rekindle rumors that some gold has disappeared from Fort Knox, and that unscrupulous politicians have stolen it.

Remember the 1973 accusations. At that time, a committee of Congressmen visited the vaults at Fort Knox and were shown

*the gold through heavy grilles bearing seals as evidence that
they had not recently been opened. It is not expected that the
doors of Fort Knox will be reopened again to Congressmen.
But if they were, they would again only be shown sealed
doors. I don't believe that the gold bullion have been counted
and the inventory checked since 1971.*

*In any event, as it is a known fact that most Arab countries
are withdrawing their gold from Fort Knox, the presence of
Iran Air planes at the airport would confirm the fact that
another Arab Emir is taking his gold out. No one will suspect
that the gold being removed, in fact, is the property of the
United States Government."*

"Smart agent you have there, Beauchamp," remarked the
President.

"One day, with your permission, Mr. President, I would
like to introduce her to you. Perhaps, next time you visit your
property in Vence? Baroness de Rivoli expects to spend many
weekends nearby, in Mougins."

"Is it where you also own a villa?" ask the President,
winking.

A shy smile outlined Beauchamp's mouth. "Shall I go
on?"

The President nodded.

*"The Secretary of the Treasury signed an agreement
guaranteeing the Sheik that upon the reopening of banks, on
Monday, the funds − the ten billion dollars − appearing
in the books of Grand American Bank in my name, will
be transferred to the name of the United Arab Emirates.
The marriage certificate, accompanied by my power of
attorney was recognized by the Secretary as proper and
valid. Surprise was expressed that the marriage had not
been announced publicly, but the Sheik covered us well
by quoting Moslem rules concerning the passive role of
women. The divorce petition may now be filed. I beg you*

to do it immediately. How much longer must I read the Quran ?

"You have lost me," said the President.

"Confidential code and procedures," answered Pierre. "As you know, some of our methods are rather unorthodox. I would prefer to keep this one a secret, even from you."

"Provided the security and reputation of France are not endangered."

"I assure you that it does not affect our security. As to our reputation, Frenchwomen were always..."

"I know, I know," smiled the President. "Continue."

"Now here is the shock for you. Finally, the Treasury Department confirmed in writing to the Sheik that, effective next Monday, the United States Government would reestablish the convertibility of its dollar into gold but at the unheard of price of one thousand dollars per ounce."

"They are completely out of their minds," exclaimed the President.

Beauchamp continued.

"In return, Sheik Al-Madir, on behalf of the Emirates, undertook to convert into gold no more than ten percent of his dollar holdings in any one calendar year."

"How was he repaid the balance of his money? His other eleven billion in Treasury Bills?" asked the President.

"Some of them had yet to mature, but they agreed to repay them immediately, if the Sheik would accept cash."

"Worthless paper for worthless paper," answered the President.

"Not exactly, sir. New paper convertible into gold at one thousand dollars per ounce."

"But that's equivalent to only thirty-three cents for each dollar. Gold is only worth three hundred dollars per ounce."

"Exactly," said Pierre, "but the Sheik is a shrewd and suspicious character. His paper money is no longer valueless. It is now worth something. He would rather take this new paper now, than be stuck with worthless paper forever."

"Anything else in your report?"

"Yes, and very interesting. Listen."

"Another important fact emerged from the Sheik's discussion with the Secretary of the Treasury. It is expected that today or tomorrow the U.S. Government will re-impose the law of 1933 and confiscate all gold privately held by US citizens."

"There is going to be an uproar over that one," mused the French President.

"They have no choice, sir. If they are going to reopen the gold window, they will need all the gold they can find. Even at one thousand dollars per ounce. Poor US citizens, it's only three and a half years ago that they were again permitted to buy and own gold. Talk about freedom. Talk about the pursuit of happiness."

"Beauchamp, you are such a gold addict that you believe the ownership of gold is a source of happiness."

"I don't. But the security of one helps achieve the other. One needs an anchor in a civilization of traders. You can't anchor the ship of your life to a piece of paper."

"Beauchamp, I wish to thank you very sincerely. Please convey to the Baroness the expression of my deepest admiration for the excellence of her work." He added knowingly, "I hope the two of you are very happy."

"She has not said yes, yet." He jumped suddenly from his chair. "My God! I forgot to file the divorce petition!"

"You have my permission to leave," said the President, amused. "I must work on my speech for tomorrow."

The Concorde landed at Nice airport at fifteen minutes to six. The flight from New York had taken less than four hours. Pierre had met the plane accompanied by an immigration officer. "Sheik Al-Madir, welcome back to France."

"Mr. Beauchamp, it is a pleasure to be back here in less surprising circumstances than those of our last meeting in Bordeaux."

Simone appeared at the top of the ramp. She was beautiful. The famous dimple was again visible at the side of her smiling mouth. She stood on the platform dressed in the same cream colored chemise she had worn in Montreal at the Ritz Carlton, the high collar framing her proud head, caressed by the warm July Mediterranean breeze. She walked down the ramp, feeling like a victorious queen returning to her subjects, pleased with herself, splendid in the setting sun. Her lips formed his name the way she had at Orly airport, many years ago, when she had returned from Vietnam.

When she reached the foot of the ramp, he took her hands and lifted them to his lips and kept his head bowed over them like in a prayer. "Welcome home".

She turned slowly to Sheik Al-Madir. "Thank you for the use of your jet. I have taken my decision. It is with regret that I must refuse your offer. There is not enough gold in the world to make me leave France again."

"That's a very big statement, Madame de Rivoli," replied the Sheik. "I'm sorry. It is my loss. I don't know where I can find an investment manager with your competence."

"What's going on here?" asked Pierre.

Simone looked at him mockingly. "Final report, sir. Sheik Al-Madir has been elected Chairman of the United Arab Emirates. Thus, he is being rewarded for his astuteness in foreseeing the collapse of the American banking system. The Rulers also wish to express their admiration to him for having converted a good percentage of the Federation's funds into gold and for having exchanged a large part of their dollar assets for other strong currencies before the closing of the banks. Finally, they are demonstrating their admiration for his ability and diplomacy which resulted in the reinstatement of the convertibility of the dollar into gold. While the rate of convertibility today does not appear interesting, in return, the value of their existing gold holdings have multiplied by more than three fold. They also recall that the value of gold has increased more than eight times in the last eight years and, therefore, it is not impossible to conceive that its price might triple in the next five years. Sheik Al-Madir's reign over the wealth of the Emirates, to which he contributed so much, will start Monday, on the day when the world is expected to inaugurate its new banking era, that of National banks.

"The Sheik has very generously invited me to become the new investment manager of the Emirates. It is a most flattering compliment. He has offered to pay me in gold and to let me determine the amount of my reward. It is an unusual demonstration of trust. I have chosen to decline the opportunity. It is written: 'To Allah belongs whatever is in the heavens and whatever is in the earth.' I disagree. If there is anything in heaven, the gods and the angels can keep it. As to what is in the earth, I believe that it belongs to those who have the imagination, the intelligence and the ability to find it, to extract it and to subjugate it to their needs and aspirations."

Sheik Al-Madir extended his hand to Pierre and then to Simone. "I must respect Madame de Rivoli's decision although she should remember another quote from the Quran: 'On the day when He will gather them all together, He will say: O company of big ones, you exploited the people.'

The ramp was removed and within minutes the sleek

Concorde purred as it glided away on an easterly course over the Mediterranean towards the soon-to-rise sun over the land of Allah.

"I had never thought he could express such socialistic ideas," remarked Pierre.

She linked her arm to his and walked to the limousine. "Arabs are the most advanced socialists on earth. If you were as rich as they are, you could also afford to be, even without the preaching of Allah."

"Madame, Mademoiselle, Monsieur, bonsoir. As your President, I shall talk to you tonight about the banking crisis that has hit France and the world this week. I shall also talk about the international monetary system whose deterioration has brought upon us the banking crisis. I shall propose solutions that in my opinion and the opinion of my advisers, shall reestablish order in the monetary system, confidence in financial institutions and trust in Governments. They shall also greatly contribute, I hope, to curing a number of ills, which have attacked our civilization, particularly the constantly widening gap of wealth between the developing nations and the industrialized world."

"But first, the situation in France, which concerns especially each of you. Our banks are closed. They were closed in order to protect them during this forced bank holiday declared by the United States, soon followed by every other country in the world. We expect our banks to reopen on Monday. When they do, the world of banking will have changed considerably. In every other country in the world, all private banking institutions have been nationalized. In those countries, starting Monday morning, citizens will no longer have a choice of banks. They will have to bank with the National bank of their country of residence. With the Bank of Canada, in Canada; the Bank of Mexico in Mexico; the Bank of Italy in Italy; etc., etc. As I said, this new rule will apply to every country but to France. Why will it be different in France? Because I believe in the right of our citizens to a choice of bankers. Otherwise, their freedom of action is seriously impaired. After all, banking is at the start and the end of every trade activity

between two trading partners. Removing the choice of banks is removing part of the freedom to trade."

"In France, our three largest banks have been nationalized for many years. Those of you who wish to bank with your Government banks are welcome to do so. Those banks are the Crédit Lyonnais, Banque Nationale de Paris and Crédit Commercial de France. Naturally, the Bank of France is also state owned and offers also the same guarantee of security as the other three, that of the unconditional support of your Government. But for those of you who wish to bank with a non-government institution, we have our private banks and we have decided to keep those banks private. This is not a new policy. French citizens have always been given a choice between a state owned industry and private enterprise. For instance, you can purchase a car from Renault, which the government controls or from Peugeot, which is a private manufacturer. You have a choice. In matters of banking, we want to protect that choice. Therefore, France will now find itself in the unique position of being the only country in the world where private banks have not been nationalized."

"Naturally, after the recent events, we are concerned, as you are, about the safety of your money when entrusted to our private banks. In order to protect you, the Council of Ministers has approved today a new set of regulations governing private banking in France. Higher capital ratio to liabilities, higher reserves on deposits, new and stricter ratios of short-term liabilities to assets, new lending limits, new investment guides and so forth. With these new regulations, we have not eliminated the risks of dealing with private banks but we have reduced them to an acceptable level. Those of you who wish full security can bank with Government banks. Those of you who wish a higher return but are prepared, in order to achieve it, to accept a risk; you have the option to bank with private banks. It is equitable. It is just. It is within the spirit of freedom of action which we wish to protect in France."

"I have treated the situation of banking on a national level, as it

affects each of you. I shall now discuss the international situation. While it does not concern you individually, it has a heavy bearing on us as a nation, because it conditions the ability of your Government to take decisions. I have mentioned the deterioration of the monetary system. In fact it is more than deterioration. Let us call things by their proper name. It is the destruction, voluntary and systematic, of what was an orderly system. It has opened the gates of hell upon the world. There was a time, not so long ago, when Governments and politicians acted within the boundaries of a certain discipline, the discipline imposed upon them by money. The supply or lack of it. Budgets needed to be balanced. Loans repaid. Electoral promises restrained. Obligations honored. Money was the result of production. It was a substitute for goods to alleviate the awkwardness of barters. Those who had no goods to bring to the market place, because they were not producers, could not barter. If they came with money, their money had to be backed by value, value stored in the vaults of their governments, which could at any time be transferred elsewhere in exchange for paper money. In those days, a nation lived according to its means."

"But enters the century of credit. Of mortgaged futures. Of accelerated consumption. Of planned obsolescence. Of record gross national production. Of faster for surer. Of bigger for better. Of irresponsible promises made by even more irresponsible politicians. Of bureaucrats servile to their elected Ministers. Of economists obsequious to the omniscience of their country's President."

"Birth was proclaimed a right to own, not to produce. To own a right to spend, not to save. To spend a virtue, not a sin. Maximum spending became synonymous with maximum growth. Spending at any cost. The cost of pollution of nature, depletion of the value of money. Spending was also decreed the source of money. Consumption, the source of production. The capacity of production, the store of value.

"Confusion had entered the rigid monetary system. Its discipline, claimed some, no longer answered the right of all citizens to an

equal standard of living, now granted to them, as a right by birth they professed and not a right earned by rational human beings through the production of their arms and brains. So, rules were disregarded. International agreements broken. All money printing presses were thrown into action at the same time."

"A solution had to be found. Driven to the wall of bankruptcy, unable to control its politicians, unwilling to balance its budgets, incapable of controlling its production, the United States proposed a solution which, despite the warnings of General de Gaulle many years ago and eventually the protests of Georges Pompidou, was quickly adopted by a number of other nations, also ruined, also unwilling to live within the discipline of their true wealth. Gold was demonetized."

"You know the sequel and the consequences. That terrible cancer called inflation set into the economy of every country in the world, sapping gradually at the earnings and savings of each citizen. Being paid with worthless paper money, its artificial value constantly eroded by inflation, countries rich in natural resources such as oil, gas, coal, nickel, copper, tin, iron ore, bauxite, phosphate, uranium, timber, tripled and quadrupled the price of their products to maintain their purchasing power. Unfortunately, they were still trading value for paper. Having purchased from producing countries what they needed, they were left with surpluses of worthless paper money. When they asked the issuing Governments to repay their dollars or liras or pounds, they were told "with what?" Money, which at one time had been a certificate of value, a proof of wealth, had become a promise. A politician's promise. A promise to pay nothing."

"Money had been demonetized the same day that gold was demonetized. Because you cannot separate one from the other, the same way you cannot separate life from the sun, water from wetness, and smell from odor. You cannot separate money from value. Money from gold. The world tried and, in less than a decade, the world went bankrupt. At a time when the growth of

the world made it necessary to expand the monetary system, we chose to destroy it. We chose to destroy the system upon which for the last ten thousand years the world had been built. The twentieth century shall be remembered in history as the century during which the world nearly self-destructed."

"Earlier this week, the world placed one foot in the grave. As I am speaking to you, I know that our friends, the United States, have already lifted the second foot towards the same grave. Is it too late? Is it too late to stop them? Is it too late to stop the end of the world?"

"Frenchmen, your President says no. A very loud no. Because I believe that the world can be saved. I believe that the world can be made a better place to live in. I believe the world's resources can be better distributed. I believe that men will always possess the ability to correct the mistakes made by other men. Only the mistakes of God might be beyond our power of rectification but God, I am told, does not make mistakes."

"Therefore, I have a series of proposals which I offer humbly to the Presidents, Kings, Governors, Prime Ministers, Chairmen and other Leaders of the world who are listening to me, tonight. These proposals are based on my belief that it is possible to conceive a world that is peaceful, disciplined, healthy and free. Not perfect but striving for justice. Not absolute but striving for equality. Not flawless but striving for happiness."

When the President of France stopped talking, one hour later, one billion people in the one hundred and forty five countries reached by satellite television, stood in their castles, their palaces, their houses, their apartments, their tents, their huts, their igloos, their hospices, their shacks, their tenements, their sampans and, in a hundred and ten different languages, they cheered; their pessimism replaced by hope, their sadness by joy, their dejection by pride.

Pierre and Simone sat on the same shag carpet in front of the same fireplace in Mougins where their adventure had started nine years earlier. But they were no longer recollecting the escapades of their youth. The last nine years were too full of cherished experiences, painful sacrifices, immeasurable happiness, and unmentionable humiliations. Too full also of an indestructible love which, now that their mission was accomplished, they could relish at leisure, contented, blessed with the bondage of their rediscovered happiness.

They had listened scrupulously to every word of the address by the President of France, following the logic of his exposé, anticipating his words as if they had written them. In fact, they had provided the tools, they had created the environment, they had brought about the crisis, and they had stopped the world in its race towards oblivion.

Rich with that knowledge, they experienced this deep and indefinable joy given only to those who contribute to the rethinking of the world. The joy of the New Creators.

Gone were the years of studying, of waiting, of planning. Gone were the nights of loneliness, of torture, of degradation. Gone were the days of danger, of excitements, of risks. Gone were the characters of their drama: the schemers, the bankers, the robbers, the spoilers, the adulterers, and the liars. Gone were the Hardrocks, the Robertsons, the Whites, the Al-Madirs, the Ferranis, the Watsons, and the Sterns. The play was over. The curtain had fallen. But there would be no applause for Pierre and Simone, for they were unknown to the billions of anonymous spectators. Only the two of them could share their success. They needed no one else. They had each other.

"I love you," she told him and buried her face in the cradle of his shoulder. She wanted reassurance. "Promise me you will never leave me again."

He lifted her head, gazed into her pleading eyes and kissed her mouth long and adoringly. She abandoned herself to the ardent passion of her love, kissing him back, her tongue reaching for his heart, her nails digging into the flesh of his neck. She remembered their passion of nine years ago but, before she had a chance to speak, he kissed the top of her breast through her chemise and begged her, "let's go to our room."

She remembered the source of their happy years and she knew she had never ceased to be an idolatress. Her hands plunged between his legs in a supplication and she exposed again the metronome of their past sexual symphonies, the source of all her passion. She paid homage to him and feeling gay and young again she asked him, "what's wrong with here?" She rose to her knees, undid the buttons of her chemise and offered her breasts to his expecting mouth, a holy communion in flesh and blood. They undressed each other with kisses, discovering thousands of pores that had never been touched, hundreds of nerves that had never been excited, and an array of love caves that had never been explored. As they rolled on the carpet, the champagne bucket crashed and wine sprayed over them. They became hysterical with pleasure.

He pointed at her. "You are bubbling."

"I was before the champagne." She became his glass of enjoyment, his cup of satisfaction. He emptied both to the last drop.

The crackling of the fire kept the beat of their moaning. She looked at the flame, "I'm warm."

"You are burning."

"Douse my fire."

"It is an eternal flame."

"Then burn with me."

Their legs were intertwined and they wished they possessed more arms in order to embrace in a permanent caress. Their bodies had blended into each other and they wished their flesh would melt into one soul. And when the crest of waves of pleasure hit them and carried them miles away, down the long beach of happiness, they shouted gaily in unison, "I love you."

In New York, on Saturday, at ten a.m., the delegates to the General Assembly of the United Nations sat in an extraordinary meeting to debate the banking and monetary crisis and to study the French proposals. While speakers followed each other on the rostrum, Heads of Nations, Ministers of Finance and Central Bankers were converging on New York to be on hand for the negotiations and decisions.

The Board of Governors of the Bank for International Settlement transferred by exception its monthly meeting from Geneva to New York at one p.m.

The International Monetary Fund convened its members for a two o'clock session. The board of the World Bank had been sitting since eight in the morning. The hallways of the United Nations, the various Embassies and Consulates and all New York hotels were crowded with representatives of foreign countries, a single purpose on their minds: to solve the Problem.

Except for foreign diplomats moving hurriedly from one building to another, the streets of New York were empty. The World sat, glued to television screens, awaiting the Miracle. A few men were debating the fate of four billion. Two thousand individuals gathered in New York were deciding the future of Humanity.

The French proposals rested on three premises. One: the only true money is gold. Two: the natural resources of the earth belong to the world. Three: the monetary systems of all countries are interdependent.

There were bitter discussions. Those without gold kept

calling it a vile metal. Those blessed with large holdings were not inclined to share. Those with natural resources claimed the sovereignty of their territories. Those without claimed that all men had been created equal with equal rights to the resources of earth. All defended their monetary policies, objected to the idea of their neighbors supervising their spending, unprepared to trust a supreme mediator.

In the end, reason prevailed, mitigated by political factors, assailed by ideological radicalism, compromised by moral considerations, but still reason prevailed and the Assembly approved by majority vote a series of recommendations:

Any natural resource considered to be a world resource by a two thirds vote of the General Assembly of the United Nations would be classified as a World Resource and its management entrusted to the International Monetary Fund for the benefit of the world.

All natural resources declared World Resources would be nationalized, the nationalizing country retaining seventy-five percent of the ownership.

The ownership of the other twenty-five percent of such World Resources would be vested by the possessing nations into the International Monetary Fund as trustee for the "have not" nations.

The exploitation of World Resources would be controlled by the International Monetary Fund with the right to set prices, to fix levels of production based on estimated needs of consuming countries and to impose rationing and quotas in case of fast depleting resources.

The International Monetary Fund was invited to create a World Resources Bank to finance the exploration, funding, proving, development and marketing of World Resources.

The Assembly recognized that gold was the only acceptable store of value at that moment but asked the International Monetary Fund to study this particular problem as there was not sufficient gold to support the existing levels of world trade and currencies in circulation. Furthermore, since the "demonetization of gold", many countries found their vaults empty of the precious metal or others like Italy found their full stock of gold pledged to others as collateral for loans.

A giant step forward had been taken by the world. A step thought impossible before the speech of the French president the previous day. At five o'clock on the same Saturday, the International Monetary Fund finally issued its press statement:

"After an all day session, the Governors of the International Monetary Fund have come to certain conclusions initiated by the Minister of Finance from France and in line with the desires expressed by the United Nations in their morning resolutions. The principal conclusions are as follows:

a) The name of the International Monetary Fund is immediately changed to the Bank of the World. (B of W)

b) The existing World Bank becomes the International Fraternity Fund.

c) The Bank for International Settlement is abolished and its functions taken over by the new Bank of the World.

d) Effective immediately, the issue of money is confined to and controlled exclusively by the Bank of the World.

e) All money issued must be backed by gold. All such gold must be deposited with the Bank of the World.

f) The production of gold in all countries is to be nationalized.

g) *Ownership of gold is recognized as a right. Now that money and gold have again become synonymous, there is no valid reason to continue the prohibition of personal ownership of gold, where it exists. Citizens must be free to hold gold and to pay with gold or, at their choice, to hold paper money and to pay with printed money, since it is backed by gold.*

h) *Twenty-five percent of the existing gold stock of each country is to be given to the Bank of the World forthwith for distribution to the "have not" countries pro rated to their population.*

Note: This shall permit each country to start with a minimum stock of gold without affecting too harshly those who hold gold as they are mostly countries with large reserves.

i) *All national budgets must be submitted to and approved by the Bank of the World. Budget deficits are equivalent to an overdrawn account at the Bank and will only be permitted when prospects of surpluses in the near future are apparent and again only with the approval of a majority of the Governors of the Bank.*

j) *At the request of any member country, money may also be issued against those national natural resources which have been declared World Resources by a two thirds vote of the Assembly of United Nations, such money to be issued to the extent of ten percent of the estimated value of the said natural resources. World Resources are being declared a new acceptable store of value ranking with gold, to the extent of ten percent of their estimated worth.*

k) *The World Resources Bank is created immediately as a subsidiary of the Bank of the World.*

l) *Loans granted by the World Resources Bank are repayable in money or at the choice of the borrowers in World*

Resources. In such a case, repayment in resources shall be distributed to the participating countries pro rata to their capital participation in the Bank.

m) The World Manpower Pool is established immediately in order to rationalize the world's resources of manpower. A better utilization of capital and natural resources can only be successful if coupled with a better understanding of the role of citizens in production and a more efficient distribution of labor and know-how throughout the world.

n) The price of gold, under the new system, is fixed at US one thousand dollars per ounce.

Note: A number of citizens and countries are bound to realize a substantial profit from the new fixing of the price of gold. It was felt very strongly by certain members that they were entitled to this windfall as a reward for their long and continued faith in gold.

o) To simplify international exchanges, all currencies will adjust their parity to the new dollar parity of one thousand dollars per ounce of gold. It is recommended that as soon as possible new currency be issued by those countries in order that one thousand French francs or one thousand pound sterling or one thousand marks or yens, for instance, be worth one ounce of gold or one thousand dollars. Afterwards, no change in parity will be permitted. None will be necessary as no budget deficits are permitted. All money will have the same backing: Gold and World Resources.

p) A number of these conclusions require the ratification of the shareholders of the Bank of the World. They are respectfully submitted for immediate consideration.

The world had taken a second giant step.

As radio, television and newspapers repeated the highly technical conclusions to the population still frozen around the world in its expectation, the leaders of the world started their debate in New York Saturday night. All international communications were reserved for calls by Heads of Governments to their advisers and colleagues in their countries of origin. Emergency cabinet meetings were arranged thousands of miles away around conference telephones. By four o'clock Sunday afternoon, the President of the United States, Barry Hardrock, alone on the rostrum, spoke to another extraordinary meeting of the United Nations. Every country in the world was represented not only by its regular delegates but by its Head of State.

President Hardrock had paused to make sure that all microphones were functioning, that all television cameras were focused on him, that all eyes here and in front of all television sets in the world were fixed on his mouth.

"The second foot of America, which the President of France thought we had directed towards the grave, has jumped over the grave, drawing the other foot with it, and America got the hell out of that cemetery!"

When the delegates laughed, the world knew that it was on the verge of salvation.

"In summary, every recommendation of the United Nations and every conclusion of the Bank of the World have been accepted and approved by the one hundred and forty-five Nations assembled here during this historical weekend. Not without difficulties, not without recriminations, not without sacrifices, not without concessions, not without forfeitures of national pride, policies, philosophies, ideologies and wealth, but we have done it."

"Tomorrow, the banks of the world shall open again. The monetary system shall work again. No one expects all citizens and all countries to be equal, but under our revised system of money, resources and labor management, everyone shall at least be given a fair chance."

"The world can walk again."

EPILOGUE
THE VALLEY OF GOLD

"There has been a battle of wits going on with the CIA leaking secret Soviet gold figures... whether the CIA underestimated the Soviet gold hoard and production on purpose, or whether it was misled by figures obtained from Colonel Alex Penkovsky who defected to the West with some photographs of gold statistics in the Soviet Union, is difficult to ascertain... Colonel Penkovsky, who was a double agent, is now dead, having been allegedly executed by Soviet operatives."

(From "CIA, Russians seen in Gold War." Paris International Herald Tribune, Saturday/Sunday, January 18/19, 1975.)

Simone stood in front of the French doors overlooking the terrace, the pool and the garden. Pierre was walking slowly through the flowerbeds seemingly lost in meditation. Roses seemed to bow to him, their master, while the carnations and the daisies danced slowly under the Azure breeze. Further back, the marigolds vibrated with the buzzing of the bees and the tulips balanced on their long stems, lost in the enchantment of their own perfume.

She turned and her eyes dropped on a folder protruding from Pierre's briefcase on his desk by the window. She was not paying much attention to it until she saw her name, handwritten in big black letters, on a slip of paper clipped to the folder. She pulled it out and read the cover: "The Moscow File." She opened it. Attached to the first page was an old newspaper article... "the Russians have three or four times more un-mined gold than South Africa, the world's biggest gold producer. Therefore, the Russians want a prominent role for the metal in the world's monetary system in order to be sure of a big market for their gold...."

She recognized Pierre's handwriting at the bottom of the story. "How much gold has Russia? How to find out? Whom to send?" Then below, many pencil scribbles. "Monti as contact? Move from New York to Moscow? Carpenter as support? Move from Cairo? Head agent? Dubeau? Landrieux? de Rivoli? de Rivoli? de Rivoli?"

She closed the file. On top, on that sheet of paper, she saw her name again written by Pierre. 'Simone?' and a series of drawings, meaningless lines, broken arrows and circles. She stepped out on the terrace and watched him walking slowly amid his flowers until he turned and saw her. His face burst with a smile of happiness. He raised his arms in a theatrical gesture and addressed his garden. "If flowers be the food of love, grow on, give me excess of it that surfeited my appetite may sicken and so die...."

"It's 'music' not 'flowers'," she shouted to him. "You don't know your Shakespeare."

"The sweetest music on earth is that of my flowers. Come. Listen to them." He bent over a row of tulips and undulated with them as if rocked by a melody. She joined him. He enlaced her and her body followed his in a movement of ballet to the music of their shared felicity.

"Pierre, why do you love gold more than you love me?"

He answered her with a question, his eyes glimmering strangely under the morning sun. "Have you ever seen gold in its natural state? Gold in the ground under tons of earth? Pure gold, untouched by man, waiting to be released to take its place as the real god of the world? Have you?"

"No."

"Come."

They drove along the Autoroute towards Nice then took a back road that took them to Vallauris.

"Where are you taking me?"

He kept driving, silently, his mind concentrating on a problem far away from the accidents of the road. They drove by the hundreds of pottery shops that line the main street of Vallauris, the pottery capital of France, and turned east towards Juan Les Pins and Antibes. The car slowed down, entered a steel gate and followed a long alley leading to an ordinary farmhouse surrounded by rows of greenhouses. A man came out of the house. Pierre removed his wallet from his back pocket and presented an identification card. "I wish to inspect gallery number four."

"Et Madame?" Asked the man as he returned Pierre's wallet.

"Agent Iris 24."

"You may proceed."

Pierre turned the wheels to the right and drove between the hot houses until they reached one bearing number four on its door. It sat at the foot of a series of terraces climbing towards the road to Vallauris, three hundred feet above them. The terraces were covered with flowers and orange trees.

"Where are we, Pierre? Please talk to me."

He took her hand and led her into the number four hot house. At the back of it, resting against the lowest terrace, Simone saw a huge stainless steel tank. Two guards stood in front of it. "Mr. Beauchamp, nice to see you again, sir. You wish to enter number four?"

"Yes. May we have hats?" replied Pierre.

One of the guards presented two golden hard hats, bearing large initials S.G.N. Pierre placed one on Simone's head and covered himself with the other. In front of the two men, Simone chose to remain silent.

"You may open up," suggested Pierre.

Another guards unscrewed a large wheel at the end of the tank and soon the whole end opened, revealing a long lighted tunnel leading under the terraces into the mountain. The door of the metallic container closed behind them.

"Pierre, where are you taking me?"

"What is dearest to you, Simone?"

"You," she answered.

"Then swear on my head that you will never reveal what you have just heard and what you are about to see. That you have never heard of Iris 24. That you have never been here. That you don't know where we are and that you are unaware of the existence of this installation."

"What is it?"

"Swear first. Solemnly."

"I swear on my love for you, my beloved, my dearest, that I shall never...."

"Follow me."

"Where?"

"To the Valley of Gold."

The entrance tunnel lead to a large chamber from which radiated a number of other underground passages penetrating deeper into the heart of the mountain. Pierre touched one of the walls and showed is hand to Simone. "This is gold. Gold in the purest form ever discovered on earth. Gold in the largest quantity known to exist in this world, possibly ten times more than the proven reserves of South Africa. Possibly, two or three times more than the admitted reserves of Russia. But perhaps the Russians are lying. Perhaps they doctor their statistics. We don't know, but we shall soon find out."

"Who discovered this?"

"The Service Géologique National de France, the SGN. With my assistance," he added proudly.

"I did not know that you were also a prospector."

"I discovered it sitting in Mougins reading about Vallauris. Think. What does it mean the name Vallauris? Come on. Remember your Latin studies. Vallauris. Vallis Aurea. The Valley of Gold. Two thousand years ago, the Romans gave that name to a valley which ran from Biot on the slope of the Alps to the Mediterranean ocean at Antibes. Today, we find that a thick layer of calcareous sandstone and variegated clay covers what must have been at one time a valley much deeper than its present elevation. We extract from it the clay that is used by the pottery artists in Vallauris."

I asked myself "why would the Romans call Vallauris the Valley of Gold if it contained only ordinary clay which was plentiful elsewhere in their Empire? Why call it Valley of Gold unless there was really gold here?"

I put the question to the SGN and they embarked on an extensive program of boring through this area. Very deep borings, through the layers of clay and sandstone. And there it was, buried three hundred feet deep, gold bearing material. Large voids in the underground walls seem to indicate the presence of caves that eventually proved to be man made galleries. We rediscovered the forgotten Roman gold mines of Vallis Aurea which were buried under a bed of clay that must have slid from the Alps sometime in the later part of the fifth century. In the middle of the Dark Ages. We rediscovered the Valley of Gold.

"Pierre it's fantastic. But I don't recall this discovery having ever been reported."

"It was not. It will not. Never. It's a secret. A top secret. We don't want the world to know. But, Simone, listen to what this discovery means. With the new gold standard adopted by the Bank of the World during the weekend, one thousand dollars per ounce, France is now the richest country in the world."

In the evening he said, "Let's celebrate."

"What?"

"Our wealth. Where would you like to go?"

"What about that Russian restaurant in Cagnes-Sur-Mer?"

"The Douchka?"

"Yes. I love the songs of Georges Valentinoff and the gypsy violin of Gulio Kokas."

"You feel romantic?"

"I feel elated and terrified at the same time."

"Don't worry, I am taking good care of our treasure."

"Our love or your gold?"

For a while, during dinner, she forgot the gold and he became her man again. Christine Valentinoff brought them flaming "chachliks" grilled in the open fireplace. With her beautiful Slavic smile, she suggested, "I hope you enjoy them. I cooked them especially for you, using secret spices I brought back from Moscow."

Koka's violin attacked the introduction to the Russian song, 'Two Guitars', and the room reverberated from the clapping of hands. The clapping died only to be born again to the melody of 'Dark Eyes'. Pierre poured more Roderer Crystal champagne in their glasses and watched the bubbles swim to the surface, remembering their love of yesterday. "Simone, I want you to marry me."

She looked at him and her eyes reached the bottom of his heart. "I knew that you would ask me and I want you to know that I have never been happier, but I can't."

"Why not? he asked suddenly anguished.

The voice of Georges Valentinoff rose and the soul of Russia invaded the restaurant.

"Because you need me."

"Yes, I need you and you should know that never before have I needed anyone so much. Or loved anyone so much. Why will you not marry me?" His heart agonized. He knew her answer, even before she murmured it.

"Because you need me…in Moscow."

Gulio Kokas interposed his violin between them. His bow wailed the music of 'Dark Eyes', as if he knew the torment in their hearts. When the words of the beautiful Russian ballad came back to her, Simone placed her hand on the face of Pierre, "You Tebya Lioubliou."

"I did not know you could speak Russian?"

"I started to learn this morning," she answered, forcing herself to smile."

His eyes were pleading. "Simone, those are words of love. If you love me so, why are you planning to leave me again?"

He kissed her hand and closed his eyes and for the first time she discovered his tears. She leaned against him, her cheek resting on his wet face, and she cried with him in the crescendo of violin music.

She kissed a tear, "Ya Vernouss, Ya Vernouss."   She repeated as if to convince herself, "I shall come back."

"I shall come back".

WORLD ALERT

Immediately upon publication, the author intends to offer a copy of this novel to the following persons of authority, among others, in the hope they can identify the causes of the horrendous financial calamity that is said, in this unusual love story, to have hit the world in the mid-seventies, and prevent its repeat in the current century, if it's not already too late.

Readers are urged to provide those persons with whatever assistance they can muster that would protect their own freedom to trade, ensure the integrity of their bank accounts is never again placed in jeopardy by incompetent bankers and unscrupulous foreign agents, and restore gold as the ultimate store of value or, at least, acknowledge the power of love. **Time is of the essence.**

- The President of the United States of America
- The President of France
- The President of Russia
- Mr. Valerie Giscard d'Estaing, former President of France
- The Secretary General of the United Nations
- The President of the World Bank
- The President of the International Monetary Fund
- The President of the Bank for International Settlements
- The President of the American Bankers Association
- The Chairman of the U.S. Federal Reserve Board
- The President of the Bank of France
- The President of the U.S. Federal Deposit Insurance Corporation
- The Financial Secretary of the Cayman Islands

Jean Doucet, the author, at the time the action is said to have taken place.

During a nine month sabbatical, spent in the South of France in the mid-seventies, Jean Doucet drew on his years of experience in commercial, investment and merchant banking to draft his first novel "When All the Banks FAILED". He kept the story buried in a filing cabinet at home for 35 years.

Recently, encouraged by friends and family members, and with time on his hands as a new retiree, he has retrieved the long forgotten manuscript whose theme is now more contemporary and apropos then ever: Banks are failing all over the world, as his novel predicted 30 years ago. Who was listening?

Who is listening now?

Important Facts

According to John Downey, chief national bank examiner at the U.S. Currencies Comptroller's Office, in March 28, 1985 there were more than 800 US banks requiring special supervisory attention. The list was expected to "swell to about 900 banks" by the end of the year. It did. How many banks are on the list now? How trustworthy is your own bank? How safe is your money? Reading "When All The Banks FAILED" might provide you with some answers. Is it too late?